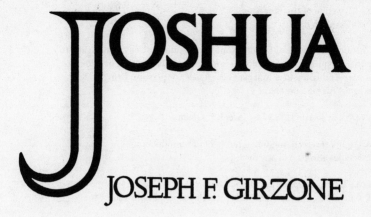

JOSHUA

JOSEPH F. GIRZONE

A TOUCHSTONE BOOK
PUBLISHED BY SIMON & SCHUSTER
New York London Toronto Sydney

Touchstone
Rockefeller Center
1230 Avenue of the Americas
New York, NY 10020

First Touchstone Edition 2003
Published by arrangement with Richelieu Court Publications, Inc.

TOUCHSTONE and colophon are registered trademarks
of Simon & Schuster, Inc.

For information regarding special discounts for bulk purchases,
please contact Simon & Schuster Special Sales at
1-800-456-6798 or business@simonandschuster.com

Manufactured in the United States of America

30 29 28 27 26 25

The Library of Congress has cataloged the Macmillan edition as follows:
Girzone, Joseph F.
Joshua.
I. Title.
PS3557.I77J6   1987
813'.54   87-10274

ISBN 0-684-81346-7

Dedicated
to
My Mother and Father

I wish to express deep appreciation to my friends and family, whose assistance and suggestions were most valuable.

I am particularly grateful to Maureen Conners Moriarty, Neal Merkel, Peter Ginsberg and Michelle Rapkin for their persistent faith in "Joshua," which was critical in bringing about this present edition.

This story is fictional. The characters in the story are also fictional, and any similarity to persons living or dead is coincidental.

The author does feel, however, that what takes place in this book could very easily happen in real life.

JOSHUA

IT WAS a quiet, sultry afternoon in Auburn. People were gathering at Sanders' store for news and the latest gossip. The weather had been sticky and hot for the past few days, just like before a thunderstorm. It was the kind of day that puts people on edge, when mosquitoes and biting flies invade from the nearby woods and annoy everyone in town.

The Persini brothers had given up laying pipe for the day; the ground was too soupy from recent rains and the site was infested with mosquitoes. Why waste time working mud? They had already left the job and were walking toward Sanders' when they met Pat Zumbar, who had also taken the afternoon off.

Pat greeted them with his usual friendly attack: "What the hell are you guys doin' away from the job? When are you gonna finish that pipeline so we can use our sinks? The women are furious you're taking so long."

"Cool off, Pat, it's too hot to work today. You took off, didn't you, and all you do is sit on a bulldozer. You should be in that mudhole, then you'd have something to bellyache about." That was big Tony. He never took much of Pat's guff. And today was no time to horse around. It was too hot and everyone was on edge.

As the men walked along the sidewalk their heavy work

boots pounded the wooden planks like rolling thunder. The men liked to hear that noise. It made them feel important. Pat reached Sanders' first. He opened the squeaky screen door and let the others enter, then followed them as the door slammed behind him. The noise startled Katherine Sanders, who was cleaning the counter. "You guys back again? I thought I just got rid of you," she said as she continued working.

"It's too hot to work today," Ernie said matter-of-factly. "I should have gone fishing like I wanted to."

"Never mind your fishing," Katherine shot back, "you better finish that water main so we can clean up around here."

At that point George Sanders came out of the back room. He was a mild-mannered man, recently retired from the county highway department, where he had worked for the past thirty years. He now spent most of his time around the store, even though his wife, Katherine, had been running it efficiently for years without his help.

This wasn't just a store, and these fellows weren't just customers. They had been friends since childhood and knew each other better than brothers and sisters. There were few secrets among them. They knew everything there was to know about each other and they were still friends. The store was the natural meeting place when there was nothing else to do, and even though the small counter was hardly adequate, the men were content to just stand around and drink their coffee or eat their sandwiches. Good-natured banter and needling was ordinary fare, and at this they were experts.

The current topic of conversation around town was the new fellow living in the old cottage at the edge of town. No one knew much about him except that his name was

Joshua and he was a plain man. He kept pretty much to himself, which piqued everyone's curiosity. Once or twice a week he would walk up the street to the grocery store and buy food and other things he needed. He wasn't particularly shy, though he didn't talk much. He just went about his business and smiled hello to whoever he met along the way. He dressed simply, wearing khaki pants and a plain, loose, pullover shirt that was a lighter shade brown than the pants. The shirt was tucked in at the waist and open at the neck. In place of a leather belt he wore a belt put together from carefully braided strings that formed a flat rope about an inch and a half wide, with a loop and large knots that hooked together in the front.

Joshua looked tall because he was slim and athletic. His long graceful hands were used to hard work and were pleasing to watch when he gestured. His face was thin but with strong, rugged features. His blue-green eyes were striking in the deep feeling they expressed. When he looked at you you had the feeling he was looking into your soul. But the look was not critical. It was filled with compassion and seemed to say "I know all about you and I understand." His walnut-colored hair was thick and wavy, not recently cut, so it gathered about his ears and neck.

Joshua was an object of intense curiosity because no one knew anything about him, and there was no way to learn anything about him. He didn't seem to have a family. He didn't have a job that anyone knew about, yet he didn't seem to be well-off enough to live without working. According to the mailman he wasn't getting any dividend checks or social security checks, no pension checks or government mail. How did he live? That's what had everyone baffled. Whenever he came into town to buy food, what he bought was meager: a loaf of unsliced French or

Italian bread, fresh fish, when it was available, pieces of chicken, some fresh ground hamburger, a few cans of sardines, fresh fruits and vegetables. It rarely varied and never amounted to much. Usually after leaving the market he would walk across the street to the liquor store and buy a gallon of table wine. Then, with arms loaded down with packages, he would walk back to his cottage.

But all this revealed little about the man except that he was orderly in his schedule, regular in his diet, and moderately well-disciplined. Beyond that he was still a mystery.

The cottage he lived in was small, not more than three rooms: a kitchen, a living room, and a bedroom. There was a back room off the house that Joshua used as a workshop. In front of the cottage, near the street, was a homemade mailbox. There was nothing like it anywhere. It was made of wood and constructed like an old-fashioned fishing boat in such a way that the keel could be pulled out like a drawer and letters inserted. There was a fish net hanging down the side to collect small packages.

Along the front of the house was a white picket fence, broken by a gate in the middle, which turned at the corners and went partially down along the sides of the property. Joshua had removed sections of the fence at the rear of the house so that the backyard opened out into a sprawling meadow, which was part of the nearby farm where sheep and cows grazed. Joshua never had to mow his lawn; a few stray sheep wandered regularly into his yard and did the mowing for him, leaving only clumps of wildflowers here and there which created a natural, attractive setting.

These were the few obvious facts about Joshua that were familiar to the townsfolk—just enough to whet their appetite to learn more about him.

It was George who brought up the subject of Joshua. "That new fellow from the *Little House on the Prairie* came in just before you guys got here. Katherine gets butterflies every time he stops in for a cup of coffee. I think she's got a crush on him," George said, with a big laugh.

Katherine was furious. "That's not true," she retorted sharply. "I just get nervous when he's around. He's not like other people, and I get tongue-tied when I try to talk to him. And George is no different. He just stands there gawking at him like a fool." George just laughed good-humoredly.

"You know, he really is a likable guy once you get to know him. And he's not stupid either," George went on. "I asked him what he thought of the Israelis invading Lebanon, and he answered that everyone has a right to live in peace. That was a shrewd answer. He wasn't taking one side, but he took both sides when you think of it. He knew I was feeling him out, and he was polite in answering but didn't reveal a thing about what he really felt."

At that point Moe Sanders came into the store. "All right, you guys, how come the water main's not finished? Everyone's wondering where you went. I tried to help you out, so I told them you probably went fishing. Are they mad! They said they haven't had running water since yesterday afternoon."

"You're a big help," Tony Persini said. "We worked in that hole all morning and couldn't get a thing done with all the mud. The pipe is broken in six different places. If the pump works and it doesn't rain, we may be able to get it finished by tonight."

Changing the subject, Moe remarked that he had just bumped into that new guy, Joshua. "He was leaving the liquor store and was on his way home. I walked over to him and started a conversation with him, and, you know, he's not a bad fellow. He's got a good sense of humor too. He wanted to know who the roly-poly fellow was with the big mouth. I told him he must have been talking about Pat."

"He didn't say that," Pat burst in. "He don't even know who I am."

"He didn't actually use those words," Moe said, "but he did describe you so there was no mistaking who he meant. You do make a big impression on people who don't know you. And there was no way he could have missed you coming down the street. I could hear you all the way around the corner."

"We were just talking about him ourselves before you came in," Tony interjected. "George had been talking to him. He seems like a friendly guy."

Moe agreed and added that Joshua had even invited him over to his house whenever he's free and told him to bring his friends too. "I asked him where he works, and he told me he just repairs things for people, wooden objects and things around the house. It doesn't bring him much income, just enough to pay his bills. He doesn't need much anyway, he said."

"Boy, what a way to live! I wish my life was that simple," Ernie said.

During this exchange George was looking out the window. "Looks like it's going to rain," he said.

Ernie turned and looked out the window. "We'll never get that pipe fixed. I'll see you guys tomorrow," he said as he walked toward the door. One by one the others followed. Katherine took their cups and cleaned the counter as the squeaky door slammed shut.

The main street was quiet. Everyone had gone home

to escape the impending storm. There were only a few cars and pickup trucks along the wide street. Auburn was an old town, built around the late 1700s, tucked away in the foothills of the mountains that sprawled out into the distance. The village, with its surrounding fields and hamlets, had kept its own identity. Its six churches attested to the varied backgrounds of the inhabitants, the names on mailboxes graphically pointing up the wide diversity of nationalities, and the antique houses and stores painted a vivid picture of life here two centuries ago.

The people were warm and friendly, once you got to know them. Being off the main flow of highway traffic, the village was isolated and well insulated from the current of change that was sweeping the big city. The people were more true to the old ways, and change came slowly, if at all.

THE RAINS came hard and furious and finally broke, allowing the Persinis to finish their work. It was a big relief when the sun appeared and blue sky replaced the heavy, leaden clouds. The feel of dampness still clung to one's bones because the long rains had left the ground wet, but it was warm and one could smell summer. The birds started singing and the flowers in everyone's gardens were bursting into bloom. The sweet aroma of lilacs pervaded the whole town, causing delight to some and asthma attacks in others. Customers who came into Sanders' store to transact their daily business were in high spirits, like school kids who are given a day off.

Even Charlie, the testy mailman, was in a cheerful mood and got the courage to knock on Joshua's door one day under the pretext of asking what he should do with any large packages that he might have to deliver. Joshua was so friendly that he caught Charlie off guard. He even invited him inside to have lunch with him, which made Charlie forget why he had gone to Joshua's in the first place. And even though it was against regulations, Charlie couldn't resist. He accepted Joshua's invitation and followed his host into the house, where he eyed everything in sight, cataloguing them and tucking them away in his memory so he could tell every detail to the folks at Sanders'.

What Charlie actually saw wasn't much, but the very simplicity of the furnishings was a story in itself, and with Charlie's vivid imagination that would provide enough to create a whole story. Charlie could hardly contain his glee over what he had accomplished.

He followed Joshua through the living room and the little hallway into the kitchen. It was a simple kitchen. The first thing that caught your attention was the hand-made, square wooden table in front of the picture window. It was solid and strong, and the top an uncovered two-inch slab of wood. The three chairs around the table were also handmade, and though not fancy, they were sturdy and expressed the personality of the maker. The chair facing the window was the one most used, as that was pulled away from the table while the others sat snugly in place, with a towel draped over one and a rope slung over the other. In front of the table the picture window gave a view that opened out onto the vast meadow, spreading out as far as the eye could see.

Joshua pulled out a chair and offered Charlie a seat. He sat down and continued to eye everything in sight, much to the amusement of Joshua, who knew he was being given a thorough going-over.

"Would you like a bowl of soup?" Joshua asked. "I'm just having lunch, and I'd be happy if you would have some with me."

Charlie was shocked by this casual familiarity of someone who was almost a total stranger. "No, well, yes, I think I will," Charlie stammered as he rubbed his chin and cheek with the palm of his hand.

The aroma of fresh chicken soup filled the kitchen. Joshua took the loaf of bread lying on the counter, cut two thick slices with a sturdy butcher knife, and placed them on the table with no dish. He dished out the soup in two heavy pottery bowls, then took the jug of wine and poured some into two water glasses. Not used to repressing his curiosity, Charlie asked bluntly, "How come you had everything ready? Were you expecting someone?"

Joshua chuckled. "I had a feeling someone might stop by so I thought I'd put on a little extra, just in case."

"You're beautiful," Charlie said in bewilderment as he sipped his soup. "You don't put on airs or act like a snob, and everybody's curious. Would you mind if I brought some of my friends over to visit sometime? You'd like them; they're real people. They're related to practically everybody in town, and if they like you, you're really in, if it means anything to you."

"I'd like that very much," Joshua said with an appreciative smile. Joshua took a piece of bread as Charlie watched. He broke the bread in half and offered a piece to Charlie. The mailman was amazed. How unusual! Here was a total stranger offering a piece of his own bread as if he had been a friend for years. Half embarrassed at the intimacy of the gesture, Charlie took the bread and blurted out, "Thanks, Josh," as if Joshua had given him a hundred-dollar bill.

"Like being a mailman, Charlie?" Joshua asked.

"Most of the time. The pay is good, but the bosses are miserable. They're always on your back for something or other."

"But you make a lot of people happy, and that's a wonderful thing. That's more than you can say for most jobs."

"By the way, Josh, everyone in town is wondering what you do for a living. Do you work?"

"Of course I work. How do you think I feed myself?"

"What do you do?" Charlie asked.

"I make things for people and repair wooden objects

like broken chairs and other household items. Sometimes I make toys for little children, nothing grand, just little things. Children like simple things, you know."

"Do you charge much?" Charlie asked bluntly.

Joshua smiled at his simplicity. "Not much, just enough to buy a little food and pay the bills."

"Maybe I'll have you make something for me sometime. Where's your shop?"

"In the back. It's just a small place. I do everything by hand so I don't need much space."

Joshua got up and asked Charlie if he would like to see his shop. Of course he would. He was dying to see it. What a scoop to tell his friends about!

The shop was indeed simple, with tools neatly arranged on nails along the wall. The chisels were set in slots according to size. At the back of the room was a workbench set beneath a wide window that looked out across the field. Sun was pouring through the window and provided all the light needed to work. On the bench were two or three partially finished objects; one looked like a small wooden wheel for a child's wagon, the other a setting for an antique clock. Lying next to them was a hammer, a chisel, and a small saw. None of the tools were sophisticated, but the workmanship of the pieces was exact and creative. Even Charlie could see that, and he was impressed, more at the ability to make such objects with such simple tools than at the artistic quality of the objects themselves. Charlie was far from being a connoisseur of fine art, but he was genuinely impressed and had more than enough information to take back to the gang. He was getting impatient to leave, not only because he had accomplished his purpose, but also because he was afraid someone might complain about getting their mail late.

Joshua could sense his uneasiness and started walking out, with Charlie behind him.

"That lunch really hit the spot," Charlie said as he shook Joshua's hand, thanked him for his hospitality, and started across the lawn to his jeep. As he was getting into the jeep Joshua yelled out to him, "By the way, Charlie, if I should ever get any big packages, you can just put them here on the porch. They'll be safe enough here."

Charlie scratched his head in bewilderment. He hadn't remembered asking Joshua, and that was why he stopped in the first place. He waved, got into his jeep, and drove off. Joshua watched him and smiled, then went back into the house.

Charlie couldn't wait until he got up to Sanders' store. When he went in with the mail it was lunchtime, just as he had planned it. The whole crew was there: Moe and George and Katherine, as well as the Persini brothers, and Pat Zumbar, the roly-poly character made of solid muscle whose voice could be heard clear across town. Herm Ainutti was there as well as a few others, a formidable lot, but jovial, good-hearted, and totally loyal to each other.

When Charlie appeared in the doorway his figure filled the whole space. He was a huge man. His face was flushed, as it usually was, a few strands of silvery hair hanging over his red forehead. He had unusually large feet, which pointed outward when he stood still. Charlie liked to play cat-and-mouse, and this time he knew everyone was waiting for what he had to tell them. They all knew he had been at Joshua's house, since Pat had seen his jeep parked outside. It was clear from the look on his face that he couldn't wait any longer to tell them about his visit, and no one would give him an opening, so finally he tried for one himself.

"Anything interesting happen today?"

"Nothing," George answered. "Everyone's tired from partying all weekend."

"Hear about Pat winning the daily double?" Herm interjected.

"No," Charlie said. "How much did it pay?"

"A hundred and forty-five dollars," Herm answered.

"Whew, you really hit it good. When you gonna buy us lunch?" Charlie asked, looking at Pat.

"Next Tuesday, right here. So make sure you're all here," Pat said in mock generosity. Everyone knew next Tuesday was a holiday, and the store would be closed.

Finally Katherine slipped and gave Charlie the opening he needed. "What are you having for lunch, Charlie?"

"I already ate lunch," Charlie blurted out. "That new fellow, Joshua, invited me in to eat with him. I had a great time. You should see the inside of his house. Fascinating."

Everyone was curious anyway, so they all shot questions at him. Katherine asked about the furniture. Moe asked about the shop. Herm asked what they had for lunch. Charlie told them everything, then some. You would think he and Joshua had been friends for years. And he told them they were all invited to stop in anytime. He reassured them that Joshua was a nice guy and would fit well in their little club.

This revelation made Charlie the hero for the next few days. He had broken the ice with Joshua, and now the door was open for the rest to visit him and get acquainted.

3

AUBURN seemed immune to the current turmoil in society. It was peaceful and people there lived simply. They owned their own houses, and though not pretentious, they provided security. When bad times hit the economy Auburn was little affected. Its inhabitants were well insulated from the problems that distressed other people. About the most stirring news in town was usually about changes taking place in the various churches.

There were six churches: the Methodist, which had a warm and friendly pastor named Reverend Joe Engman; the Presbyterian, whose minister was a very proper person; the Episcopal, whose pastor was a born actor; the Lutheran, whose pastor was rigid and pompous; the Baptist, which had a simple but likable man for a pastor; and the Catholic, whose pastor was aloof and inflexible.

Major changes in the Catholic Church had affected and shaken that whole congregation loose from the crusty customs and traditions that had shackled them for generations, to say nothing of the prejudices that had marred everyone's social relationships in one way or another. As usual, people were more willing to make the changes than were the clergy. The clergy become insecure when changes are discussed. They may seem brave enough about changes in ceremony, which don't really affect people's public lives, but when it comes to things that affect life-style and people's relationships with other religions, they often get nervous.

Since everyone was supposed to be ecumenically minded, the clergy did get together on occasion. They scheduled interfaith services once or twice a year. They even met for coffee and doughnuts once a month and talked about all kinds of irrelevant topics. But when members of their congregations attended another church, they were highly indignant and, indeed, personally offended that someone would think another church might have more to offer than theirs. In fact, the clergy became upset when they saw their people even socializing too much with members of other congregations. So ecumenism was more window-dressing than a serious attempt to bring the people closer together.

As friendly as the people of Auburn were, they were, by family tradition, clearly marked packages and knew just where they belonged. Occasionally individuals had, over the years, developed strong friendships that went a lot deeper than denominational loyalties, as was the case with the crew who hung around Sanders'. They were all of varied nationalities and religions and formed a veritable ecumenical movement, except they weren't overly interested in religion.

Because relationships were so tightly knit in the village, a stranger had little hope of ever becoming a part of it. And a stranger was anyone who had lived there for less than fifteen years. In Auburn relationships were established in childhood. You grew up together as friends.

Joshua's living in a cottage on the outskirts of town was not just a geographical fact. It was a symbol of where he stood in relation to the community: outside. He was the focus of everyone's attention and his solitude intensified their curiosity. Charlie's uncharacteristic intrusion into his privacy was an expression of the townspeople's curiosity about this quiet man. Most newcomers in a town make desperate attempts to be accepted, but Joshua gave the impression he couldn't care less. He was the talk of the village precisely because they couldn't get to know him.

But now that a beachhead had been established, and Joshua had made everyone welcome, he could expect a steady stream of visitors in the days to come.

Herm Ainutti was the first. The weather had been pleasant, and people were walking around town again, chatting with neighbors. It was not unusual to see Joshua working his vegetable garden in the backyard. Herm had been out to the liquor store to buy his bottle of "medicine," which he needed for his heart. He had to pass Joshua's place the way he was going, though he could have saved three blocks by going the other way. As he passed, he called out to Joshua. Joshua turned and waved. When Herm started to talk to him, Joshua dropped his hoe and walked over to the fence. He was always ready to stop what he was doing and spend a few minutes socializing. It was almost as if that was his real business.

Herm was a friendly fellow. He had a little printing business, which he worked at mostly for his friends now that he was retired. He had taken a liking to Joshua ever since he first saw him walking down the street with his bag of groceries. Like everyone else, he was curious about the newcomer and wondered what he really did with his life. He asked Joshua about his garden, and, as Joshua was quite proud of his little garden, he invited his visitor to come in and take a look at it. It wasn't much, Joshua told him, just big enough to raise a few vegetables for the summer.

Herm was surprised at how orderly the garden was: about four hundred square feet, with everything arranged in mathematically precise rows. It was a work of art, with perfectly straight furrows between each row to provide drainage and aeration. There were rows of tomato plants and different kinds of lettuce. There were beets and radishes and peppers and a few cucumber plants. There were also onions, but they were arranged in a peculiar manner, all along the outside edge of the garden, in two rows and close together. Outside the onions was a perfectly arranged row of miniature marigolds. Herm was fascinated. "How come you got the flowers and the onions planted like that?" he asked.

"For protection," Joshua answered. "Rabbits don't like marigolds and sheep don't like onions, and, as much as I like rabbits and sheep, I don't like them eating my vegetables."

"Clever," Herm remarked with a smile. "I notice that all the plants you have produce in early summer and by the fall they're all dead. How come you didn't plant vegetables that last till the end of the season?"

Joshua looked at him. The look seemed to penetrate right through him and far beyond as he answered simply, "I may be busy then, doing other things, and I don't want to waste the food. It's a gift of God."

Joshua also told Herm that he was welcome to take any vegetables from the garden, even if he wasn't at home. Herm liked that offer very much and thanked him. Then he took his leave and started for the gate. Joshua followed him. That was a nice gesture, which the mailman had also noticed. For someone so obviously strong and manly as

Joshua, he seemed remarkably refined. Little gestures like this gave his guests the impression they were really important to him. It made them feel good, as if he was really glad they came to visit him, even if they were unexpected and uninvited.

As the days went by and people became acquainted with Joshua, he rarely had time to himself. People enjoyed visiting with him and just listening to him talk. He was a good talker, not about trivial things, but about things he noticed during the day—interesting things in the lives of the people, or fascinating things he noticed in nature, details that other people were often too busy to notice. More and more people were coming to him with their problems. Joshua proved to have a rare insight into human nature, and those people who took his advice usually fared well. Most people's problems are of their own making, and making people more aware of themselves would frequently provide the key to the solution. Between visits Joshua did his work. He worked fast, so he didn't need much time to finish a job. Most of the jobs were uncomplicated, so they didn't require great imagination or planning. Even when he was busy he was never too busy to sit and visit when someone came to see him. His happiness and pleasant nature seemed to draw people, and his spirit was contagious. When a person left him it was usually with a deep sense of peace and a renewed enthusiasm for life. Joshua's own view of life was so simple and uncomplicated, and his rare understanding of the goals and purpose of life was so healthy, that people would walk away free and lighthearted until they complicated things for themselves all over again. But it was tiring for Joshua to give so much of himself, and when evening came he needed to be by himself to recharge his energies.

Joshua looked out across the valley and into the distant hills. Behind them, through the slight haze, he could see the tops of tall buildings in the neighboring city. "All these will I give you, if only you will fall down and worship me" crossed his memory as if it were only yesterday. He reminisced as his mind crossed the centuries; buildings change, architecture changes, styles of dress change from time to time (though women still enjoy wearing the furs of animals), modes of travel become more sophisticated, tools evolve into complex machines and robots, but man fails to learn much from the lessons of the past. In spite of all the knowledge that has been amassed through the ages, people would still rather learn from their own limited experiences so their responses to life remain just as primitive as those of people a thousand years ago. Can man change? His memories are only from his childhood. He has no memories of things that preceded him, yet it is memory that conditions and shapes responses to life and determines patterns of growth. Is man forever doomed to invent ever more sophisticated technology but never mature sufficiently to comprehend and control his own inventions?

Joshua thought long and hard, intermittently envisioning his own place in the long-term plan his Father had laid out for him eons ago and for the whole complex course through which humanity would evolve. Always optimistic, always positive, always understanding and patient of what had to be, Joshua maintained a simple and happy attitude toward life, looking to distant goals rather than to momentary and immediate satisfactions, realizing that, in spite of appearances, his Father's will would ultimately triumph.

The cawing of a crow on a limb above him distracted him. It was quiet, even more quiet than before. Shadows were deepening as they stretched farther across the field, and Joshua felt a twinge of loneliness. As strong and self-reliant as he was, and as much as he enjoyed being by himself, at times he realized poignantly just how different his life was and how separated he was from the intimacy of other people's lives. They came to him and enjoyed being with him, and drew inspiration and strength from his vast and seemingly endless source of wisdom and strength, but they left and went back to their own world of family and friends and life in the village. He was very much alone, and at times like this realized how unhealthy it is to be alone. He wasn't a part of others' lives. He wasn't unhappy about it, it couldn't be any different, but he still could not help but notice how life went on all about him and he stayed very much the stranger. It had always been that way. This time was no different. He was here for a purpose, a clear and carefully delineated objective designed by his Father, and intimacy in the life of the people was not germane to that plan. It would prevent the easy maneuvering that had to be part of his life.

On the bench in the workshop lay a beautifully carved bird. It was difficult to tell what kind of bird it was, since it was not colored, but it looked very much like a sparrow or a finch. It was so perfectly carved that it looked real—it even looked soft to the touch.

Next he took a large block of wood, approximately a foot and a half long and about six inches thick. It was an almost perfect piece of cherry wood. Laying it on the bench under the fluorescent light, he took the hammer and large chisel and began chipping away with quick, easy strokes. He first carved away the upper corners, and gradually worked his way down the sides. After about half an hour the outline of a lamp base began to emerge. It seemed

people were fascinated by the unique wood-carved lamps
Joshua made, and each day new orders would come in.
The orders came and were simply addressed:

> Joshua
> Mountain Road
> Auburn

No state, no zip, nothing else. The mailman knew. The
objects Joshua made were cheap enough, fifteen dollars for
a lamp base, two dollars to fix a broken chair leg, twenty
dollars for a lawn chair. The birds were free. Little children asked for them, and he was delighted to make them.
Some were resting, with their heads tucked under a wing;
some had wings spread wide as if landing; others held their
heads high as if chirping; each was different and each was
perfect.

Joshua didn't work late. Shortly after the sun went
down he quit for the night, put away his tools, cleaned up
the shop, and went to bed. Going to bed was a ritual. He
would kneel at his bedside for the longest time talking to
God, sometimes silently, sometimes out loud. When he
prayed like this it would frequently last far into the night.
His position would rarely change, though occasionally he
would raise his hands as if pleading. Most of the time his
hands would rest on the bed, relaxed, one hand resting on
top of the other, his face peaceful, his open eyes looking
into the dark as if seeing something no one else could see.
To him God was not just a phantom humans concoct to
fix their imaginations on, but a real being present before
him who responded to every thought and plea. Nor was
praying for Joshua drudgery. It was as if he was enjoying
a dialogue with a dear friend, with someone he loved intensely, and someone who was intimately involved in his

life, who controlled circumstances, made decisions, even decisions with which Joshua sometimes strongly disagreed. It was almost as if he and God planned the next day in every detail.

When Joshua finished praying he was always tired, and this night was like any other night. He knelt, talked to God, then crawled into bed and slept peacefully the whole night through.

The next morning he woke up to the accompaniment of the rising sun and the singing birds. He sat up, stretched, yawned loudly and sensuously, then got up, washed, and went into the kitchen to prepare breakfast. For breakfast he had an orange or a banana, a piece of bread, which he fried in bacon grease, and a cup of black coffee. Lately, as he was becoming acquainted with more people, he would just have a cup of coffee. Then later on, when the coffee shop opened at seven o'clock, he would have breakfast there with some of the men. On those occasions the breakfast would be much heartier, consisting of bacon and eggs or pancakes and sausages, which he seemed to relish most. He mixed in well with the men, even though he was quiet and reserved. Mary, the shop owner, always took care to wait on him herself and was annoyed if one of the other girls got to him first. He seemed to notice how hard the girls worked, and in his own quiet way, when no one noticed, would tell them how much he appreciated their good cooking and their friendly hospitality. A couple of the girls were boisterous, but they were good-hearted and Joshua would laugh at the funny remarks they made. Even when sometimes they were off-color, he'd still smile at their good nature. Joshua was no prude. He genuinely enjoyed people and felt comfortable with the lively banter and earthy ways of these ordinary folk. Nothing would change them, but beneath the exterior was a goodness and a kindliness that covered a multitude of sins. He liked them, and they knew it and responded.

This particular morning Joshua ate at home. He had a busy day ahead, with more than the usual number of orders to get out. People would be stopping to pick up their pieces, and he wanted to have them ready. After breakfast he put on his sandals and went out.

His walk took him past Joe Langford's house. Mary, his wife, had spotted Joshua walking up the road and called out to him, asking him if he'd like to come in and have a cup of coffee. Mary had spoken to Joshua on occasion when he would be taking his early walks, but this was the first time she had gotten enough nerve to invite him in. Joe was just coming back to the house for breakfast. He usually milked the cows before he had his breakfast. This way he worked up a good appetite.

Joe liked Joshua, and showed it by his broad grin as he spotted Joshua walking up the path to the house. "Up early again, I see," Joe yelled over to Joshua.

Joshua smiled and quipped, "I guess I'm just an ol' farmer who'd rather be up and around than sleeping away the most beautiful time of the day."

The two men met at the front steps and Joe held the door open for Joshua to go in first. Joe and Mary's was a quaint brick house, not large, but big enough for their needs.

Mary had breakfast all ready for Joe, and she asked Joshua if he would like to join them.

"Where are you from?" Mary asked Joshua.

"From Bethlehem," Joshua said simply. Since Bethlehem was a nearby town, Mary and Joe thought nothing of it.

"What brings you up this way?" Mary continued. "It's certainly dead enough in Auburn."

"It's quiet here and the people are friendly," Joshua answered. "I am a simple man, and my needs are modest, so whatever I make on my wood carving is sufficient."

"What do you make?" Mary asked him.

"Whatever people like. I made a lamp for a family the other day. I'm making little birds for some children who came to visit me yesterday."

"You'll have to make something for us when you get a chance," Mary said.

"I'd like to."

"Thanks for the coffee," Joshua said as he got up from the table. "You are good neighbors."

"You're welcome anytime," Mary said as she walked him to the door.

Joe and Joshua walked out the back door together, chatted for a few moments in the driveway, then separated.

Joshua was back home in less than fifteen minutes. It was still early, and even though he had stopped off at the Langfords', he was still able to get an early start at his work.

The workshop was bright on sunny mornings as the light shone through the side window, making the room a cheerful place to work. Joshua picked up his tools and began work on the lamp base he had started the night before. He chiseled away bit by bit until, by ten o'clock, he had finished the job. He took it out of the vise, stood it up to see if the base was level, shaved the bottom on one side, then stood it up again. It was perfect. Next he took fine sandpaper and smoothed every detail, felt it with his fingertips, then put it to one side and began work on another piece. You could tell Joshua was proud of his work. By eleven-thirty he had finished his second job for the day.

The next job was more demanding, and, since he didn't have the wood for it, he had to make a trip to the mill on the other side of town. He walked out, not bothering to lock the door behind him.

On the way he met a group of children playing on the sidewalk in front of the candy store. "Hi, Joshua," a little freckle-faced girl called to him. The other children turned, and when they saw it was Joshua, ran over and grabbed his hands. A pretty blond-haired girl looked up at him admiringly and asked him if he finished carving the little birds.

"Yes, they're all finished," he said. "If you come by when I get back from the mill, I'll give them to you." They all let out a cry of glee. "Oh, I can't wait to see mine," one girl said as the others chimed in.

The children went back to playing as Joshua continued walking up the street. The sun was high in the sky, and it was getting hot. Joshua looked handsome in his own rugged way. His skin was turning bronze from his continued exposure to the sun. His hair was a bit tousled, the long curly strands hanging down over his forehead as he walked briskly along, his arms swinging slightly. His slim, elegant figure radiated a carefree grace. It was a pleasure to watch him move. There was no doubt he was different. Watching him, one couldn't help but wonder what he was doing in Auburn. Half the young girls in town already had their eyes on him. Even the married women secretly admired him.

Joshua turned the corner at the end of the main street and arrived at the entrance to the mill, the only real in-

dustry in town. Huge trucks rolled through town all day
long, bringing logs to be cut into boards for lumber. Joshua
was probably their smallest customer, but the manager
liked him because he wasn't pushy and he didn't mind
waiting until others were waited on.

"Hi, Josh, what's on your mind today?" the manager
called out to him.

"Nothing much. I just need a cherry log if you have
one. No rush, Phil," Joshua replied.

"Give me five minutes and I'll take care of you myself,"
Phil shot back as he walked across the yard with a customer.

"Sorry for keeping you waiting, Josh," Phil said when
he returned. "What did you say you need?"

"A cherry log about five feet long and twelve inches
thick," Joshua told him.

"That's going to be a tough one. Did you see any out
in the shed?"

"No."

Phil yelled to one of his assistants, "Do you have a five-
foot cherry log twelve inches thick?"

"I don't remember seeing one," the man hollered back
across the huge room.

Phil took Joshua out to a pile of logs that had been
lying in back of the shed all summer. "Maybe we can find
an uncut log that's dried out enough for you to work with."
They walked through the pile trying to find the right one.

"How about this one?" Joshua said, pointing to an almost perfect log with hardly a knot in it.

"You sure do have a good eye," Phil said as he sized
up the piece of wood. "Let me have the men bring it in
and cut it up for you. It'll only take a few minutes." Phil
marked the log and he and Joshua went inside.

"My kids really liked the little duck you carved for them last week. It's such a beautiful piece of work, my wife doesn't like to let them play with it. She's afraid they'll break it. How's your business doing, by the way?"

Joshua replied matter-of-factly, "As well as I'd like it to; enough to make a living. I don't need much."

"What are you going to do with that big log? If you're going to carve that, you'll have a job on your hands. That's a lot of wood. And you won't be able to charge no fifteen or twenty dollars, either. The wood itself is going to set you back about fifty dollars."

"This job's a little special. Some Jewish people from the synagogue asked if I would carve a figure of Moses for their social hall," Joshua answered with a smile.

"I didn't know you did jobs that big. That's going to be quite a piece of work. How long will it take you to do it?"

"Actually, it's easier than working on the little birds. There's more detail in the wing of a bird than in the whole five feet of Moses. There's just more wood to be chipped away. It'll probably take me three or four days working steady."

"Will it be cash, Josh, or shall I hold off until the synagogue pays you?"

"I'll pay for it. I've been saving for it, so I should have enough. How much is it, Phil?"

"Fifty-six dollars even."

Joshua took the money out of his pocket, counted the exact amount, and gave it to Phil.

"That log is going to be heavy, Josh. How are you going to get it back to your place?" Phil asked, concerned.

"I'll carry it."

"That's a heavy load. If you don't mind waiting a couple

of hours until the truck gets back, I'll drop it off on my way home."

"Thanks anyway, Phil, but I'll be able to carry it," Joshua said appreciatively.

At that point the men brought in the log. It was all cut and planed, a beautiful piece of wood. "I'd like to see that statue when you finish," Phil said as Joshua went to pick up the log.

"Come down Friday morning on your way to work," Joshua told him.

"Okay. See you Friday morning, first thing."

Joshua picked up the log, hoisted it over his right shoulder, and walked toward the door. Through the yard and down the street he went, seemingly unaware and unconcerned about the weight of the heavy log he was carrying. But as he got halfway down the main street he put the log down and rested. It was a hot day, and he was sweating heavily.

One of the men from Sanders' store spotted him and came over. "What d'ya got there, Josh?" he asked.

"Oh, just a cherry log for something I have to make," he answered.

"It looks heavy, want a hand?" the man asked. It was Mike Charis, a quiet young fellow.

"No thanks," Joshua answered, but Mike had already picked up the piece of wood.

"My God, what is this thing made out of, lead? This is heavy," Mike said as he tried to carry it. Then, putting it down, he apologized. "Sorry, Josh, you'll have to carry that yourself. It's a little too heavy for me."

Joshua smiled. "Thanks, anyway, but I'm used to carrying these things. It doesn't bother me."

"You're a lot stronger than you look, fella," Mike said

in bewilderment as Joshua picked up the log and put it over his shoulder. The two men walked down the street together.

"What are you going to make with that piece of wood?" Mike asked.

"I've been asked to make a statue of Moses for a synagogue in the city."

"Are you Jewish?"

"My family was, a way back."

"I saw you in church last Sunday. I thought you were Catholic."

"You're right, I am Christian."

"You mean you're a Jew and a Christian too?"

"Jesus was a Jew and a Christian, so were the apostles."

Mike seemed mystified at this latest revelation. He liked Joshua, and even though this bit of information was a surprise, it didn't really affect how he felt about him. Everybody liked Joshua for what he was, and if he happened to be a Jew, that wasn't his fault. He was still a good guy and a good friend.

In no time at all the story got around town about the "three-hundred-pound log" Joshua had carried all the way from the mill as if it were a piece of cardboard. As the story spread the weight of the log increased, and with it Joshua's stature in the eyes of the people, particularly the young men and boys. Their fascination with this likable stranger knew no bounds, and everyone was curious to find out all they could about him.

After Mike left Joshua at his house Joshua carried the log around to the yard, since it was too big to work on in the house. He placed it carefully on the ground and looked it over closely, analyzing the grain in an attempt to determine which side he should use for the front and which side for the back of the figure. After looking at it from different angles, he finally made up his mind and set to work at once. With a heavy black pencil he outlined the figure on the surface of the wood, stood back, looked at the sketch, made a few changes, drew the arms in two sections so he could carve them separately, then, taking a saw, cut those sections off the block and set them aside.

Then he set to work carving the main part of the figure. His hands worked fast, and in no time at all the wooden log was no longer a piece of wood but was beginning to show signs of life. The outline of a head began to appear. The neck was partially formed. The upper portion of the shoulders joining the neck already showed a character of great determination. In his enthusiasm to work on the piece, Joshua forgot lunch and worked straight through the afternoon.

By five o'clock he had made remarkable progress, and you could see the well-delineated figure, with depth and strength of personality emerging more and more with each stroke of the hammer and chisel. But Joshua was growing tired. He had worked all day, ever since he got back from his morning walk.

Finally he stood up, stepped back from the figure, and looked at it critically. He seemed content with the progress he had made and walked toward the cottage, deciding to call it a day.

As he was leaving the workshop to go into the kitchen, there was a knock at the front door. He opened it to see the four little children he had met earlier in the day.

"Joshua," one of the girls said, "you told us to come over this afternoon to pick up the birds you made for us. So here we are."

Joshua laughed. "I was just thinking about you, wondering if you would come. Please come on in."

The children followed Joshua through the living room, the kitchen, and into the workshop. They were all eyes, trying to absorb as much of the inside of Joshua's house as their vivid imaginations and memories could hold. Joshua walked over to the workbench, took the four little birds he had made, and gave them to the children. They gasped their delight. As young as they were, the children still appreciated the beauty of these handmade creations. They looked at them from all sides, fascinated by their gifts. "Oh, thank you so much, Joshua," the freckled brown-haired girl said. The others chimed in, "Thank you, Joshua, they are beautiful." One of the boys looked intently at his, meditating on it for a long time.

Joshua watched them, smiling, with obvious satisfaction at the simplicity of the children's delight. Then, at once, they turned to Joshua, hugged him, and told him how much they loved him. He bent down, put his arms around them, and told them that he loved them too. "Your Father in heaven has given you many presents, just like these little birds, but all alive and free and singing songs for you all day long, and even at night, like the nightingale. You should notice these beautiful creatures and let them remind you of how much your Father loves you."

"Do you know God, Joshua?" the blond-haired girl asked him.

"Yes, I do know him. We are good friends," he replied, then added, "You had better run along now and let Joshua cook his supper."

"Good-bye, Joshua," they all said as they walked out the front door and down the pathway to the street. Joshua watched them as they walked away, talking excitedly about their presents, admiring them and pointing out how each bird was different from the others. Joshua smiled faintly and walked into the house, closing the door behind him.

It was a long time since breakfast, and Joshua was hungry. He thought of a day long ago, when his mother and her relatives were looking for him, concerned about his health. It seemed some gossips had told his mother he was pushing himself. He had been preaching all day long and had not taken time to eat. They got his mother all upset, so she came looking for him. He blushed as he thought of his response. "Who are my mother and my brothers? They who do the will of my Father in heaven are my mother and my brothers and my sisters."

Just before he ate dinner that night he sat for a moment and raised his eyes slowly, as if in deep thought. He did that before each meal. It was brief and casual, nothing showy. One couldn't tell whether he was thinking or praying. But that was the way Joshua was. His rich inner life rarely burst out on the surface, and his intimacy with God was evident only after one got to know him and could interpret the little things that betrayed the intensity of his feelings.

Joshua was not a pious person in the disparaging sense that people tend to associate with individuals who like to show their religion. He showed none of that kind of behavior. It wouldn't even occur to anyone to think of Joshua as a religious person. He was just an ordinary person who radiated an enthusiasm for life and for everything that had life. He loved the beautiful colors in nature. He was fascinated by the animals, and found humor and playfulness even in the most forbidding of the four-legged creatures. But he wasn't a dreamy-eyed nature lover who got himself all disconnected from reality. He was too balanced for that. He was, indeed, a most fascinating kind of person, with an inner beauty that contrasted remarkably with the external simplicity of his life. Even though Joshua was physically attractive, and possessed a grace that was charming, when one came to know him more intimately all that seemed to pale beside the richness and depth of his personality.

It was a rare person who got to know the real Joshua, either because most people didn't have the ability to see beneath the surface or they couldn't capture at one glance all the facets of his rich inner life.

It was getting late, almost eight-thirty. The sun was about to settle down behind the hill in the distance, and a cool breeze was blowing in from the hills. Joshua decided to call it a day and retire for the night. He usually went to bed at sunset and rose at sunrise. Maybe this harmony with nature was the secret of his excellent physical condition.

Joshua went inside, and in a few minutes his lights were out.

CHAPTER 4

AT ABOUT the same time as Joshua retired that night a party was just beginning at the Sanders' house. The whole crew was there with their wives. Most of them were not heavy drinkers, probably because they talked so much that they didn't have time to drink. The conversation at these parties usually ran the gamut of everything from world politics to the economy. Eventually, in the late hours, the topics would come around to more local items of interest, like Joshua, for instance. "Has anyone seen him lately?" "We should have invited him over tonight. He's quick-witted and would have been fun."

"Did you see him carrying that big log down Main Street this morning?" George asked. "That guy's strong."

"Mike Charis tried to help him, but could hardly lift the thing," Herm mentioned. "How much do you think that log weighed?"

"Must have weighed at least two hundred fifty, three hundred pounds," Charlie said.

Pat disagreed. "That's impossible. He couldn't carry anything that heavy. He's too fragile."

"You haven't seen that guy," George said. "He may look fragile, but he's as strong as a bull."

"I don't believe it," Pat continued to object.

Then Moe added in his own quiet way, "I don't think the log weighed three hundred pounds, but it had to weigh at least a couple of hundred, and that's still a pretty good size piece of wood."

"I don't know about that guy," Pat said. "I like him, but I can't figure him out. He doesn't have any girlfriends. That's not natural. Do you think he's gay?"

"That's terrible," his wife, Minnie, interrupted. "He's just a quiet person." Pat's wife still, quite miraculously, had a patient disposition even after over forty years of marriage to Pat.

"Well, why doesn't he go out with girls?" Pat continued, pushing his point.

"That doesn't mean a thing," Herm said, annoyed. Herm had liked Joshua ever since their conversation a week ago. And if Herm liked you, you couldn't do any wrong. He'd defend you against his best friend.

"Maybe he just likes to keep to himself," Charlie, the mailman, put in. "Maybe he's divorced, who knows. He seems normal enough to me. Maybe he loves his work, and is content just being alone."

"Sometimes I don't understand you guys," Jim Dicara added. "You come up with the weirdest theories. You find a fellow once in a lifetime like Joshua. He's a nice guy. He's intelligent. He's friendly. He's got everything going for him, and you tag him as a weirdo. To me he's a very normal person. He loves what he does, and he's just content to be by himself. Personally, I envy him."

Since everybody respected Jimmy, that ended the conversation. It was decided that Joshua was a good guy. They also agreed that they would invite him to their next get-together.

* * *

The next morning, at the crack of dawn, Joshua woke up to the sound of birds singing outside his window. By the time he had finished breakfast, it was only six o'clock. But today he was so excited about finishing the figure of Moses that he didn't take his daily walk, getting right to work instead.

The wood was wet with the morning dew, which Joshua rubbed off easily with a rag. He stood back for a moment to view the object, then went to work with hammer and chisels.

By eight o'clock he had the outline of the whole figure cut deeply into the wood. Only a master craftsman could work with the ease and economy with which Joshua plied each stroke. Every movement had meaning. Each cut with the chisel brought new life into the dead wood. By eleven o'clock the figure had been cut free from the block of wood and had its own independent existence. To an untrained eye, it looked finished, but there was still much work to do.

Joshua picked the figure up off the ground and rested it against the trunk of the fat maple tree that grew near his workshop. He stepped back, looked at the figure, turned it around from side to side, stepping back a little farther each time to view it from a distance. Then he got down on his knees to do the fine details of the face with a tiny chisel. First he worked on the eyes, carefully giving them a well-rounded look while setting them deeply beneath the brow. This was a difficult job, because the artist had to consider the effect of light from different angles on the deep-set eyes.

When he finished they looked almost alive, as if they would blink at any moment. Next he worked on the nose and nostrils. Soon they began to flare, as if venting great emotion. The lips, which seemed soft and sensuous, were slightly parted, as if about to speak. Even the locks of hair, which he worked on next, were so delicately carved that it seemed the slightest breeze would blow them free.

By noon Joshua was tired. His hair was hanging down over his face, which was lined with beads of perspiration. His body was covered with wood chips. He raised his hand and put it through his hair, and then stood up, holding the hammer and chisel in one hand. He enjoyed working on this project. Indeed, his enthusiasm for it inspired him to work with an intensity that didn't show when he was working on other pieces. It was as if he was doing the sculpture of a dear friend and wanted it to be perfect.

All that was left to do were the arms. Placing the hammer and chisel on the table near the grill, he went inside, humming a tune that was totally unfamiliar, and which didn't sound like anything of our age. But it was joyful and lighthearted, and one could imagine people dancing to it.

When he came back outside he was carrying a bag and had a towel thrown over his shoulder. He walked straight past the sculpture without even looking at it, out into the meadow. Reaching the pond, Joshua stripped and put his clothes in the water to soak. Then, walking into the water, he dived under and disappeared. When he came up he was far out in the middle and swam across the surface heading for the opposite shore. When he reached it he stood up and looked about, just drinking in the beautiful landscape.

Soon Joshua plunged into the water again and swam to the far corner and back. When he finished he went back to his clothes and, with a piece of soap he had brought with him, started washing and scrubbing them. After rinsing them out he hung them on the willow tree to dry in the hot sun. While he waited he went back into the water and swam until he was totally relaxed.

Then he came back to shore, got out of the water, dried himself, and put on his clothes. As he took them off the willow branch the thought of other willows long ago flashed across his memory: "By the willows of Babylon, there we sat and wept, when we remembered you, O Zion. There we hung up our harps; how could we sing in a foreign land?" The thought brought on a melancholy mood as his mind wandered back across the ages thinking of that lonely exile.

Joshua dressed quickly. It felt so good just walking with nothing on, but, then, human beings can't cope with the problems they create, so he adjusted his thinking and realized how good it was to put on fresh, clean clothes that don't stick to your body. The old robes, he thought, were a lot cooler, but their sheer weight was oppressive.

It was almost two o'clock when he headed back across the field. He still had to finish the arms of the statue.

When he reached the cottage he went out into the yard. He worked on the arms for almost two hours, giving them a form and a plastic look that made them appear like real limbs poised for action.

By four-thirty he was finished. He took the two arms, placed them in holes he had carved into the torso, and set the figure in an upright position on the ground. Then he looked at it from various angles. He touched up a few spots here and there with a small chisel, then glued the arms in place. After letting the glue set he sanded the figure from top to bottom and applied a dark stain. After an hour he applied a second, then a third coat, each time making the figure richer and more beautiful. Even though it took

Joshua a short time to complete his work, no one could say it was anything but a masterful, beautiful piece of workmanship. The strength of feeling and conviction in the expression on the face, the taut neck muscles showing the vehemence and insistence of character, the shape and positioning of the hands and fingers, with the left hand partially closed, clutching his breast, and his right hand gesturing with muscles tense made the figure appear alive.

In meditating on the statue one could easily sense the zeal and power of the man, and also the not so quiet desperation as he tried to bend the will of his listeners. The people at the synagogue would either be honored and delighted to possess such a powerful work of art or they would be offended by the message it so graphically delivered. Joshua smiled as he anticipated the various reactions. But it was his intention to deliver a message that could ill afford to be ambiguous: Moses insisting on a way to God that so many of his people resisted.

The figure was now complete except for the wax, which would give the stain a soft sheen. Joshua waited until the stain dried, then rubbed in the wax, making sure every crevice was smooth and clean. Then he picked up the statue, placed it upright on the table, and looked it over. He was proud of his work. He caressed the figure almost affectionately, as if it were the real Moses and not merely a piece of wood. Then, picking up his tools, he took them into the workshop and went out to clean up the yard and rest for a few minutes before preparing his supper.

Joshua's idea of rest was to look over his garden and pull a few weeds. The garden was growing nicely. There had been good growing weather so far, and all the gardens in the neighborhood were lush with healthy growth.

While Joshua was preparing supper a loud knock on

the front door interrupted the almost monastic silence of the cottage. Joshua wiped his hands, went to the door, and opened it. There stood Pat and Herm. Joshua grinned as Pat shot out loudly, "Hope we didn't come at a bad time. Herm and I thought we'd stop over to say hello."

"Come right in," Joshua said with a laugh. "It's never a bad time. I was just putting some things on for supper. If you don't mind my cooking, you're more than welcome to have supper with me."

"No, no. Our wives would kill us if we didn't show up for supper," Herm said apologetically but not too convincingly as Joshua proceeded to add more meat and vegetables to the pan. He got out a bottle of wine, a chunk of cheese, and a loaf of bread and prepared a snack while waiting for supper to cook.

"What brings you all the way over here?" Joshua asked the two guests between sips of wine.

"We had a party at Jim's last night," Pat answered, "and your name came up. Herm and I decided to stop over and visit you today. Also the guys wanted us to invite you to our parties from now on. They thought you'd have a good time. They like you for some reason or other. I don't know why," Pat finished good-humoredly.

"That's why we're here," Herm added, "to give you a standing invitation to our parties. We're having one next week, if you'd like to come."

"That's very thoughtful," Joshua replied. "I would be happy to go," but he added with dry humor, "Does Pat always come to the parties?"

Herm picked up the humor and came back quickly, "We invite his wife. She's a nice person, but he always comes along. We make him behave, so he's not much trouble."

Joshua enjoyed the friendly banter between these two men who had been friends since childhood and whose conversation would have been grossly insulting if spoken by someone else. But between these two, and the others in the group, it was just ordinary fun. If one didn't insult the other like this, the other would think he was mad at him. That's what Joshua liked about this whole earthy crew. They were crude at times, hotheaded, always shooting from the hip, but honest men you could trust, never phonies or two-faced, saying one thing to your face and something entirely different behind your back. If they gave you their word, you could count on it. They would stick up for each other against an army, and even if they lost they would at least lose together. Their wives were good women, long-suffering and tolerant to a fault of their husbands' loyalty and total, unspoken commitment to one another.

By this time they had already half finished their meal, but they were so engrossed in their conversation, as usual, that they hadn't paid much attention to eating.

"You know, Josh," Herm said, "you're a mystery. You've got everybody in town trying to figure you out. What is it about you?"

Before Joshua had a chance to answer, Pat jumped in. "Yeah, everyone thinks you're a real smart guy, and yet all you do is cut wood. It makes everybody wonder. If I'm not prying, were you ever a priest or something like that? You got class and refinement like you might've been a priest."

Joshua became serious. "I'm just God's son," he answered simply, without elaboration. "We're all that," Pat responded, "but there's something different about you. There's more to you than meets the eye, and that's what's got us curious. And yet you're a humble guy, and you act just like the rest of us, and maybe, in your own mind, you're not different from us. And that's what everybody likes about you. You don't have the slightest idea the impression you made the other day when you came walking down the street with that huge log on your shoulder. Everyone's still talking about it. They were not only impressed with the weight of the log, but that you're not afraid to work like the rest of us."

Even Herm was impressed that Pat got out so much of what everybody in town was thinking. He just sat back in his chair eating. Joshua sat on the step with his elbows on his knees. He looked very serious while Pat was talking and listened intently, realizing that Pat's question had struck at the heart of Joshua's identity. He knew there would be some whose simple faith would pierce the mystery surrounding his appearance, but it was important to keep the secrecy of his identity and his mission intact. Joshua didn't like being evasive. It was against his nature, yet he had no right laying bare truths that would not be understood and which were really no one's business. Those who should know would find out in their own simple way. They would gradually come to a realization and would then understand. He also knew there were some who could never understand. They would always be the ones who would, in the end, try to destroy. They could not be content to see goodness and enjoy its presence. They have to twist and distort and see evil in the simplest acts of goodness until, in the end, they have painted such a warped image in their own minds that they are really convinced that what they see is evil and have to purge it from their midst. That has been the fate of many good people throughout history. No, there was no way he could take the chance and tell them the naked truth.

But Joshua still listened to Pat, and when he finished he responded by saying, "Pat, in all truthfulness I am just myself. You will get to know me more and more as the days go by and, in time, you will come to understand what you have seen. And there are others who will understand, but not all. It has never been otherwise. This is because your faith is simple, and so is Herman's, and you see what others cannot see. All I do is bear witness to the goodness and love God has placed in creation."

Joshua had not talked this way before, and both Pat and Herman were taken back by the seriousness of Joshua's answer. But while Joshua was in the mood, they figured they'd ask him some more pointed questions.

"Josh," Herm asked, "what do you think of church and religion?"

"Real religion is in people's hearts, not in buildings. Jesus tried to teach this lesson once before when he told the woman at the well that the time was coming when men would worship neither on Mount Garizim nor in Jerusalem, but would worship the Father in spirit and in truth. Unfortunately, that lesson never caught on. Religious leaders always felt they had to organize people and structure the practice of religion in such a way that they would become the highly respected mediaries with God, and religion then became the practice of doing what religious leaders told one to do and deteriorated into the measurable observance of manmade laws.

"Religion doesn't have to be like that. Jesus taught that people are free, free to enjoy being God's children, free to grow and become the beautiful people God intended. But this is impossible in the presence of rigid authority that needs to control people's thinking and their free expression. Jesus would be very unhappy over the way many religious leaders enjoy exercising authority. He tried right up to the end to dispel that tendency by washing the feet of the apostles, telling them to be humble and serve rather than dominate and dictate, like pagans enjoy doing to their subjects."

Pat and Herm were not ready for all this, and they were quite surprised at the bluntness of their host. Yet he did not appear bitter, just honest and straightforward. They both agreed that what he said was right. Herm went a step further and asked what he thought about the man who had been their pastor for over twenty years.

"He's not a bad person," Joshua answered. "He just doesn't know how to love. He hurts without intending to because he knows only law and not love. The law is ruthless and unbending, and breaks people under its weight. A kind shepherd will put people before the law, like Jesus did. 'The sabbath is made for people and not people for the sabbath,' is the way Jesus put it."

When Joshua finished he took another bite and washed it down with a mouthful of wine. At about that time Joshua's animal friends appeared near the big tree in the yard, too timid to come closer. Joshua spotted them, put some food on his plate, and took it over to them. The two men enjoyed seeing the friendliness of the animals, how they came over to meet Joshua and climbed all over him when he bent down to feed them. "Look at that! Even the animals like him!" Herm said.

"Why wouldn't they? He probably feeds them every night," Pat said.

Joshua came back with the empty plate as the animals

walked away. "They're my regular guests," he said as he put the plate on the table.

"Hey, Josh," Pat said, "Phil said you were making a statue for the synagogue. Is that true?"

"Not exactly for the synagogue. Statues are not allowed, you know. I was asked to carve a figure of Moses for their social hall. In fact, I finished it just before you came. Would you like to see it?"

"I'd love to," Pat said.

Joshua got up to lead them into the workshop, which they hadn't seen before.

They were amazed when they went into the shop and saw the figure of Moses standing there. It was so real and lifelike.

"Can I touch it?" Herm asked.

"Go ahead," Joshua told them. They couldn't take their hands off the figure.

"It's beautiful," they both said. "You're a real artist, aren't you?" Herm said almost respectfully and with genuine awe at the masterpiece standing there before them. "You made that out of that big log you were carrying down the street?"

"In only two days?" Pat fired in quick succession and in disbelief.

"Imagine taking an old log like that and turning it into something as beautiful as this!" Herm said thoughtfully. "It's beautiful."

"Hey, look what time it is!" Pat said. "We'd better get home."

The men walked around the side of the house and Joshua accompanied them to the gate.

"I like that mailbox," Pat said as he rubbed his hand over the keel of the boat.

"Yes, it brings back memories," Joshua said almost absentmindedly, then smiled when they both looked at him.

"What do you mean 'memories'? You're hardly forty years old! They didn't make that kind of boat in your lifetime." Then he added in jest, "Maybe when Herm was a kid, but not you." They all laughed.

After they left Joshua went back into the house, not even thinking to lock the door, and after doing the dishes took a walk out in the backyard to relax for a few minutes. It had been a long day. People were getting to know him, and it was becoming increasingly difficult to control his schedule. He was fortunate to have gotten his figure of Moses finished before Pat and Herm came, because no matter how busy he was, he would have stopped everything to visit with them. He believed people were more important than schedules, and he would never make people feel uncomfortable by letting them feel they had come at a bad time. You only treat strangers or people you don't like that way. Friends are welcome anytime, and everybody was a friend to Joshua. That was another reason they felt drawn to him. They sensed he genuinely liked them, and they were flattered.

When Joshua was ready for bed he knelt down at his bedside, with his head in his hands, for the longest time. Tomorrow was to be an historic event, the first such encounter with his people in centuries. It just had to go well this time. Things were different now. They had experienced so much during the passage of time. Their mingling in with Christians, even though they were often treated miserably by them, couldn't help but give them a chance to see the beautiful aspects of Jesus' spirit and love of humanity. It had to rub off. He prayed intensely that things would go well. He hoped they would like his figure of Moses. Things have changed. In the past it would have been unthinkable for Jews to contract for the sculpturing of a statue, even of Moses. Putting it in the social hall rather than in the synagogue was merely a subterfuge to assuage their sensitivity to the commandment forbidding the fashioning of graven images. It was ironic that the prohibition came originally from Moses himself, whose figure they were now setting up in their midst. But perhaps even Moses would be pleased at the change in spirit of his people. As Joshua prayed he could sense the reaction of Moses and Elijah as they anticipated the events of the coming day. Joshua smiled, ended his prayer, and rolled into bed, exhausted but happy.

5

JOSHUA had hardly finished breakfast when there was a knock at the door. It was only five forty-five. When he went to the door and opened it there stood Phil, the manager at the mill. He had remembered Joshua told him to come on his way to work if he wanted to see the figure he was carving for the synagogue.

"Hope I didn't come too early," Phil apologized. "I was on my way to work and didn't want to miss seeing your masterpiece. I don't think I'd ever get a chance to see it in the synagogue."

Both men went outside and Joshua placed the sculpture on the table near the grill. The sun was filtering through the trees, and its rays looked like inspiration from heaven as they struck the figure. Phil literally gasped. "God, that's beautiful!" he said, picturing in his mind the lifeless log Joshua had carried out of the shop just two days before.

"You carved that from the log you bought the other day?" Phil asked Joshua, still finding it hard to believe.

"Yes, the same piece of wood," Joshua replied.

"You seem so casual and so ordinary, Josh. It's hard to imagine you as a real artist."

"Why should a person act any different just because he can carve a piece of wood? Talent doesn't justify putting on airs. Any ability we have comes from God, and our

48

recognition of it should make us humble, not arrogant. That's the mistake so many scientists make when they think they have created what God has given them the privilege to discover. In their smallness they use their discoveries as reason to question the very existence of the person who gave them their ability. That is the modern unforgivable sin. In their blind pride they put themselves outside the reach of God's saving grace, like the Sadducees and Pharisees of centuries ago."

Phil listened intently as Joshua spoke. He liked to listen to Joshua because there was a depth of wisdom that flowed from him that was rare. Yet he wasn't arrogant or patronizing. He just had a beautiful way of looking at life and everything in it.

"I know what you are saying, Josh, but I would think you'd be proud of a beautiful piece of work like that," Phil said.

"I am," Joshua reassured him, "and I fully enjoy my work, especially the pleasure in people's faces when they see something I made for them. Yes, I'm proud of my work, but I can also appreciate the beauty of soul in a humble person who has no other obvious talent than the humility to stand in awe of the gifts God has given to others. That gift is more precious in the eyes of God than many others, don't you think?"

Phil laughed. "The way you put it, how could I think otherwise? What you say is so kind, you make even me feel good. I have no talent at all, but I have always admired talent in other people."

"You are a good man, Phil. You have the kind of talent a father needs to appreciate his children and help them grow into the persons God intended. You will be proud of your children one day, in spite of all your worry and grief."

"Thanks, Josh. I needed that. Well, I had better get off to work. The men will be waiting for me. I think the statue is remarkable. The members of the synagogue should love it."

"I hope so," Joshua replied as he followed Phil around the house to the front gate. Joshua went back into the yard and brought the statue inside, then went out to take his morning walk.

He walked up the main street and down the side road that led out into the country. About two miles along the road was a patch of run-down shacks that were once houses. A group of poor people lived there, good people, no better, no worse than the rich people he associated with so freely. Some of them had just lost their jobs, others were chronic welfare cases. It made little difference to Joshua. But these poor people loved Joshua, and he particularly liked the children. They were simple and unspoiled, unlike so many children who are spoiled by having too many luxuries too early in life.

When Joshua appeared coming down the road the children would spot him and run out to greet him, grabbing his hands and throwing their arms around him. Usually he brought little things he had made, like yo-yos or little wooden dolls, or toys that rocked, or funny little figurines with comical faces. The children loved them, but they loved Joshua more, and even when he didn't bring anything they were still glad to see him. They loved the stories he told them, stories about life, and about using God's gifts to do good for others, and bringing happiness into others' lives so God could be proud of them. Each of them could be real miracles of God's love by overcoming the hardships of life and making something of their lives. He told them that God had a special love for them because they didn't have all the nice things that others had, and that they should never be envious or bitter because they didn't have a lot. He told them he had nothing and he was very happy because he could enjoy all the beautiful things in nature that belonged to God, like the sunshine and the beautiful skies, and the little birds and animals and flowers in the field. You don't have to possess them to enjoy them. Being free is the secret of peace and happiness. Always be free, and not possessing things is part of being free.

Of course when Joshua talked this way to the little children it was always when the parents were around. He knew they could understand what he was saying better than the children, but the children, too, would remember one day all the things he had told them, and it would affect their lives long into the future.

As Joshua approached the patch of houses a mutt broke the early morning quiet by his harsh, raucous bark. He was tied by an old knotted rope to his dilapidated dog house, so he couldn't go far. He looked harmless anyway. A screen door squeaked open and a child in undershorts appeared in a doorway at the side of the house. He spotted Joshua and went back inside screaming. In no time there was a crowd pouring through the doorway, some clothed, some partly dressed.

"Joshua, what are you doing up so early? We're just getting out of bed," a little girl called out to him.

"I'm taking my morning walk. Sometimes I take the other road. This morning I thought I'd walk up this way," he responded as he approached.

"Can you come in our house and have breakfast with us?" a sandy-haired boy with one sock on asked Joshua.

Joshua ran his hand freely over the top of the boy's disheveled head. "I've already eaten my breakfast," he replied, but all the children joined in, asking him to come into their house, one pulling on his right hand, another pulling on his left.

A middle-aged man appeared in the doorway. He had obviously just got up too. When he saw the children tugging at Joshua he laughed. "You're not going anyplace," he said, "you might as well resign yourself to having at least a cup of coffee with us. They're certainly not going to let you go."

Joshua laughed and let the children pull him into the house. In the kitchen was an old-fashioned stove, more valuable as an antique than as a heating unit. In the middle of the spacious kitchen was a long homemade wooden table with benches built into either side. The children all ran to their places at the table, the little ones vying with one another to sit next to Joshua, whom the father had directed to sit in his place at the head of the table. He sat on the bench next to Joshua. The children tried to sit near Joshua, but found it too hard to maneuver, so the tiniest one ended up with no seat, crying that he wanted to sit near Joshua. Joshua picked him up and put him on his lap as the child stuck his tongue out at his bigger brother, grinning with glee over his accomplishment.

A young-looking mother came out from another room, pinning up a large strand of her fading blond hair. She looked tired and worn for her young years, but smiled broadly when she spotted Joshua. Walking over to him, she bent over and kissed him. Joshua told her how joyful and radiant she looked so early in the morning. She blushed, but clearly enjoyed the compliment. People in her station don't receive many compliments, and she didn't know quite how to react, so she merely smiled a thank-you, then proceeded to ask if he would like a bowl of raspberries. She and the children had picked them the day before over across the field, and they have been waiting ever since to eat them.

Joshua's eyes widened. "I'd love some," he said.

All the while the children were in turns arguing, pushing, eating, and trying to get Joshua's attention, which was quite impossible while their father was talking to him. Only the little one sitting on Joshua's lap benefited. He kept picking the berries out of Joshua's dish. The father tried to stop him once or twice, but Joshua enjoyed the child doing it so much that he gave up.

"Mommy, I'm still hungry," one of the children cried. Margaret tried to ignore him, but then one of the other children chimed in and she became embarrassed. She apologized to Joshua for the children's rudeness and then told the children they would have to wait until she went to the store. The children knew, and Joshua also realized, they had nothing else in the house. Hank's unemployment check didn't go very far, and it would be another few days before they could get anything else at the store. That was why they went berry picking. They would probably do the same thing today. If the father was lucky, he might be able to get a couple of rabbits or woodchucks for supper for the next few days, which the kids really hated but ate anyway because they were so hungry.

Joshua didn't stay much longer. He wanted to get back home and get to work. He was expecting the people from the synagogue but didn't know what time they would come. He thanked the couple profusely for their generosity, kissed Margaret when he left, and shook Hank's hand. The children asked him if he had to leave and he told them he had a lot of work to do. He put his hand on each of their heads, silently blessing them, then walked out the back door. As he was leaving Margaret slipped a small package in his hands, kissed him again, and closed the door behind him.

Down the road a ways, Joshua opened the package and saw a small jar of raspberry jam. Tears appeared in his eyes. "The poor never have enough for themselves," he thought, "but always have enough to give away."

It was only nine o'clock when he reached home. He put the jar of jam on the counter and took the figure of Moses and put it on a small stool in the kitchen, where there would be plenty of light and it would be all set up for his visitors. With a soft cloth he rubbed the wax veneer until it glistened in the sunlight. He looked at all the folds in Moses' robe to see if he had missed anything. No, it was perfect. All he had to do now was wait for the people to come and pick it up. He couldn't wait to see the look on their faces when they first saw it. Their first reaction would tell the story and reveal their true feelings.

He didn't have long to wait. He had just executed the finishing touches when there was a knock at the door. His heart fluttered. He knew he shouldn't be nervous, but he was. He wanted so much for the people to be pleased with what he had done for them. These people were special to him and so was Moses. He answered the door and was faced by four well-dressed people, three men and a woman.

"Shalom!" one of the men said to Joshua.

"Shalom alechem!" Joshua responded, to everyone's great delight and with an accent that was authentic.

"Where did you learn Hebrew?" the woman asked.

"I learned it a long time ago," Joshua replied simply, then welcomed them into his house.

The woman was very attractive and well-dressed. She was wearing a light blue skirt and blue silk blouse. She had soft black hair and an olive complexion that blended with her greenish-blue eyes. Her thin features were further refined by a delicately shaped nose, arched eyebrows, and soft, sensuous lips. She was beautiful. Whenever Joshua looked at her he seemed pleased. She held out her hand as she was introduced. Her name was Marcia Klein.

The men were, judging from appearances, all businessmen, well-dressed, sharp-looking. One was wearing a gray pin-striped suit. His features were thick and earthy, accentuated by heavy black-rimmed glasses. He was introduced as David Brickman. The second man was thin and looked like an intellectual. He was dressed in a light tan suit with a white shirt and bow tie. His name was Aaron Fahn. The third gentleman was meticulously dressed, wearing a dark blue suit, perfectly tailored, with a custom-made shirt and a dark blue tie decorated with gold fleurs-de-lis. The tie was held precisely in place by a gold tie clip with a diamond inset. His shoes were Italian imports, made of alligator skin. A stunning gold ring on his right ring finger sparkled with a brilliant sapphire. On each side of the sapphire were three small diamonds arranged in a triangle. The man introduced himself as Lester Gold.

"We can't wait to see our masterpiece," Aaron said enthusiastically. Everyone agreed. After shaking hands and exchanging pleasantries, Joshua ushered them into the kitchen, where the sun was still streaming through the window. As they entered, the kitchen they were caught off guard, not expecting to see the statue there. But there it was, with the sun radiating the face of Moses as if he had just come down from the mountain. Marcia gasped with delight, "My goodness, that's beautiful!" then caught herself, as she had not intended to betray her feelings before she had made a thorough examination of the workmanship. But the surprise at coming upon the figure so suddenly had startled her, and she'd reacted before she realized it.

The reactions of the others were more measured. "I never imagined it would look like this," Lester said. Aaron looked at it carefully and showed obvious delight, then proceded to finger the nose, lips, and locks of hair. "This is a masterpiece," he finally decided. "I have never seen a work of art with such lifelike qualities. I wouldn't be surprised if it moved."

The woman, who was without doubt an artist herself, looked at the statue more critically. She asked Joshua if the figure was done in one piece. Joshua told her no. He could not get a piece of wood wide enough. The woman looked for the seams in the arms but couldn't find them. "Where did you attach the arms?" she asked impatiently, unable to find them herself.

Joshua walked over to the statue, looked under a fold in Moses' robe, and found the seam with difficulty. The seam didn't show, and even after showing the woman, she still could not see it. She shifted her gaze to the nostrils and touched the ear lobes, which seemed soft. She knew they couldn't be—they were made of wood. She looked at the eyes and the details of the eyelids. They were carved to perfection. Satisfied, she stepped back and looked straight into Joshua's eyes and said, "All I can do is thank you for the remarkable piece of art you have sculptured for our hall. It is one of the most beautiful pieces of art I have ever laid my eyes on. It will be a treasure in our midst."

Joshua beamed his simple and unconcealed delight and thanked her.

"By the way, Joshua," Lester said to him, "are you Jewish, by any chance? With a name like Joshua and the feeling you put into the statue—you must be!"

Joshua smiled and answered cryptically, "Yes, I am very closely related."

"We'd love to have you visit our synagogue if you'd care to. You'd be most welcome," Lester assured him.

"I'd like that very much," Joshua replied, "but it's quite a distance from here and I walk."

"That's no problem," Aaron said. "I'd be more than happy to pick you up. How about tonight, so you can see the people's reaction to your masterpiece?"

Joshua was thrilled. "That would be wonderful," he responded excitedly.

"I'll pick you up at six-thirty sharp," Aaron promised.

"I'll be ready."

Lester reached into his pocket and took out an envelope. He presented it to Joshua. "I feel embarrassed giving you a check for only a hundred dollars for such a beautiful work of art. The wood alone must have cost most of that."

Joshua accepted the envelope and thanked the group, assuring them that he was very happy to have done this work for them. He then picked up the statue and carried it toward the front door as the group followed.

As they walked to the sidewalk each one took his turn admiring the figure, saying how impressed the rabbi would be when he saw it. Reaching the van, Lester opened the door for Joshua to place the statue inside. He stepped in and placed the figure carefully on the thick blankets covering the floor.

As he stepped back out Marcia put her hand on his arm and urged him warmly and emphatically not to miss the services that evening. Joshua looked at her, smiled, and said, "I'll be there."

After they exchanged good-byes the van took off and left Joshua at the gate of his cottage. He closed the gate and went inside, but only to emerge a few minutes later and walk up the street toward the grocery store.

The owner welcomed him and asked what he could do for him. Joshua ordered a variety of meats and groceries and vegetables and fruits. He also picked out an assortment of candies. The man tallied the bill, which came to $72.56.

While Joshua was taking the money from his pocket and counting it, the grocer put everything into bags. Joshua paid the bill and asked the man if he would be kind enough to deliver the food to the family down on the back road. He knew the people Joshua was talking about and told him they were very nice people and he would be happy to do him the favor. To save the people's pride, Joshua wrote a note and put it in one of the bags: "With grateful appreciation for all your kindness, please accept this small token."

The proprietor promised to deliver the order himself so no one would know about it. He'd have it down there within the hour. Joshua thanked him and left.

AARON arrived promptly at six-thirty that evening, and Joshua was ready. His hair was neatly combed, with the semblance of a part on the left side, though his hair was too free to tolerate a perfect part. He had washed and pressed his pants and shirt, so he looked neat. He also wore a light sweater vest, which one of the women in the patch of houses on the back road had knit for him. It was brown, like the rest of his clothes, so he looked presentable, though no match for the elegantly dressed people who had picked up the statue earlier in the day. He was clearly a poor person by worldly standards. The sandals he wore were also plain but sturdily constructed to give good support to his feet.

Aaron parked in front of Joshua's cottage, right in front of the gate. As Joshua walked toward the car Aaron got out and met him on the sidewalk. He shook his hand and opened the door for him. Joshua seemed a little embarrassed by all the fuss, but accepted it graciously. It was a good twenty-minute ride to the synagogue, which was located in the city, but they had plenty of time to arrive before the service started.

It was a few minutes before seven when they got there. Aaron parked the car and the two men walked to the building together. They were cordially greeted by an usher who offered Joshua a yarmulke. He placed it on his head while the usher talked to Aaron. Aaron was obviously quite active in the congregation, which was clear from the greetings he got as he entered the vestibule.

Aaron introduced Joshua proudly as a friend and the artist who carved the figure of Moses for the hall—and, half-jokingly, as a potential member of the congregation. Everyone greeted him warmly.

Since it was almost time for the service to begin, Aaron brought Joshua into the synagogue proper. As Aaron had duties to perform, he asked Joshua if he would mind sitting by himself until he got back. He didn't mind at all. In fact, he felt right at home.

As soon as the rabbi entered, everyone stood and the service began. The rabbi welcomed everyone, especially guests from out of town, and in particular the special person who had designed the beautiful work of art for the congregation. A couple of people not too far from Joshua looked over at him and smiled warmly. Joshua blushed.

He became totally absorbed in the service, thoroughly enjoying the singing of the hymns, the psalms, which were so familiar and so precious to him. Being by himself, his voice stood out as he prayed unashamedly and sang with all his heart. He was not embarrassed or self-conscious, and when a few heads turned to see whose voice it was, he didn't even notice. His voice was a rich and mellow baritone, hearty and full of enthusiasm.

When the service ended and everyone filed into the vestibule on their way downstairs, a few people came over to Joshua and told him how much they had enjoyed his singing during the service. Joshua was really embarrassed but managed to thank them, blushing all the while. He didn't realize he was singing so loudly, he said. They told him he needn't apologize, his voice was beautiful.

In the vestibule the four people who had been at Joshua's house earlier in the day found him in the crowd and came over to rescue him. He was easy to pick out; everyone around him was well-dressed, while he looked like he just came in from the fields; and even though he had washed and pressed his clothes, he still was not what one would call elegant. In fact, he looked rather pathetic, though it didn't seem to bother him. He was not at all self-conscious about how he looked. No one seemed to care anyway. He was accepted for what he was and not for what he wore. And he was clearly a highly gifted individual who had a lot to give people. Those who knew him and grew close to him were proud of his friendship and cared little for what he wore. Besides, people were used to artists. They all seemed to dress strangely, so what he wore seemed quite normal for an artist. As a matter of fact, no one paid much attention to what he was wearing anyway. They were curious to see the sculpture, about which they had heard rumors all afternoon over the telephone.

Joshua's four companions flanked him as they walked downstairs together, telling him how impressed the rabbi was when he saw the figure. They were sure the congregation would love it.

When they entered the large hall they immediately spotted a group of people standing up front. In front of them was the figure of Moses, as if speaking to the crowd watching him, gesticulating and urging them with all the force of his mighty personality. As Joshua and his friends walked closer they could hear the comments. "What a powerful work of art!" "Do you think they really gave him as hard a time as his face betrays?" "I have no doubt they did. He was forever calling them names, like 'stiff-necked,' and 'hard-hearted,' and 'rebellious.' He certainly doesn't look like too patient a person from that statue."

The social committee had put out coffee, tea, and pastries on several tables in the room. The crowd began making its way to the food while some stayed on to look at the sculpture. At that point the rabbi came in with two women who were talking excitedly about something. One of the women, a Mrs. Cohen, was telling the rabbi she had been sitting near the visiting artist during services and had heard him saying his prayers and singing the hymns in Hebrew. The rabbi was skeptical, but the woman insisted and her friend agreed with her.

The rabbi tactfully ended the discussion by saying, "Perhaps he is Jewish. One never knows. If he is, I'll find out discreetly." That seemed to satisfy the women, and they settled down to a more relaxed dialogue as they walked closer to the statue.

As they approached Lester walked over to the rabbi, gently took him by the arm, and led him over to Joshua. The rabbi's face showed excitement, a departure from his normal composure. He had been pleased with the figure since he had first seen it earlier in the day, though he was overwhelmed with the power of the piece and did not miss the unambiguous directness of the message it conveyed. He could see it was not merely a representation of history, but carried a profound message to the modern Jewish community. He felt proud that the figure belonged to his congregation, and although some criticized him for erecting a "graven image," even in the social hall, he felt the figure's powerful message more than justified his decision. But as proud as he was of the statue, he did feel a certain annoyance, and, indeed, an embarrassment, that the statue should be delivering a message to his people and not just representing a plea to the ancients. However, his people were no different from the Hebrews of old and they, too, needed strong messages from above. Thinking of these things, the rabbi began to see in the statue all the messages he should have delivered but was afraid to, and his original annoyance over the statue's message was replaced with gratitude to the artist. At least by commissioning the artist the rabbi said through the artist's hands all the things he felt God wanted him to say. And his conscience felt soothed.

"Rabbi Szeneth," Lester said, "this is Joshua, the artist who carved the figure of Moses for us." Then, turning to Joshua, he introduced the rabbi as their esteemed spiritual leader. The two men shook hands.

"I am deeply grateful to you, Joshua, for the beautiful work of art you have created for our people. And you did create. It is not just a piece of wood, or even just a figure. It speaks loud and clear. I heard the message. I must admit that at first I didn't like what you said, but as I thought about it, I realized you were saying all the things I should have said but didn't have the courage to, and I am grateful. It is masterful," the rabbi said to Joshua.

"Thank you, Rabbi. You do me honor," Joshua said politely, then continued, "I want it to be a permanent testimonial of my love for my people."

"Your people?" the rabbi asked, surprised, remembering what the two women had been telling him.

"Yes, my people," Joshua answered, "I love them deeply."

"You are Jewish, then?" the rabbi asked.

"Yes."

"Then please come to our synagogue whenever you like and feel at home," the rabbi said, then quickly added, "I don't feel so bad now that the message in that figure came from one of our own."

Joshua chuckled as Rabbi Szeneth and the delegation accompanied him to the place where the statue was erected so they could all get a closer look. One lady glanced over at Joshua and, suspecting he was the artist, asked coldly, "Are you the artist?"

"Yes, I am," Joshua responded politely.

"Why does Moses seem so insistent? He looks almost desperate in his frustration."

"He was, after all, only a human," Joshua replied courteously, "and when you think of the task he had to accomplish, and the obstacles he faced daily for forty years, he couldn't have been any other way. What he endured would have broken a lesser man, so just looking frustrated isn't too unrealistic an expression, do you think?"

"I guess not, but it makes you feel almost guilty when you analyze it."

"Is that bad?" Joshua asked.

"Perhaps not, but when I look at a work of art I like to enjoy it. This one makes me feel uncomfortable. As a piece of art it is well done, and I'm sure most people will love it."

"I'm afraid many of our people are picking up the same impression I did," the rabbi said. "It certainly is not going to be ignored or be treated as just a decoration. And maybe it will be a constant sermon to all of us when we are tempted to stray from God's law."

By nine-thirty the social hour began to break up. Aaron came over to Joshua and asked him if he was ready to leave.

"I think so," Joshua replied, and the two men started to leave, saying good-bye to various people as they walked toward the front exit.

"What did you think of our congregation?" Aaron asked Joshua when they were leaving the parking lot.

"They seem like a friendly community," Joshua answered.

"Were you pleased with their response to your sculpture?"

"Yes, their reactions varied, as I thought they would. But I wanted to leave a lasting impression that would provoke a thoughtful response so the work would have a personal and lasting value for everyone. It is difficult, Aaron, for people to think in spiritual terms. The world of the senses is so vivid and so real. The world of the spirit is real to God, perhaps, but to human beings it is hard to believe it even exists. For someone to talk about it makes people feel uncomfortable, yet it is important that they be reminded of the spiritual world."

Aaron listened as Joshua spoke. He was captivated by what Joshua said, but also by the calmness of his manner. He wasn't critical of human behavior, but spoke as if the world of the spirit was very real to him. He moved with such ease through an area of thought that was a tangled jungle for most human minds. He let Joshua continue without even asking questions as he drove his luxurious automobile through the city streets and out into the country roads toward Auburn. The road looked like a long tunnel as the headlights cast beams far ahead under perfectly arched tree limbs.

The night was quiet. A cool breeze swept across the countryside as they drove along with open windows to breathe in the fresh air. Aaron was silent. Only Joshua spoke. Aaron was a worldly man, and Joshua mystified him. Aaron's father owned a steel factory, and Aaron, since childhood, had spent most of his time around the plant.

Now he was president. His father had retired over a year ago and placed his son in charge of the whole operation. Aaron was a kind person; he spent much of his free time helping the rabbi with the many administrative chores around the synagogue. He was not a particularly spiritual man but donated money to various charities. His fascination with Joshua came from his inability to understand a man with the intelligence of Joshua who walked through life as if material things were worthless. He knew Joshua could have any position in life he set his mind to, but he was content being simple and having practically nothing in the way of worldly goods. This confused Aaron, who was taught at an early age the value of material things. He had position, bank accounts, stocks, real estate investments, and a happy family life, all that is really important to a man.

Joshua confused him because he had none of these things and didn't even seem interested in them. And yet he was happy and peaceful, which Aaron was not. Underneath all the material bliss and the good life he was living there was an emptiness, a gnawing void that gave him no rest. His money and investments were like a child playing monopoly. It was a game that fascinated him, and which, at one time, was exciting but now bored him. In quiet, lonely moments the thought that that was all there was to life frightened him. Perhaps that was why he enjoyed being with Joshua. He felt a certain peace when he was with him and a calming serenity that he could not find elsewhere. Aaron wished he could be like Joshua. He wished he had his peace. He felt good and clean inside, as if walking through a new atmosphere with a rarified, enriched environment.

"Joshua," Aaron finally said, breaking his long silence,

"how did you become the way you are? Who taught you all the things you believe in?"

"Why do you ask?" Joshua questioned curiously.

"Because I can't understand how anyone could develop the vision of life that you have. It is so foreign to my way of thinking, and so different from the thinking of everybody I know."

"I experience what I believe, Aaron, so I know that what I believe is true."

"What do you mean, you experience it? How come I don't experience it?"

"Each person looks at life through a different vision. Three men can look at a tree. One man will see so many board feet of valuable lumber worth so much money. The second man will see it as so much firewood to be burned, to keep his family warm in the winter. The third man will see it as a masterpiece of God's creative art, given to man as an expression of God's love and enduring strength, with a value far beyond its worth in money or firewood. What we live for determines what we see in life and gives clear focus to our inner vision."

"Who taught you to think that way?"

"It is what I see. You could see it, too, if you could detach yourself from the things you were taught to value. They do not give you peace, nor do they give you lasting satisfaction. They leave you empty, and filled with a longing for something more."

"That's true, how do you know?"

"I know how man was made and understand what he really needs if he is to grow and find peace."

"Joshua, you are a strange man, but I really feel close to you. I would like to have you as a friend."

"I am honored, and I will treasure your friendship."

They had already arrived in the village. Aaron turned down Main Street toward Joshua's cottage. The streetlights were partially hidden in the foliage and the village looked quaint, like part of another age. The shadows hid from view all the modern additions to the village, showing only the shapes of buildings as they must have looked two hundred years before. There was a loneliness to the setting, and Aaron felt sorry for Joshua, living alone in the midst of everybody else's world but not being a part of all the joys and heartaches of family life. He couldn't help but feel alone.

CHAPTER 7

THE NEXT MORNING Joshua lay in bed, propped up against his pillow, as he listened to the patter of raindrops on the roof. It was restful, almost musical, as it fell in measured cadence against the window-panes. Joshua's mind seemed far away, and for the longest time he was completely absorbed in his thoughts, as if contemplating a vision of distant times and places. He left the house and walked up the main street to the diner.

Moe Sanders was walking toward the diner from the opposite direction. He was with Pat Zumbar and Herm Ainutti. "Hey, look who's comin'!" Pat cried out in a voice that shattered the early morning silence. Joshua couldn't help but hear, and since he was still almost a hundred and fifty feet away, he merely waved slightly and smiled at the unexpected recognition. As the men approached Moe greeted Joshua. "Good morning, men," he returned as the three men filed into the diner.

Part of the gang had already gathered, and the place was noisy with the clanging of dishes and silverware. The smell of frying bacon and eggs whet the appetite and put everyone in a good mood. "Look at Joshua's girlfriend beam now that Josh is here," Herm said jokingly about Mary, who owned the diner. Everyone knew Mary liked Joshua a lot. She couldn't keep it to herself, because every time

Joshua came in she would get all flustered and blush. It was a dead giveaway, and there was no way she could hide it. Joshua was aware of it and smiled at her with a knowing twinkle in his eye.

She continued to blush and stood at the place where she knew Joshua was going to sit.

"Good morning, Mary," he said to her affectionately, then added quietly, "You look bright and pretty on such a gloomy day."

She blushed even more. "I guess I always brighten up when you come in. At least that's what everybody tells me. What'll you have for breakfast?"

Joshua looked up at the menu hanging on the wall above the stove and, after pausing a few seconds, gave his order. "I think I'll have pancakes and sausages, with orange juice and coffee."

Mary wrote it down and then put a cup of steaming coffee at his place. The others watched with feigned envy. "Boy, look at the service he gets. Privileged character," Herm said good-naturedly.

Moe reached over the counter and grabbed the pot of coffee. He filled everyone's cup, saying as he did, "I guess we'll just have to wait on ourselves if we want to get anything to eat." Before Moe finished a waitress came over and finished pouring the coffee. "If you guys were as nice as Josh, maybe you'd get special treatment too," she said as she poured the last cup.

It was only a little after seven, and a Saturday morning, so the diner was half empty. Pat's voice dominated the room, making everyone else's conversation a mere undercurrent. "Heard you were at the synagogue last night," he said to Joshua. "What were you doin' over there?" There was no offense intended. It was just the way Pat talked.

Whatever passed across his mind automatically expressed itself.

Joshua had just taken a mouthful of hot coffee and almost choked on it over the abruptness of Pat's remark. The men laughed. "Yes, we had quite a time. You'd love it there," Joshua replied.

"I doubt it," Pat countered. "What were you doing at the synagogue?"

"I had been asked to carve a statue of Moses for them, so they invited me for the viewing. I felt quite at home. We're all Jews, spiritually, you know."

"I'm no Jew," Pat protested. "Maybe Moe is, his brother even looks like one."

Mary put the piping-hot pancakes and sausages in front of Joshua. She also put a few extra pats of butter with the order and winked, as if to say "Don't thank me; they'll make fun." Joshua smiled back. He had a warm spot in his heart for this good-natured girl. But Mary's gesture didn't pass unnoticed. Moe, who was sitting right next to Joshua, spotted the action and immediately complained, "See that. She even gives him extra butter. All the special treatment. She wouldn't do that for us, and we've been coming here for years."

Mary just ignored the noise and went about her business.

Herm had been unusually quiet, but finally came to life. "You go to our church, don't you, Josh?" he asked.

"Yes," Joshua answered.

"I thought I saw you there, but I never saw you go to Communion, so I didn't know whether you belonged or not."

"I do go to Communion in my own way, which would be difficult to explain," Joshua replied.

Pat picked him up on that. "What do you mean 'in your own way'? Either you go or you don't."

Joshua laughed and tried to explain. Fortunately he was saved by the waitress bringing out Pat's breakfast. That distracted everybody for the moment, but Moe remarked that he had seen Joshua going to the Methodist church one Sunday.

Joshua nodded. "I feel at home wherever people sincerely honor my Father." Simple enough, and everyone seemed satisfied, but whenever Joshua said "my Father," it was so different from the way people spoke, it made everyone wonder. Joshua spoke those words with such deep affection, no one knew whether it was just a peculiar mannerism or whether he felt a special relationship to God. For the next few moments it was so quiet in the diner that all you could hear was the clashing of dishes and silverware. Everyone was busy eating.

When the gang had finished they filed over to the cash register and paid their bills. Joshua left a generous tip under his cup before he left. Then they all walked outside.

The four of them walked down the street to the corner and took the turn to the back road.

"What possessed you to move out this way?" Herm asked Joshua. It seemed all they did was ask Joshua questions, but he didn't seem to mind.

"It's quiet and peaceful here, and the people are friendly," he answered honestly.

"You should be a politician," Moe said, "you know just what to say."

"You seem like such a happy person, even though you're all alone. Don't you get lonesome living by yourself?" Herm asked.

"No. I like being by myself. And I'm never really alone.

People stop in all during the day and talk to me or ask me to make things for them. And besides, God is with us all the time, and He's real, though we don't think of that very much."

"God's with everybody, but it still gets lonely. When you finish work at night what do you have to look forward to but an empty house?" Pat objected. "Wouldn't it be nice if you had someone to cook for you and take care of you when you finish work at night?"

"Yes, I suppose, but I'm quite content, and I enjoy cooking my meals and eating in peace, and taking a walk across the meadow. The beauty of nature is endless in its fascination. And it's so peaceful. Wouldn't you like to be by yourself at times?"

"You're damn right I would," Pat said, "especially when my wife's after me for something I did or for shooting off my big mouth. But, no, she's good. I guess I got it made."

"You seem to be an intelligent fellow, Josh," Herm said, moving to a serious vein, "what do you think of religion?"

"What do you mean by religion? Do you mean the way it is or the way God intended it be? There's a big difference, you know."

"Well, the way it is, the way the churches run it."

"God never intended that religion become what it is today. Jesus came to earth to try to free people from that kind of regimented religion where people are threatened if they don't obey rules and rituals invented by the clergy. Jesus came to teach people that they are God's children and, as God's children, they are free, free to grow as human beings, to become beautiful people as God intended. That can't be legislated. Jesus gave the apostles and the community as a support to provide help and guidance and consolation. Jesus did not envision bosses in the worldly sense. He wanted his apostles to guide and serve, not to dictate and legislate like those who govern this world. Unfortunately, religious leaders model themselves after civil governments and treat people accordingly. In doing this they fall into the same trap that the scribes and Pharisees fell into, making religion a tangible set of measurable religious observances, which is legalistic and superficial. In doing this they become the focus of religious observance rather than God, and it is their endless rules and their rituals rather than love of God and concern for others that occupy the people's attention.

"Customs and practices and traditions then replace true service of God, and these become a serious obstacle to real growth in the love of God. If people take religious leaders too seriously, they become rigid in their thinking and afraid to think for themselves, and must always refer decisions to the clergy. Even as adults they will still cling to the religious practices of their childhood, and when even ceremonies and mere customs change they panic, because they have been lead to believe these things *were* their faith. With that kind of mentality all growth stops, because growth means change and holiness means an ever-deepening understanding of God and what he expects of each one of us. If a person is not open to the inspirations of the Spirit, because it goes beyond what priests allow him, then even the Holy Spirit cannot work in him and he remains stunted. What is worse, he frustrates the work that God wants to accomplish in him. That's why the prophets of old were such great men. They had the boldness to see beyond the limitations of human religious traditions and provide guidance to God's people. They had the courage to break out of the sterile rigidness of religious forms, and incurred the wrath of religious leaders who hated them for this, and persecuted them, even killing some of them in the name of religion. Religious leaders constantly fall into this pitfall of wanting to control religion and people's practice of religion, and not allowing people to think for themselves for fear they will lose control over them."

Joshua's companions listened intently, spellbound by the intensity and insight of this man who was ordinarily so gentle and calm. When Joshua finished they were very quiet, unable to add anything or even ask a question. Finally Herm broke the silence, saying to Joshua, "You really feel strongly about this, don't you?"

"Yes," Joshua answered, "because Jesus never intended that religion do the damage to people that it has. It is horrible how many religious leaders have persecuted and even had people tortured for their beliefs. Even God respects people's freedom, and faith is a gift. People must believe freely. The function of religious leaders is to set an example, to draw people to God by their own deep faith and by the beauty of their personal lives, not intimidate people into sterile external observance. That is not religion. That mocks true religion.

"True religion comes from the heart. It is a deep relationship with God, and should bring peace and joy and love to people, not fear and guilt and meanness. And worship has meaning only when it is free. God is not honored by worship that is forced under threat of sin or penalty. Nor is God honored by subservient obedience to religious laws devoid of love. God is pleased only by the free expression of the soul that truly loves him. Anything less is counterfeit and serves only the short-term needs of religious institutions."

The men weren't ready for such a discourse, but they

were delighted to hear Joshua say what he did. In their hearts they believed what he said, but could never in a lifetime express it in the words he used. Moe reflected the feelings of the others when he told Joshua, "You should be a priest. We need to hear things like that. It is something we all feel, but we have never heard it expressed in church. In fact, I don't think any preacher would dare to speak like that. He'd be thrown out on his ear."

"Where did you get all your knowledge from, Josh?" Herm asked with almost respect in his voice.

"When you think about things and feel strongly, it is easy to express what you feel. Understanding God's love for us is something everyone should feel strongly about, and we should not allow anyone, even religious authorities, to take that from us."

The men were glad they took this walk with him. They had never talked like this with anyone before, and yet these were the things each of them thought about in the privacy of his own soul but never dared to share with anyone. They were delighted to hear Joshua speak so freely and unashamedly.

As the foursome started back to the village Pat asked Joshua if he'd like to come to the party he was having that night at his house. Joshua was delighted and readily accepted. Before long they reached Joshua's place, stopped at the gate for a few minutes, then broke up, each going his own way.

Joshua went into his house and, after relaxing for a minute, entered his shop and started to work. The sun was shining through the windows, bringing to life all the partially finished objects lying here and there around the room, some on the bench, others on little shelves, some resting on stools, or on the floor. Some were finished, though most were in different stages of production.

Since people were coming in shortly to pick up articles, Joshua knew where he had to start—the antique chair in the corner of the room, with the broken leg and the pieces missing from the back. The new leg and pieces were resting on the chair. He had made them at odd times during the week, when he wasn't working on the statue. They were easy to fashion, so they didn't take long. All he had to do now was sand them and glue them in place.

He finished that job by ten o'clock and set it aside. The next piece he took up was an old wall clock with beautifully carved molding around the sides, most of which was chipped or broken off. He stood the clock up against the wall behind the bench and wound it up so he could listen to the chimes. They were primitive but charming. They sounded almost like someone striking crystal. As the chimes played Joshua sat back on his stool and dreamily absorbed the mood created by the antique-sounding tones, his thoughts wandering off into a meditation on time and eternity and the ingenious invention of the clock to measure slices of time in an almost perfect relationship with the movement of the planets. He thought, with a twinkle in his eye, that few have yet grasped the reality that time is not real but only a figment, an illusion, that there is no past or future, only the present. The human mind invents the past because it can experience the present only in small, momentary slices. When the experience ends it is gone. To record the experience man invented time. We catalogue experiences and call them the past and place them in various time frames. To the human mind the future is a blank, a void. Though it is already present to God, it is not yet within the focus of man's experience, so it is called future. Will the mind ever be able to understand that the past is still present and that the future already is?

The chimes stopped and the abrupt silence broke Joshua's dreamy mood. He picked up the clock, looked it over, then set it on the bench and began to work on it. With a few deft movements of a tiny handmade saw, he cut off the broken decorations and laid them aside. He then drilled holes into the molding. The next step was more difficult. He had to recarve the broken pieces and make them look exactly like the damaged ones. It took time, but he seemed to enjoy this painstaking and tedious kind of work, which demanded perfection. One by one he recarved the broken pieces and drilled tiny holes in the back of each. Then, making equally tiny dowels, he dipped them in glue and inserted them into the holes. He then fit the decorations into place. It took a good part of the day, but the finished product was perfect, so perfect it was impossible to tell it had been repaired.

The day went by fast. Joshua interrupted his work only twice, once for lunch and again when an old couple came to pick up their antique chair, which turned out not to be an antique to them but simply one of the few chairs they still had in their house. They had sold off most of their furniture to pay bills, and this chair, along with a few other pieces of furniture, was all they had left. When they saw the chair all fixed their eyes widened with excitement. It was beautiful and sturdy. The old lady sat in it; it was solid and firm. Joshua smiled his own satisfaction. When the old man went to pay Joshua asked if they would do him a favor. He knew they were poor and didn't want to take any money from them, but he didn't want to hurt their feelings either, so he brought them out into the kitchen and asked the lady if she would teach him different ways to cook chicken. She taught him a couple of recipes and insisted on writing them down for him. While she was doing this the old man noticed the grill in the yard and gave Joshua a recipe he had for barbecued chicken. When they had both finished Joshua showed such obvious gratitude that, when he refused to take any money for fixing the chair because they had been so kind in helping him, they both felt as if they had done Joshua a favor and left the house happy. Joshua offered to carry the chair down to their house, but they wouldn't hear of it.

When they left Joshua watched them. They took turns carrying the awkward piece of furniture as they walked up the main street toward their house.

By four-thirty Joshua had finished for the day. It had been a long day and he had worked hard, and even if it was not hard work, it was tedious, and he was tired. The sun was still hot and high in the sky, so he decided to go and take a swim and maybe a nap. He had to go to the Zumbars' for supper, and as that would probably go on into the late hours, which he wasn't used to, he really should rest first.

THE WHOLE CREW was at the Zumbars' that night. Their small house could hardly contain the crowd, but that was no problem. They never stood on ceremony. If they wanted the whole gang over, they would invite the whole gang, and it was up to them to shift for themselves. They were used to "roughing it" at each others' houses. And this night was special. No one wanted to miss this occasion. Joshua had been too much of a mystery since he appeared in town almost three months ago. Though he seemed friendly enough, only a few individuals had had encounters with him, and he was known more by rumor than by hard facts about his real life. This party was a good chance to meet the real Joshua.

Joshua walked to Pat's house. It was a beautiful evening, a grand finale for a fickle weather pattern all day. Pat was standing on the porch talking to George Sanders, Herm Ainutti, and Charlie, the mailman, when Joshua approached. It was the mailman who noticed him first and cried out, "Hey, look who's comin'!" The others turned and loudly hailed his entrance, which embarrassed Joshua. He smiled and continued walking up to the house, greeting each one as they came over to welcome him. The mailman shook his hand, saying with a certain satisfaction,

"Welcome, buddy," as if he had prior claim to his friendship, since he had been the first to make his acquaintance.

They all ushered Joshua into the house, where there was already a crowd. For a brief moment everyone just stood and stared. Joshua's sharp eyes scanned the crowd, locking the impression of each one in his memory. He had seen most of them before, at least the men. Most of the women were strangers. Pat was so proud of his guest that he swelled up like a peacock as he introduced each one to Joshua, who just looked deeply into the eyes of each as if peering down into their very souls and greeted them warmly with a simple hello.

This was not a sophisticated group. What you saw was what they were, nothing was hidden. They were down-to-earth, good-hearted people who had played together as children, studied together as students, and now worked and socialized together as adults. When they were at gatherings like this there was no ceremony. People just stood up and walked around or went outside into the yard while eating or talking to one another. Some sat down to eat, but they were mostly the women. Most meals turned out to be buffet style whether they were planned that way or not. This particular one was planned that way.

Pat finally remembered to introduce Joshua to his wife, Minnie. She was a kindly, understanding woman, and was taller than Pat. Minnie also had a good sense of humor, and when her husband introduced her to Joshua as his wife she looked at Joshua and said good-naturedly, "Yes, for over forty years, and I don't know how I put up with it."

"What are you talkin' about? You got it made," Pat said in self-defense.

"I sure do," Minnie added.

Joshua smiled and said, "I can tell you two were made for each other."

"Let's get some food, I'm starved," Pat said as he ushered Joshua over to the table, where there were platters and serving bowls filled with all sorts of Italian pasta and meat dishes. Though not too many drank liquor in this crowd, they knew that Joshua drank wine, so they offered him a glass of homemade wine to see if he liked it. It had been made by a little man with a big soul, nicknamed Shorty. He used to be a boxer, and even though he was now in his sixties, he was still in good shape. He wasn't there that night, but had sent two bottles up for Joshua. Joshua tasted the wine, swished it around in his mouth, then looked at Pat and said, "Not bad at all. In fact, it's very good."

"You can thank Shorty for that. He wanted you to have it," Pat told Joshua. "You can take it home with you. Nobody here drinks it."

After allowing Joshua to talk to the women for a few minutes, the men started pulling him out into the backyard, where they were holding court. This was their big chance to ask Joshua all kinds of questions. Even though Joshua knew this was one of the reasons they were happy to see him, he realized they also had a genuine good feeling for him, so he didn't mind their intense curiosity.

"Josh, sit down here," Herm said as he motioned for Joshua to take the lawn chair next to him. Joshua walked over with the plate of food one of the women had dished up for him and sat down, trying at the same time to balance his dish and the glass of wine.

"Josh, tell the guys about your visit to the synagogue last night," Moe suggested.

"There really wasn't much to it," Joshua answered. "In fact, I felt very much at home. The congregation had mixed feelings about the statue I carved for them. Some thought the message conveyed by the figure was too graphic and critical of people of today. I suppose the work is vivid, but I intended to communicate a message and not just represent a dead figure from out of history. Most of the people seemed to like the work and they were very cordial and warm. They even invited me to come back whenever I liked, which I thought was very nice of them."

"It sure was," Herm said jokingly, "especially since they're not going to get rich on you."

"God never gave a penny to anyone, yet he enriches the whole world with gifts that cannot be calculated in terms of money," Joshua shot back none too gently. Herm seemed embarrassed over what he had said. He hadn't intended to hurt Joshua, but hadn't been able to resist making the remark.

"What do you think of the Jews, Josh?" Pat asked. "They still think they're God's chosen people. How long are they going to push that line?"

"They *are* God's chosen people," Joshua answered. "God has no favorites. He blesses all equally, but chooses everyone for a different work. The Jewish people were chosen for a special work, to be prepared for the coming of the anointed, so they would recognize and accept him when he comes and give him to the rest of the human family. That Jesus was born from the Jews is an honor that can never be taken from them. They still share that glory, a glory that they will one day realize. Unfortunately, Christians have not helped. By their cruelty and intolerance they have kept Jews away from Jesus and will one day have to answer for it."

No one had heard Joshua speak like that before. It was with an air of authority, and not like the congenial stranger they had come to know. But he was not offensive in what he said, nor in the way he said it, although he left very little doubt as to how he felt. The men, sensing this, backed off.

At that point a young man came walking up the path. He was a priest. He was wearing his clerical garb but no hat. He looked too young to be already balding, but he was still a good-looking man. Jim noticed him first and remarked, "Oh! Here comes Father Pat."

The crew turned and boisterously greeted the priest. As he approached he seemed a little unsteady. Pat got up and gave him his chair, telling him jokingly, "Here, Father, sit down here. You need it more than I do." Pat sensed the priest had been drinking and that he would feel more comfortable himself if the priest were sitting.

Father Pat sat down, thanking Pat as he did so. As soon as he sat back in the chair he looked over at Joshua, who was looking directly at him with a look that seemed to pierce his soul. The priest lowered his gaze momentarily, feeling a slight embarrassment in the stranger's presence.

"My name's Joshua," Joshua said to break the ice and make the priest feel more comfortable. As he did the two men reached out to each other and shook hands. "Father Pat," the priest said, "pleased to meet you."

Again their eyes met. This time the priest could not take his eyes off Joshua. It was as if he had been hypnotized. The priest's instinctive analytical sense saw something more in Joshua than just a mere stranger. He noticed the kindness in his eyes, and the sadness that came from being hurt, but a sadness unspoiled by bitterness or cynicism. He felt in his handshake an extraordinary strength that belied the apparent delicacy of his appearance. He had to force himself to keep looking at Joshua because he could tell Joshua's eyes saw more than just the surface. He knew Joshua was looking into his very soul, but he could not see criticism in his look. He saw a warm and gentle affection radiating from his glance and felt drawn to him immediately.

As the priest was analyzing Joshua, Joshua was doing the same thing to the priest. Priests can be a critical group, wary by experience, and frequently selfish, conditioned to be this way, perhaps, by the loneliness of their lives. Some priests are haughty, and look upon people as beneath them, as subjects to be kept in their place or told what to do. But Joshua saw none of this in Father Pat. On the surface he saw a man who liked to drink, but underneath a man almost overwhelmed and frightened by life, a man desperately lonely but struggling hard to observe the kind of life that was expected of him. Joshua could tell he sincerely loved people and enjoyed making them happy and doing nice things for them. Joshua had spotted him coming up the sidewalk long before the others had and noticed the children running over to him and grabbing his hands, happy to see him as he handed out little things he took out of his pockets. "Here was a real priest," Joshua thought, "a man after the heart of God, in spite of his drinking." Joshua's eyes, and the faint smile on his face, betrayed the love he immediately felt for this frightfully vulnerable man of God.

This whole exchange of glances took but a brief moment, which was unnoticed because everyone was too busy talking and vying for the floor.

"I'm glad you could come," Pat said to the priest. "We wanted you and Joshua to meet each other. What'll you have to eat, Father?"

"A glass of scotch with ice and soda," the priest said with a grin.

"Hell, I was going to get that anyway," Pat said, then added, "But what'll you have for a chaser—ravioli, lasagna, or sausage and peppers?"

"Lasagna sounds good," the priest answered as Pat entered the house, letting the back door slam behind him.

Father Pat Hayes was the assistant at the local Catholic church. He had come to town less than a year ago and almost everyone in town had taken to him immediately. His warm personality and engaging sense of humor put people at ease and they enjoyed being with him. Since they liked him so much, his drinking problem was easily over-looked. Father Pat was a far different kind of person from the pastor, who was a humorless, pompous man who could rarely say anything that didn't have a sarcastic edge to it. He was very conscious that he was pastor and thoroughly enjoyed being administrator over this rather widespread territory and every Catholic in it. He even treated Father Pat more as an altar boy than a highly intelligent profes-sional with a much finer mind than his own. Father Pat's weakness left him vulnerable to chronic verbal abuse from the pastor, who seemed to be almost happy his assistant had a problem so he could give vent to his sadistic delight in humiliating him. The pastor treated the parishioners the same way. He was sole master of his parish and every-one in it. His sharp tongue kept everyone in his place. No one dared to cross him for fear of becoming the target of his cutting sarcasm. The spiritual state of the parish seemed to be of little concern to anyone except Father Pat. This was why the whole parish rallied around him, which totally exasperated the pastor.

Attending parish parties, like the one this particular

night, was Father Pat's escape. Life in the rectory was intolerable. Supper was formal and joyless, and during each meal both sat in silence, and on the rare occasion when there was talk, it was about parish business. This was difficult for Father Pat. He came from a happy family and was used to good-humored banter. He wasn't a spoiled boy, so he learned at a young age how to get along with people. But no matter how hard he tried, there was no way he could develop a pleasant working relationship with the pastor. The fact that he was clearly more intelligent than the pastor didn't help matters.

Pat brought out the priest's supper and sat down near him on an old tree stump, which Minnie used as a planter. "How's our pastor?" Pat asked cynically. Everyone knew Father Pat's life must be hell, and even though he was loyal to the pastor and never talked about him to the parishioners, the people knew and joked with him about it. The priest would just laugh occasionally when someone hit the mark.

Joshua sat and listened intently to the conversation, picking up odds and ends and putting the pieces together to form a rather clear picture of the spiritual state of the Christian community. At one point George came over and asked Joshua what he thought of their parish. As usual, Joshua was honest and blunt.

"As I said this morning, Jesus' care is for people, not for the clergy's need for authority. Jesus preached a message of freedom, the freedom of God's children. Religious leaders should help people understand life and enjoy being God's children. They must resist the temptation to run the parish as a business and lord it over the people like the pagans do. Jesus never intended to start a business, but to lay the foundation for a closely knit family of people caring

for one another. As it is, the Church has become a structure superimposed on the life of the people, and the people
are not really allowed to be part of it. Their role is just to
support the structure. In a real community of Christians
the people are the heart of the community. They are allowed to live freely and plan their own lives as Christians,
and to build up their own lives as God's people. The pastor
is for them a gentle guide, offering advice and counsel and
direction when needed. There is a genuine love that in-
spires a community like this. That is what Jesus intended."

Father Pat sat listening with a look of awe. When
Joshua finished the priest asked him how he knew so much
about the Church and the Christian life. Joshua just smiled.
The priest told Joshua that what he said was beautiful but
a dream that could never become a reality. "Priests are too
stuck on their own authority to allow the people to be free
and to function as mature Christians," the priest said.
"There was one priest, a beautiful person, who tried to
set up a Christian community styled after the pattern you
just described, and the bishop himself took the priest out
and replaced him with a priest who would get the people
back in line. What the Church preaches and teaches is
one thing, what the Church officials will allow is an entirely different matter. They become very nervous when
they see the people having too much freedom to do things
on their own. The Church is great on preaching justice
and love, but they are also among the worst violators."

Father Pat usually didn't mouth off like that, but Joshua's insight into the life of the community had unleashed
the priest's pent-up frustrations and he poured out, for the
first time, his own feelings about the Church. The little
group sitting around was taken aback but glad to see Father
Pat expressing such strong convictions. He hadn't done

that before, and people were getting the impression he was just a nice guy who liked to sip scotch and tell jokes. This outburst revealed a more serious side of his personality, a facet, perhaps, that expressed his real self, which was never allowed to surface in his work as a priest.

Joshua listened as the priest spoke and agreed that priests exist to serve the people, but they, too, frequently would rather rule them instead. Unfortunately people tolerate this because they are afraid of incurring the priest's wrath. The problem seems to be just the opposite with the Protestant churches. There the problem ministers face is too much control by the people, so the minister is often afraid to preach the real message of Jesus and compromises his ministry so he can keep his job.

The conversation gradually drifted to lighter topics. Father Pat told a joke about a contractor who was dying. The man's wife asked the parish priest to visit her husband in the hospital and try to put him into a more spiritual frame of mind. He certainly wasn't prepared to die. The priest went and talked to the old man. In the course of the conversation the priest suggested the man make a donation to the church in atonement for his sins. The church needed a stained-glass window. He even promised to allow the man to inscribe on the bottom of the window anything he liked. And this perpetual memorial would cost only ten thousand dollars, which, after all, wasn't much for a man of his great wealth. At that point the doctor came in and started making out the bill for taking care of the patient for the past two months. The bill came to almost fifty thousand dollars, at which the poor old man almost had a stroke. But realizing the end was near, and he couldn't take the money with him, he decided to oblige the two men.

Asking for his checkbook, he wrote the check for the doctor. Then, while writing the check for the priest, he reminded him of his promise to allow him to inscribe whatever he liked on the window. The priest reassured him. The old man then told the priest in a firm and steady voice just what he wanted: "In honor of Patrick J. Murphy, who died like Christ . . . between two thieves."

Everybody laughed at the priest's ability to poke fun at his own profession. For the rest of the evening the conversations stayed in a light vein. Joshua went inside and spent time talking to the women. They were thrilled at his interest in their families and felt proud when he praised them for the good job they did at keeping their families so close and preserving such a healthy spirit in the neighborhood.

Joshua left the Zumbars' at close to eleven o'clock. Father Pat was standing near the door when he left, his scotch in hand. He was in a jovial mood when he said good-bye to Joshua, promising to stop over to Joshua's house after his last Mass tomorrow. Then he told him, with a twinkle in his eye as he looked at the glass of scotch, that he could see Father Pat was deeply spiritual. The priest smiled good-naturedly at the subtle dig and watched Joshua as he walked down the steps to the sidewalk, wondering what kind of a man Joshua really was. His priestly intuition told him that he was not just a simple wood-carver. He'd find out tomorrow when he had a chance to talk to him alone.

9

THE SUN'S RAYS shimmered through the needles of the tall pine tree overhead, and the grass glistened with dew as Joshua walked through the meadow, deep in thought. Sunday morning was quiet in Auburn. No noisy traffic broke the peaceful silence of the Sabbath rest. Sunday should be that way everywhere so people could give their wearied souls a rest from the nerve-shattering noise of their workdays. The quiet of nature is God's tranquilizer.

From the village a melancholy church bell called out across the fields for people to come to worship. Joshua returned from the fields and walked down the main street to the Catholic church. He had been to the Presbyterian church the week before, which he found a very proper place and the people well-dressed and polite, although they weren't overly friendly. A teenaged boy had sensed Joshua's embarrassment and introduced himself to make him feel welcome. After the service the minister had politely suggested that Joshua wear clothes that were more formal to the worship service, since it was God's house. Joshua told him these were the only clothes he had and suggested God was more concerned about the adornment of his soul. The minister was a little annoyed at being preached to but said nothing and turned to the other people standing nearby.

In the Catholic church he got lost in the crowd. The sheer number of people blurred styles and fashions, and a stranger could remain a stranger in the sea of faceless people. Joshua walked in with the others, smiled at the elderly, distinguished-looking usher in the threadbare suit, and took a place in the last pew.

His eyes scanned the interior of the church, noting in a few swift glances every detail of the structure and decorations. He looked momentarily on the statue of the Virgin Mary and smiled ever so faintly, reflecting pleasure and understanding humor at the same time. He then knelt down, rested his elbows on the pew in front of him, and buried his face in his hands, resting his head against the tips of his fingers. He stayed that way the longest time, even after the priest began Mass. It wasn't until everyone sat for the sermon and the woman in front of him hit her head against his arms that he became aware of what was going on and sat down.

Father Pat was offering the Mass. He looked remarkably recuperated from the party and was speaking eloquently. He felt at home in the pulpit. He liked people and preached to them from his heart. He enjoyed sharing his own feelings about God and Jesus and about life. He seemed almost to caress the congregation with his warmth, and the people responded. There was hardly a person in the parish who didn't like this kindly, gentle man, except for a handful of individuals who seemed to delight in finding fault with every priest who came to town. But no one could criticize him for his sermons. They were masterpieces of clarity and simplicity. This particular morning he was talking about the carefree quality of Jesus' life-style and that the central point of Jesus' teaching was the freedom he came to declare to mankind. It was that announcement of freedom which amounted to a declaration of war against the religious structure of Israel that got him into trouble. No one felt comfortable with what he preached except the people. They loved him, and it would be no different if he came back today. He would preach the same message, and religious leaders would respond the same way, except they might be more subtle than resorting to crucifixion.

The priest noticed Joshua sitting in the back of the church and was briefly distracted, but not long enough for anyone to notice. He caught himself and continued speaking, every now and then looking over at Joshua, trying to see his reaction. The priest went on to tell the people they should take this message of freedom to heart and should enjoy being the children of God and should feel free. They should trust God and believe Him when he talks about the birds of the air and the flowers of the field and not worry about what they are going to eat and drink or what they are going to wear. The sermon was beautiful, and everyone was moved by its simplicity. Even Joshua seemed to be extremely pleased and slightly nodded his head in approval at a couple of points.

The priest finished his sermon and went back to the altar to continue the liturgy. Joshua watched the priest attentively and was distracted only when the usher came by with the collection basket. Joshua lowered his head and the usher passed him by. During Communion time he knelt, and again became totally absorbed in his thoughts.

At the end of Mass, Father Pat went to the back of the church to greet the people. Whenever *he* said the Mass the crowd hung around outside talking. As they walked past him they told him how much they enjoyed his sermon and said how beautiful Jesus must have been. When Joshua went past he shook hands with the priest and, with a broad smile, congratulated him, telling him, "One would judge, by your sense of intimacy with Jesus, that you knew him personally."

"I think I do," Father Pat retorted, then reminded Joshua he would be down to his place later on.

"I'll be waiting," Joshua replied.

A few ushers were standing around the priest. He introduced them to Joshua. The men said they had heard a lot about him but imagined him to be a much older man. They were happy to meet him. After exchanging pleasantries they parted, Joshua walking down the street while the others went back into the church.

On his way home Joshua stopped at the bakery. He couldn't resist the smell of fresh bread that filled the air on Sunday mornings. The baker was a high-strung individual but a hard worker. He was sliding the huge wooden paddle back out of the oven. On it were four fat loaves of freshly baked bread. He gave one to Joshua, who picked up a bag and put the bread in it himself, then paid the baker and left. When he got outside the store he opened the bag and tore off a big chunk of hot bread and began eating it, tucking the rest of the loaf under his arm.

The rest of the morning went fast. Joshua enjoyed Sundays. He could walk in the meadow and watch the animals, who were no longer afraid of him. Occasionally he would take bits of food with him to pass out to them when they came up to him. He didn't walk too long this morning. It was already getting late.

When he got back to the house there was a frantic knocking on the front door. He opened it and was surprised to see Margaret, Hank's wife, carrying her little daughter in her arms. It was the little girl who always ran out to meet him when he walked down the back road. The mother was beside herself.

Joshua took them inside and asked the woman what had happened. Between sobs she tried to explain. She said her daughter was dying and pleaded with Joshua to help her. She knew he was a good man and God would listen to him. Would he please help her? The girl had been getting headaches and high fevers. The mother gave her aspirin, but it didn't help. She kept getting worse, sometimes becoming unconscious.

"Did you take her to the doctor?" Joshua asked.

"We have no money."

"What about the hospital?"

"We have no insurance either."

Joshua told the mother to sit down, taking the child from her and sitting down himself. He looked down at the girl, who could barely open her eyes. She looked up at Joshua and smiled faintly, then seemed to become unconscious. She lay almost lifeless in Joshua's arms, pale, her left arm hanging limp as Joshua held her close to him. He remembered her running out of the house in her underpants to greet him, grabbing his hand and holding it tightly. She really loved Joshua.

"Can you please help her?" the mother pleaded frantically.

Joshua looked at the girl, then looked up at the mother, who was sitting at the edge of her chair, tears streaming down her drawn cheeks. "Woman," Joshua said, "you have such faith. How could God not listen to you?"

Joshua couldn't stand seeing people in such hopeless straits. He told the woman to trust God and take her daughter back home. She would be better before they arrived there. "God has heard your pleas, and your great faith," he told her. "So don't worry. Your daughter will be well. Just give her a lot of liquids for a day or so until she feels like eating again. She'll be all right."

The woman had complete trust in Joshua. She thanked him and took her daughter in her arms and walked out the front door, carrying the child all the way up the street. As they disappeared around the corner the girl opened her eyes and looked up at her mother. "Why are you carrying me, Mommy? I can walk."

The mother cried for joy. "Are you sure, honey?" she asked the child.

"Yes, Mommy, let me show you."

The woman put the girl down and she stood up straight and firm, but she was still pale and weak. Margaret felt the child's forehead. There was no sign of fever. She asked her if her head ached. It didn't. The mother threw her arms around the child and cried out loud for sheer joy. Then the two of them walked down the back road together, holding hands.

It wasn't long after Margaret left that Father Pat came over. He was dressed in casual clothes, with a friendly grin on his face.

"Come on in, Pat," Joshua said, glad to see him.

"This is a nice little place you got," the priest said as he looked around.

"Nothing pretentious," Joshua responded, "just enough to suit my needs."

"I like it," the priest said.

"Have you eaten yet?" Joshua asked.

"No, we don't eat on Sunday at the rectory. It's the cook's day off."

"Will you have lunch with me?"

"Okay, I am hungry," Father Pat answered.

The two men walked into the kitchen. Joshua pulled a chair away from the table for his guest to sit down, then went about stirring the pot of chicken soup. It was much the same meal as when the mailman came except for chicken breasts, which he had roasting on the grill in the yard, and a bowl of salad.

Joshua served the soup, then the rest of the meal. The two men didn't waste much time getting into an involved discussion. That was why the priest had wanted to come in the first place. Joshua poured two glasses of wine, which they sipped while eating. He left the bottle on the table in case his guest wanted more.

The two men enjoyed talking to each other. Father Pat was a ready talker and lost no time telling Joshua all the rumors about him in town, needling him when he finished the list. "You couldn't possibly be as bad as all the rumors I've heard. That's why I wanted to get to know you for myself."

Joshua laughed loudly. He knew he was the object of mystery and sort of enjoyed it. Not lost for words himself, he retorted with the same good nature, "You don't do too badly yourself, you know."

"Oh, don't I know it," the priest responded. "I guess I do keep them guessing. And my drinking doesn't help."

Joshua said nothing, just continued eating.

"I hear you have your own business, Josh," Father Pat said.

"Yes, it's not much. Just enough to pay my bills. I'll never get rich on it."

"What do you do?"

"I make things out of wood. Sometimes people bring in broken furniture. Sometimes they order pieces like lampstands or figurines."

"I heard about the statue of Moses you made for the synagogue. I thought Jews weren't allowed to have statues."

"They're not, but they thought it would be all right if they put it in the social hall rather than the sanctuary."

"I heard some were a little upset with the bluntness of the message in the statue," the priest said.

"I know, the rabbi told me as much."

"You know, Joshua, you're a strange fellow. You're not just a wood-carver. You have too much depth and understanding of things to be content to just carve wood. I almost get the impression you've been this way before," the priest said, looking intently into Joshua's eyes as he said it, trying to pick up the slightest change in facial expression. "You have such a beautiful attitude toward everything. When I was speaking about Jesus this morning in the sermon, I couldn't help but think of you. You seem to have picked up the real spirit of Jesus and adapted it perfectly to your own life. You're the only person I know who has done that. In most Christians, even good ones, their imitation of Jesus is just that, imitation. They zero in on one trait of Christ and practice that till it becomes almost a caricature. But you live his ways with such ease and grace. I don't think even he could be much different from you if he were to come back."

Joshua did show a trace of discomfort and started to blush.

"I embarrass you," Father Pat said. "I'm sorry, but I couldn't help telling you that because you are a living example of what I try to preach, and it's frustrating at times. When I met you I felt I had met the living ideal of what I had talked about so often. I wish I myself could be more like what I preach. I try, but it's hard."

"You're a good priest, Pat," Joshua reassured him, "but

don't allow yourself to get discouraged. Everyone has im-
perfections. That's the way God made them, and as long
as people are striving to love God and care for one another,
they are pleasing to God. Perfection is more a process of
striving than a state to be attained, so one's perfection is
measured not by success in attaining a measurable goal but
in attitudes constantly changing to ever more perfectly
reflect the mind of God."

"That's what I like about you, Josh. You make even
the most profound things simple. But what I can't understand is where you got such marvelous insight into things
most people don't even give a damn about. Where did you
learn it? Your whole life seems to be so finely attuned to
God and nature that you walk through life as easily as a
spring breeze floats through a forest full of trees."

Joshua continued to sip his wine. "I guess I just do a
lot of thinking. I try to understand people and things and
spend so much time alone that it gives me the peace and
quiet to sort things out and put all of life together so it
has meaning. That is the one thing most people don't take
the time to do, and it is necessary if you are to find meaning
to life."

"You know, Josh, I drink a lot. I wish I didn't, but I
get so lonely, and living in the rectory with the pastor isn't
easy. Sometimes I feel I'm not really cut out to be a priest,
yet I feel so strongly called to the priesthood. I love the
work. I love people. But I want so much to have a family
and I feel that my whole spiritual life needs the support
of a woman and a family if I am to grow as a person. I
don't feel I have the gift of celibacy. I even have a friend
I feel very close to and I feel guilty about it. Is it possible
that God can give the call to the priesthood but not the
gift of celibacy?"

"You have just answered that for yourself, Pat. Only the individual knows to what God is calling him. No one can dictate a calling or demand a gift that is not there. If God gives the call to the priesthood, but not the gift of celibacy, then others must respect what God has done and not demand more. Otherwise they will destroy what could be a beautiful work of God."

"But what if I know I have a call to the priesthood and also know just as strongly that I need to love someone who will love me and support me in my work? This need is so distracting that I cannot ignore it without it destroying me. It makes it almost impossible for me to do my work." Tears began to well up in the priest's eyes.

Joshua reached over and put his arm around the priest's shoulders and told him, "You are a good priest, Pat, and God has called you. You cannot compromise that. If my Father has not given you the gift of celibacy, that is his business, and your superiors should respect that. Tell the bishop and insist that he take you seriously and help you solve your problem. The Church must respect the way the Holy Spirit works, especially in the souls of priests, otherwise she will destroy her own priesthood. What Jesus has made optional, the Church should not make mandatory."

"But the Church will not allow priests to marry," the priest insisted, still pushing his point.

"Then you must struggle for change."

"But what about myself and my own situation? I want to be a good priest."

"Just try your best. God always understands if you try. Even if you fail, God still understands. But be careful not to shame your priesthood or damage the people's faith. If your conscience forces you to make a decision, God will understand. Doing the work of Jesus can be accomplished in many ways, and marriage is no obstacle to that work, and often, if a woman is spiritual, she can be a great help and inspiration. There are also many other Christians who will need you and accept you. But do not be impetuous. Sometimes God works slowly and may want you to suffer the pain of loneliness right now so you can better understand the loneliness of others and be a better priest. It may be that in time God will free you from that pain, so be patient, Pat, and walk close to Jesus. When you are sad walk out into the meadow, and on the upper meadow you will find Jesus. He will meet you there. Talk to him and let him guide you. He promised, you know, and I promise you too."

"Joshua, I can't help but feel God speaks through you. You make me feel so much at peace. As I said before, for you everything is so simple. Even now you have answered something that has troubled me for years, and finally I see clearly. Thanks, Josh."

"I'm glad I helped," Joshua said.

By this time both were finished. Joshua started cleaning the dishes. The priest dried them. Afterward they went into the backyard. Joshua showed Pat the garden and pulled a batch of tomatoes that were beginning to ripen. He also picked some cucumbers and piled them in his arms as they both walked back into the house.

As Joshua was putting the vegetables into a bag, Father Pat asked him if he had any family nearby.

"My family have all passed on, I'm the only one remaining," Joshua answered casually as he continued putting the tomatoes into the bag.

"Josh, I hear you've been attending services at the various churches and I'm a little confused. I thought you were Catholic," the priest said curiously.

"I look upon all the churches as one family. I know God has no favorites. Religious leaders of each church feel their religion is the true religion. God doesn't view religion as structures. He loves people, and where people are trying sincerely to serve him and love one another, God is with them. God laughs at petty rivalries and ignores arrogant attitudes that make people think they are first in God's eyes. He looks upon all Christians as members of the same family who have never learned to get along, and who, like the apostles, are continually struggling for primacy. Each group of Christians expresses something different in what Jesus taught, but none of them reflects completely the spirit of Jesus.

"The Catholic Church shows a beautiful tenacity to the precise letter of Jesus' teachings, but it has missed the message of freedom that was so essential to Jesus' spirit, and it has done shameful things to enforce the observance of the letter of the law in its devotion to dogma. That was what the chief priests and the Pharisees did in their time. They failed to see the main thrust of Jesus' life, which was to free the human spirit from the theological prisons that religious leaders construct for people. Fidelity to the teachings of Jesus cannot be forced by threat of punishment. Jesus never wanted that. He wanted the human spirit to find him in freedom and to embrace him joyously and spontaneously.

"On the other hand, the other churches were wrong in tearing the body of Christ apart by their anger with Church leaders. They have been just as intolerant, even though they sincerely try to teach what they feel to be an important message of the gospel. Each of them, in their own way, stresses some aspect of Jesus' spirit, though they are frequently careless about things that Jesus was willing to die for. There is also an admirable love and spirit of caring and a simplicity among various Protestant churches that the others could do well to learn. That is why I feel free visiting all the churches. Would Jesus do any differently?"

"Joshua, sometimes I wonder about you when you talk like that. I still think there's more to you than just a woodcarver. Your vision far transcends the merely human mind. Joshua, who are you, really?"

"As you said this morning, you already know who I am. What more can I tell you than what I have said?"

The priest searched his memory in vain, trying to remember what he had said to him after Mass.

"One day you will understand," Joshua continued, "and your heart will rejoice."

At that point the priest started to leave and told Joshua he was going home to visit his mother and father, who were expecting him for dinner later on. As he started for the door Joshua handed him the bag of vegetables and told him, "Give these to your mother, I'm sure she can use them. She has a fine son. Your parents should be proud of you."

"Thanks, Josh. You're a good man and I appreciate your helping me. Have a nice afternoon."

The priest then left and walked out to his car, with Joshua, as usual, accompanying him to the gate. As he drove off Joshua went back into the house. He was tired. Last night's partying was unusual and he wasn't used to it. Today was busy, and even though he had enjoyed helping the poor distraught mother and entertaining the priest, it had been exhausting. Joshua fell down on his bed and in a few minutes was sound asleep.

10

URING the short time Joshua had been in the village he had come to know a good number of people. He had, in his own way, become a celebrity, as almost everyone liked him and found his conversation stimulating. In a small village like Auburn you rarely come across exciting people, so Joshua stood out. His relationships with people were simple enough and uninvolved, but as he was friendly and outgoing, people easily engaged him in discussions about almost everything and found him knowledgeable about a wide range of subjects. And since religion is of almost universal interest, questions and discussions about religion came up frequently. It was about these matters that Joshua seemed to have the strongest feelings and spoke freely about whatever issues were brought up. But the things Joshua believed in so strongly, and which people found to be logical and sensible, were, as far as the current trends in religious thought were concerned, quite radical.

While most people found Joshua's ideas refreshing, and indeed beautiful, there were some of a more conservative bent who were deeply shocked, and even offended, by some of the things he expressed. His practice of attending services of different churches was beyond their comprehension. Some thought this to be an expression of liberalism, others thought it merely odd, and some wondered if it didn't show a lack of any strong religious convictions. The clergy, outside of Father Pat, had become familiar with Joshua more through rumor and occasional contact than by any serious encounter or dialogue. What they did see in him, or hear about him, they didn't particularly like. He came across as a free spirit who was more content to just shop around rather than commit himself to any particular church. They had heard he had carved a statue of Moses for a synagogue in the city and had even attended services there. At clergy fellowship meetings, when Joshua's name came up, he was the butt of jokes and wisecracks. It was reported that he was Jewish and might even join the synagogue. But it was surprising how well-known he had become in so short a time.

What was really troubling the clergy, however, were Joshua's freely broadcast convictions about religion. There were some well-placed lay people who were not happy with what Joshua had to say about the practice of religion in the churches, and because they were eager to ingratiate themselves, they were only too willing to bring tales back to their pastors. The reports made it look as if Joshua had criticized the pastors personally, which, of course, was not his way. However, it did serve to stiffen their attitude toward him, so for the most part they had already formed strong opinions of him without ever having met him or talked to him about any of these matters.

Joshua sensed this and realized there was nothing he could do about it. It wasn't the first time gossips had done serious damage to his work and reputation and ended up pitting the establishment against him. It is always that way with visionaries who are not afraid to think for themselves and dare to be different. They must be willing and prepared to endure misunderstanding and suspicion by those whose minds are too small to comprehend ideas that are beyond the ordinary. Their very existence is an annoyance and a threat to functionaries who are content to stick to the book without ever applying imagination to their work.

These were some of the thoughts Joshua was mulling over while he went about his work in the shop. But his meditation was broken by a knock on the front door. He put down his tools and went to see who was there. He was surprised to see two men, well-dressed, standing on the porch.

"Gentlemen, come right in," Joshua said to them cordially, then asked if he could do anything for them.

The men said they couldn't stay, just wanted to deliver a message. Would Joshua be kind enough to attend a meeting of the clergy association that was going to be held next Tuesday afternoon at two o'clock? Joshua said he would be very happy to attend. When he asked what the occasion was he was told that the clergy of the various denominations would like to talk to him. After delivering this message to Joshua the men left. Joshua went back to his shop to continue his work.

Interruptions in his work were becoming more frequent of late, and it was becoming increasingly difficult to finish his backlog of orders. As much as he disliked refusing work because of the joy his work brought people, he was beginning to let them know he could no longer keep up with the volume.

The week itself went by quickly, with nothing too eventful taking place other than a change in attitude on the part of some people who had previously been friendly toward him. He didn't know what had brought it about, but realized there was little he could do about it. He was still kind to them and acted no differently toward them than he usually did.

That Friday night he went to the synagogue as usual. His friend Aaron came and picked him up at exactly six-thirty. The people at the synagogue expressed a genuine warmth toward him and accepted him as one of their own. They did not know whether he was Jewish or not. It didn't matter. They liked him and treated him as a friend. After the first service Mrs. Cohen had told the rabbi that she had heard Joshua saying his prayers in Hebrew. The rabbi had promised to look into it, so he asked a close friend, Mike Bergson, to sit a discreet distance away from Joshua and listen to him. Mike was a Hebrew scholar and taught at the university.

At the service that night Joshua was aware of the man sitting in front of him, a little off to the side, and straining as if trying to listen to him. When the rabbi led the congregation, praying in Hebrew, only a few responded, Joshua among them. His voice was clear and unmistakable. After the service the man walked past Joshua, smiling at him as he did so. Joshua noticed him later talking to the rabbi, but was too far away to hear what he was saying.

When Joshua entered the social hall members of the congregation collected around him, forming their own little clique in the corner of the hall. The rabbi walked in with Mike Bergson. The two were still talking when Marcia, who had been a member of the statue committee, came over and stood near the two of them.

"Are you sure it was Hebrew he was speaking?" the rabbi asked Mike.

"Yes, Rabbi. I have no doubt about it. However, it is a form of Hebrew I am not familiar with. It seems to be a dialect of Hebrew no longer spoken, and if I wasn't afraid of seeming ridiculous, I would say it is Aramaic, the form of Hebrew spoken almost two thousand years ago. I can't imagine where he would have learned it."

In the meantime Joshua was busy speaking to his fan club. They had worked their way to the corner of the spacious room where there were sofas and comfortable chairs. Joshua was sitting in the rocking chair while the others formed a semicircle around him. The small group had come to know Joshua quite well, not only from the installation night, but from a talk Marcia had given to the sisterhood during the week describing the statue and discussing extensively the personality of the artist. She had done a good public relations job for him without even realizing it.

"Joshua, I know you are not a member of our congregation, but you showed such feeling in the figure you carved for us that we are convinced you are a deeply religious man," Mrs. Cohen, a plump, round-faced, middle-aged woman said to him.

Joshua merely smiled his pleasure at being accepted so readily by these people he loved so deeply. "You have all been very kind to me. You make me feel quite at home, as if I had always been part of your family," Joshua responded.

"When you carved that statue of Moses you expressd such deep religious feeling, I couldn't help but think you do a lot of thinking about God and religion. Would you share with us some of your thoughts?" It was a lady by the name of Mrs. Stern who asked Joshua that question, and it was a question that was right on target. This was just the opening Joshua needed to express his feelings about religion and what it should mean for people.

"I think it is important for people to realize that God's

prime concern is people, not religious structures. They exist merely to channel God's word to people. But it is people that God cares about. He wants them to understand their lives and to find happiness. He wants nothing from them except that they allow themselves to grow. God's law is not a code arbitrarily imposed on people to restrict their freedom unreasonably. It was intended as a guide to happiness. Over the centuries religious leaders have twisted the law into a code that is irrelevant to man's nature and thereby restricts the natural freedom people should enjoy. This is what makes religion seem like a burden to people rather than something they should find joy and comfort in. This arbitrary restriction of freedom has given religion its bad name and, in fact, has given religion its name. The word *religion* means to 'bind up,' and that is just what God did not want to do. God created people to be free and to enjoy the existence he gave them. All that God wants is that we love him and love one another and in doing that, find happiness. It is all so very simple."

"That is beautiful," Mrs. Stern said. "I have never looked upon religion in that way before, yet God could not be any different than you just portrayed him. It is so simple when you look at life that way. You must really be at peace with yourself, Joshua."

At that point Marcia walked over and took a place in the circle directly in front of Joshua. He noticed her and smiled faintly. Marcia returned the smile. A man sitting next to Marcia by the name of Bernie Hauf asked Joshua a very pointed question: "Joshua, why do our people suffer so much?"

Bernie was a middle-aged man with strong features and eyes deeply set beneath his brow. He had known pain and sorrow in his short life and was always searching for answers. It wasn't the first time he had asked this question of guest speakers.

Joshua looked at him tenderly, expressing a warm affection for what he saw in the man. "Bernie," Joshua said, "you are still God's chosen people. Your destiny has always been tied up with God, who has used you to channel his blessings to mankind. But, as in times of old, when God was pointing in one direction and your people drifted in another, you suffered the pain of your alienation, so today when God points the way for your people and you go in all directions, many even denying his existence, God still lets you know he is concerned by allowing you to suffer again the pain of your alienation. You must remember, you are not free like other nations to choose your destiny. You belong to God in a special way, and you must allow him to guide you. When you realize that you will find an honored place among the family of nations."

Joshua's eyes moved toward Marcia. He couldn't help notice how beautiful she was. Her beauty was not only physical. Her mind was quick and alert, and beneath the genuine intellectuality of a highly cultured mind was a warmth and beauty of soul that was rare. Joshua instinctively loved her, and it showed in the way he looked at her. Again their looks met. Marcia did not look away, but tried to read what she saw in his eyes. There was a depth and a penetration in his glance that prompted her to turn away, but she would not. She was determined to understand him. She knew she was irresistibly drawn to him, though she could not understand why. She did not ordinarily react that way to men. Although she was capable of strong feeling, her career as an artist and a scholar so completely captivated her that interest in men proved little distraction. But Joshua was different. She seemed to find in him the personification of everything about her work that appealed to her. He was not just an artist, that was obvious. The way he carved showed a mastery of form and principles which had taken her years to master, yet she knew he did not learn these things from books or in a classroom. His understanding of nature and people and life forms revealed a knowledge that could not have been accumulated in one lifetime. His knowledge of people was too vast for his thirty years. Like Father Pat, Marcia had the distinct feeling he had been here before. His sense of history was too personal. It was experienced, not learned.

She saw in him the embodiment of everything to which she dedicated her life and could not help but be powerfully drawn to him. She also knew he was attracted to her, and although his eyes left her, she continued to analyze him. She could see by the way he treated people that he felt an intimacy with people that even members of families rarely felt. It was as if each person in some way belonged to him, as if he had known each one long before he met them. Each person's question he answered differently, as if he understood what each needed to hear, and each one responded accordingly. His mastery of the dynamics of group psychology was easy and graceful; he seemed to empathize with people's anguish in trying to understand life.

Marcia loved the way he handled people. The very simplicity of his understanding of life she found unsettling. As she thought of him she couldn't help but wonder what his personal life was like, what he did when he went home on a night like this to an empty house without even a telephone. He must be lonely. Why does he live the way he does? He is clearly not just in love with art or wood carving. He loves people too much to be contented with just that. What does he think of in the quiet of his thoughts in that empty house? Would he be terribly upset if she came to visit him some evening after he finished his work? At that moment Joshua looked at her. She felt he read her thoughts, and she blushed. But his look also seemed to say to her, "Come." In her heart she answered, "I shall."

All during this discussion Joshua had been talking. Now there was a lull. Marcia decided to ask a question. "Joshua, what do you think of God? This question has troubled me for a long time, and I never discussed it with anyone before. I am curious as to your feelings on the matter."

Joshua looked at her and took a few moments to compose his thoughts. How could he sum up in a few words his thoughts and feelings about a part of his life that was so intimate and so far beyond words to describe? "Marcia," he said, "before all else God is one. Moses stressed that point, and he was right. But it is important to understand that the unity in God's being is not like the unity in a human person. God is not human. God is unique and cannot be compared. However, God is simple, which is a part of his unity, but his simplicity is beautiful in that it can be seen in many facets and is capable of limitless expression. Every beautiful creation expresses some facet of God's beauty. Every prophet expresses something of God's presence. Jesus possessed in himself a unique reflection of God's infinite love for his people. Every delicate and powerful force in nature reveals a facet of God's majesty. The vast expanse of space beyond the stars provides a hint of the unlimited comprehension of God's intelligence. And yet there is more to God than that.

"God's love is like the warmth of the sun, which touches every object in creation at the same moment, giving it warmth and light, and in touching knows intimately each one in the same instant. But God's love is also foolish, because he understands the difficulty we have in trying to grasp him, so he frequently manifests himself in ways we can understand, even at the risk of confusing us even more as to his identity. I think, Marcia, that you can best find God if you look within yourself. The most powerful revelation of God's presence and his love lies within you. If you take the time and talk to God, you will find him, and in finding him you will find the greatest joy of your life. He will reveal himself to you, and in possessing him you will understand all else."

"Joshua, that is beautiful," Marcia said, "but it is not easy to understand. I would like to talk to you about it again. I can see that you experience what you say and it brings you a lot of peace. That makes sense."

At that point a stocky man, an executive type, walked over to the circle. He had been watching and listening from a distance and seemed fascinated with Joshua. His name was Roger Silverman, another member of the synagogue's inner circle.

Roger stood near the outside of the circle and didn't ask any questions. He just wanted to listen. When the discussion group broke up Roger walked over and introduced himself. "My name is Roger Silverman. I already know you're Joshua. I've been hearing about you all week, and from listening to you talk I am quite impressed with your work and your involvement with people. I own one of the TV stations and would like to do a story about you if you wouldn't mind."

Joshua had mixed thoughts about publicity. Would it complicate his life and interfere with the limited purpose of his mission or would it provide good support for what he knew he had to accomplish? It didn't take long to decide.

He calculated the advantages and disadvantages and made his reply.

"Where will the interview take place?"

"Wherever you feel most comfortable."

"As I have no car it would be difficult for me to come to the city."

"I will send the crew out to your place if that's all right with you."

"Fine."

"How about tomorrow?" Roger asked.

"You don't waste time, do you?" Joshua said with a grin. "Tomorrow will be all right. How about nine o'clock?"

"Okay, nine o'clock it is. The crew will be there right on time."

As Joshua and Roger were walking across the hall with a handful of people, the rabbi approached with Mike Bergson, who wanted to meet Joshua. "Joshua," the rabbi said, "I would like you to meet another good member of our congregation, Michael Bergson. He has heard some of your admirers talking about you and wanted to meet you."

"I am honored," Joshua said graciously as he held out his hand.

"I am the one who is honored," Mike responded. "The figure you carved for us is eloquent. Every time I look at it it speaks a different message. That says a lot for the artist who could put so much into a piece of wood."

"Thank you," Joshua said humbly.

"I must say, you also speak excellent Hebrew. I couldn't help but overhear as you were praying during the service. Where did you learn to speak so well?"

"I learned it from my family."

"You are Jewish, then?"

"Yes."

At that moment Aaron came over and offered to take him home. The conversation ended abruptly as Aaron had some business to discuss with the rabbi before he left with Joshua.

As many of the people were leaving they went out of their way to say "Happy Shabbat" to Joshua. Marcia said she would like to visit him some evening if he wouldn't mind. It seemed a bit forward, but Marcia was always independent and never ordered her life on the formalities of less independent women. Being involved in highly re-spected cultural and scholarly institutes, she felt com-fortable with people so that what might seem forward to others was natural to her.

When Aaron finished talking to Rabbi Szeneth, he and Joshua walked out together. They still had a long trip home.

CHAPTER 11

THE COTTAGE where Joshua lived was no longer quiet and tranquil. People came to visit more frequently. Rumors spread about the dying girl who Joshua had cured. The television crew coming to town and stopping at Joshua's stirred enough talk for a month. He had become an instant celebrity. He was no longer the simple man who lived in the Van Arden cottage down the street. He was Joshua the sculptor and the man of vision whose ideas on religion and life had broken through to the big city. Orders for sculptured pieces came in large numbers, and his house was busy all day with visitors coming and going.

Even though he was trying to wind down his business, Joshua did commit himself to two large pieces because their influence would reach a number of people. They were works requested by two clergymen, one an Anglican priest by the name of Father Jeremy K. Darby and the other a pastor of a black congregation. His name was the Reverend Osgood Rowland. Oddly enough both men requested that Joshua carve a figure of Peter the Apostle, who was so warmly venerated by the early Christian community. Joshua told them that, although he was not taking any more orders, he would do these because of his own love for Peter and the influence the figures could have on so many people.

It was Father Darby who had approached him first. Joshua had been working in the garden, and was walking around the house with the hoe over his shoulder, when a highly polished black foreign car came rolling up to the front of the house. A chauffeur stepped out and opened the door for his passenger to exit. A huge hulk of a man flowed out of the back seat and pulled himself up to his full stature. He was a clergyman dressed in a gray suit and wearing a Roman collar. The man pompously strode over to the gate, which looked dwarfed in comparison to the man's huge frame. Joshua put his hoe against the fence and walked over to greet him.

"Is Mr. Joshua, the sculptor, at home?" the priest asked in an imitation Oxford accent.

Joshua extended his hand and, with a smile, said, "I am Joshua."

"You are Mr. Joshua?" the cleric responded with an almost hurt tone of voice. "But you are just a simple gardener. Surely there must be another Mr. Joshua who is the well-known sculptor?"

"I'm the only Joshua who lives here," Joshua responded. "I also carve wood. If I am the one you are looking for, I would be happy to assist you."

The priest looked over the simple surroundings and Joshua's very ordinary clothes. He seemed deflated.

"Well, if you are the only one, then you must be the one I am looking for. I had expected a distinguished man of the world with a certain elegance befitting his reputation," the priest said. "I am Father Jeremy K. Darby, rector of Saint Peter's Episcopal Church," he proclaimed as he put forward his hand for Joshua to do reverence.

Joshua, not knowing whether he was expected to shake it or kiss it, merely tried fitting his hand underneath it and held it briefly, then let go. The hand was listless, without character. Joshua felt a strange, creepy feeling in his stomach. "Would you like to come into my workshop?" Joshua asked courteously.

The priest bowed slightly his acquiescence and followed Joshua into the house. The chauffeur stood at attention near the gate. Joshua called to him and invited him too. The priest was taken aback by Joshua's violation of protocol, but as the chauffeur did not notice his boss's grimace, he accepted Joshua's invitation and came up to the house. Joshua extended his hand and gave his name, as the minister did not see fit to introduce a lowly inferior. "My name is Arthur, sir. I am honored to meet you," the man said with a real humility. The three men walked inside the house.

As Father Darby walked past the furniture he was careful to let nothing touch him, as if avoiding possible contamination. He looked around the room with disdain, questioning in his mind the ability of a man whose lifestyle bordered on poverty. Joshua was conscious of what was taking place but said nothing. They walked out through the kitchen and into the workshop. It was neat, but there weren't many carved pieces lying around and nothing to show off. The priest looked the place over, remarking, "Is this all you have? I thought I might see a well-appointed shop with the latest professional equipment and a room full of art work."

"Frequently real talent needs only the simplest tools to accomplish its work," Joshua said honestly and without sarcasm. "I do have all I really need."

The priest looked around and, seeing all he cared to see, turned back into the kitchen. "I hope I am not making a mistake in commissioning you to do this work for me," he said.

"I will do my best. What was it you had in mind?"

"A grand figure of the great Apostle Peter, a man for whom I have always felt a certain affinity and the greatest affection. He was the chosen leader of the apostles and was established by Jesus as the foundation of the Church. I envision him as a man of great proportions and equal dignity, not unlike myself, if I may be permitted to indulge in a little vanity."

"Yes, I can see there is a resemblance," Joshua told Father Darby with a smile, trying to be as serious as the comical situation would allow.

Joshua didn't dislike the man, but his mannerisms were annoying and, as much as he understood human nature, it was difficult for Joshua to converse with him because there was no way to break into the monologue. The priest's next remark was the payoff: "If you don't feel equal to the task, I would appreciate it if you would let me know now and I will look for someone else to do the job."

Joshua had no misgivings about his ability and assured the priest he could do the work for him. If he came back in a week, it would be ready for him.

As there was no further need for conversation, Father Darby turned and walked toward the door. "Come, Arthur," he said to his chauffeur. Joshua accompanied them to the door and walked up the path with them. The chauffeur made an attempt to exchange a final pleasantry, which Joshua did not miss, but as his employer made no similar gesture, he and Joshua just exchanged glances. The cleric did, however, manage a stiff "Good-bye, sir," before he walked over to his car.

As the car drove off Joshua picked up the hoe, which he had left leaning against the fence, and went back into the yard to finish his work in the garden. He thought about Peter for a long time, occasionally smiling to himself as memories crossed his mind. Yes, there were similarities between Peter and the priest. They were both pompous and taken up with themselves. They were both huge. But after that there was little else they had in common. Peter was a big man in other ways, too, which Father Darby was not. Peter had a big heart if not a big mind. Darby was cold and unfeeling. In his younger days Peter would have enjoyed having a chauffeur, but he was also the type who would have gotten just as much pleasure putting on the chauffeur's cap and taking the chauffeur for a ride.

During the course of these thoughts Joshua wondered how he should design the statue. He was almost tempted to use the priest as the model, but quickly dismissed the thought as mischievous. Peter certainly wouldn't appreciate it. Also, he wondered about the message the figure should project. Every work of art should have a message. Joshua thought for the longest time and, after tossing out a dozen ideas, finally decided just how he would carve the statue of the great Apostle Peter.

It was close to four when Joshua decided to take a walk up the road. It was a warm, sultry day, and he had been busier than he would have liked and needed to get away by himself for a while. Too many things were happening lately, and he had to sift through everything to see where it was all leading.

He walked up past Langford's place, but continued on so as not to break his meditation, stopping only occasionally to watch the birds playing in the trees or to look across the meadow and watch the wheat playing games with the breeze. As the gentle wind blew across the field of golden wheat it looked like flocks of sheep running through the meadow. He thought of people without a shepherd, then continued walking.

On his way back a small group of people confronted him. One of them, a woman, had spotted him from her window when he first started his walk. Like the Pharisees of old, she had been laying in wait for him and had found her chance. She called her cronies and they all gathered at the corner where they knew Joshua had to pass. The group didn't look sinister; it looked more like a casual meeting of friends. But this group had a purpose. They were middle-aged, mostly Catholic, intensely conservative, and deeply distressed about the radical changes taking place in the Church. Hearing Joshua speak on various occasions, and knowing his custom of attending different churches, Protestant as well as Catholic, their feeling about him bordered on something close to horror. He had spoken about Jesus coming to set men free, and that structured religions stripped people of the freedom God intended they enjoy. He was definitely not a healthy influence, and his lack of commitment to a particular church showed a real lack of religious conviction.

As Joshua walked down the road they came over and practically surrounded him, as if to prevent his escape. "We would like to speak with you, sir," spoke up a medium-built woman wearing blue jeans and a light blue print blouse.

"Would you like to come over to my house where we can be more relaxed?" Joshua asked calmly.

"No," the woman insisted, "what we have to say can

be said right here. We are concerned about things we have heard about you and things that some of us have heard with our own ears and we don't like it."

"That is perfectly all right. I never felt that people always had to agree with me. They are free to do their own thinking," Joshua responded politely.

"You have been here in town for only a short time, and you have disturbed many of our people with your ideas and your unusual way of doing things," said another woman. "We are old-fashioned people from the old school and we are offended by what you said about our religion, about it depriving people of their freedom. You once made the remark that people who stick to the old ideas are incapable of growth, and that Catholics are stuck more on the external observances of religion than on loving God and their neighbor."

The silent pause after the woman's attack demanded an answer. Joshua looked at her and the others sympathetically. "Yes," he said, "most of what you said is true, but not quite the way you word it. Religion in the time of Jesus was not much different than it is today. Religious leaders may have had more power to punish people for violations of religious observances, but religious leaders have always felt that in some way they had a mandate from God to control people's lives, and even their thinking. When people don't obey they are made to feel they are disobeying God, and resisting God's grace, and jeopardizing their salvation. That is not healthy. God never intended that human institutions should have such control over people's lives. God made people free. They are his children.

"It is the function of the apostles and those who succeed them to guide the flock gently and to offer what Jesus taught. But it is not their place to dictate what people must

believe or bully people into submission. That deprives people of their freedom as human beings. Nor should they
demand more of people than God Himself. Religion is most
beautiful when a person lives an ordinary life but motivated
by a great love of God. Artificial practices imposed and
added on as religion do not make a person religious or
pleasing in God's eyes. That was the Pharisees' type of
religion, which Jesus so vehemently rejected."

One lady remarked, "Well, I can go along with that.
I always felt that we should be free to make our own
decisions."

But another person took exception, saying the Church
stands in the place of Christ, and what the Church teaches,
man must obey.

Joshua admitted that the Church succeeded to the chair
of Moses and the seat of Peter, as Jesus wished, but Jesus
was also most insistent that his followers not imitate the
practices of the Pharisees, who delighted in inventing
elaborate practices for people to observe and transformed
religion into observance of human traditions. When religious leaders do this they turn people away from God
because people rightfully resent being forced to observe
rules made by people and mandated as necessary for salvation. That is what Jesus was referring to when he told
the apostles they should not partake of the leaven of the
Pharisees, nor should they be like the pagan rulers who
love to lord it over their subjects.

"Give us an example, sir," the same man insisted.

"Very well," Joshua agreed. "The Church demands
that its members marry before a priest, otherwise the marriage is invalid. There is nothing wrong with marrying
before a priest if that is what the couple choose. To demand
it under penalty of invalid marriage and the stigma of

immorality is another matter. If a couple marry without a priest, you say that marriage is invalid, and the couple lives in sin. They may be married for many years and have several children, but if one of them, at any time, walks away from that marriage, and the children, and comes with another lover to a priest, they can be married with the priest's blessing because the previous marriage was considered invalid.

"Or take a man who cares nothing for religion. He marries out of whim before a justice of the peace. Since he is a member of the Church, his marriage is ruled invalid. The same man marries five other women, and has children of each, then abandons each of them and all the children. He finally decides to marry a woman in the Church. This is easily arranged because the previous ceremonies were treated as if they never existed. It makes no difference that he left a flock of children behind. His new marriage is now blessed in solemn ceremony by the priest. Do you think this kind of legalism pleases God? It is the way the Pharisees conducted religion. Their laws and rituals were made with little reference to what pleased God.

"Or take the forgiveness of sins. Jesus intended this to be a great gift to bring peace to tortured souls. Religious officials turned that gift into a cruel nightmare that occasioned mental anguish for countless good but introverted people who found it psychologically impossible to lay bare their souls to another. Are they doomed to perdition because of this? It is this insensitivity on the part of Church officials that has taken the gifts of God and turned them into instruments of pain for people. Jesus intended forgiveness to be offered gently and with compassion, and not accompanied by humiliation from an impatient priest or in ways that would cause little children to urinate from sheer fright. What Jesus intended to be so casual and free-spirited they have encased in rigid rituals on scheduled times, as if the Holy Spirit worked on timetables dictated by humans."

The group was shocked by what they had heard. One or two listened with interest and were even inclined to agree. They had experienced similar happenings themselves, and knew Joshua was speaking the truth, but had never dared to criticize the priests or the Church for fear of committing sin. The others in the group were on the verge of rage. They had never heard anyone criticize their Church the way this man did. They had always been taught, and firmly believed, that the Church is the infallible voice of God.

"So what we have heard is true," retorted a stout, bespectacled man in his mid-forties. "You are hateful of the Church and you criticize her teachings and her laws."

"That is not true," Joshua shot back with fire in his eyes. "I love the Church, as Jesus loves the Church. It is his great gift to mankind, but there is a human aspect of the Church that needs constant correction and prodding to remain faithful to the spirit of Jesus. Mature Christians should not be afraid to speak their minds and out of real loyalty insist that the spirit of Jesus be followed. They are not servants in a household. They are the family itself, no less than those who like to rule. Jesus wanted his shepherds to be servants, not rulers, and the Christian people should not be afraid to speak. I say what I have said because I care that the Church be what Jesus intended it to be, a haven of peace, and a consoling beacon lighting the way, not a prison of the spirit or a sword that cuts and wounds."

What Joshua said did not smooth things over. They had never heard priests criticized this way before. Because it was done in the name of Jesus it was even more diabolical and cynical. He was evil, but in the guise of pretending to be a religious man. Either he was misguided or he was malicious in a devious and subtle way. One woman felt like slapping him in the face for his blasphemy. Another person expressed sorrow for the unhappy state of his soul and promised to pray for him. One of the men told him that he was a heretic and he would do all in his power to destroy his influence in the community.

One final question they had to ask him: "Why do you always go to different churches? Why don't you make up your mind and join one church?"

Even though the question was not well-intentioned, Joshua took no offense. He laughed good-naturedly, realizing that these people could never possibly understand. He answered simply. "I feel that Jesus loves people, not structures, and his people are not limited to Catholics or Methodists or Presbyterians. Wherever sincere people gather to honor God, God is in their midst, so I feel at home with them, whoever they are. Would you expect Jesus to do any differently?"

He was impossible. They couldn't make sense out of his reasoning. It was counter to everything they had been taught since childhood. They had to admit there was a certain beauty to the casual freedom he felt, but even that was dangerous because it was seductive. It was threatening to rigid concepts of faith and could weaken the faith of those already weak. His mentality would too easily appeal to the young, so they must keep their children away from him as something more dangerous than a disease. Their children already loved Joshua. That in itself was bad. They must never be allowed to go near him again. He could destroy their delicate faith. They didn't realize that he never talked about things like this to children. They couldn't understand. They were already free and beautiful, and he only wished the grown-ups could be more like them.

Joshua shook his head as they walked away, talking excitedly all the way up the street. As he watched he could see the long flowing robes of Pharisees and scribes. Their mentality was the same, only the setting was different— basically good people, but narrow and undeveloped, who must ultimately destroy what they cannot understand.

Later that evening the same group went up to the rectory and had a meeting with the pastor. Father Pat met them at the door and ushered them into the spacious living room to await the pastor's arrival. The young assistant was not one of their favorite people. He was too much like Joshua in his thinking, and it was only the good pastor's firm control that kept him straight. Father Pat knew they couldn't stand him, and the feeling was mutual. He had strange vibes about their coming to see the pastor and was curious about the purpose of their meeting. He knew it had something to do with Joshua, but wasn't exactly sure of their intentions.

However, after the pastor came and entered the room, closing the door behind him, it didn't take long before their loud voices revealed everything. It was not that Pat was eavesdropping. That was against his principles. But he couldn't help overhearing the whole conversation. His office was in the next room. The pastor's rising suspicions about Joshua gave easy play to what these people had to tell him. Pat was concerned. He knew no good would come from this. He felt torn. He loved Joshua but could do nothing to protect him from what he knew would come out of this meeting. He wished the pastor had invited him to sit in on the meeting so he could say something in Joshua's defense.

He himself knew that Joshua was harmless to a faith that was genuine. He was only a threat to a faith that was misguided and misdirected. He really loved religion and was deeply religious in a way that was authentic, even though he had none of the trappings of a pietistic person. Pat also realized that Joshua's understanding of religion was not blasphemous but, on the contrary, that he saw to the very core of what religion should be, an expression of people's healthy growth as human beings inspired by a deep love of God and humanity and all of God's creatures. As religion was, it was rarely healthy. But how could he tell the pastor that, because he wasn't healthy?

Joshua had eaten supper in the yard that night and, as usual, had entertained his four-legged guests. They were friendlier now that they were getting to know him. Even the skunk had become an accepted member of the group. But Joshua was not himself. Something was weighing on his mind, and he appeared depressed. The animals seemed to sense his depression and showed it, jumping all over him and pulling on his clothes.

But his mind was on other things. He was baffled by people. They find it so difficult to be tolerant or to open their minds to see another view of things. They cling so tenaciously to the things of their childhood, which they never dare to question. To hold to one's faith is one thing, but to hang on to mere traditional practices that do not really touch what Jesus taught shows a faith that is misdirected and also an insecurity and a fear that palsies any growth in real faith.

When Joshua finished supper and went back into the

house, there was a rap on the door. He went to answer it and was shocked to see Marcia standing there. She looked ravishing in her kelly-green dress, which was soft and light and accentuated her sleek figure. Joshua's mood changed as soon as he saw her. His face relaxed and lighted up with a broad smile. The two of them embraced lightly and went into the house.

As he closed the door behind him he noticed a group of people walking down the street. It was the delegation just returning from the rectory. They had seen Joshua and Marcia embrace and the two of them go into the darkened house. Joshua only too well realized the implications.

Joshua was glad she had come. He was fond of Marcia and knew that she liked him, and he needed the comfort of a friend. It had not been a pleasant day, and Joshua could clearly see the way things were going. The future seemed ominous, and her coming was a welcome relief from the tension of the day and helped to dispel, at least temporarily, the gloom that had overtaken him.

As far as art was concerned, Joshua and Marcia had a lot in common. She was deeply involved in art and culture and philosophy and had so many questions to ask Joshua. She was probably not at all aware of how she really felt about him, and even though she may have originally been drawn to him for purely platonic reasons, each day the attachment became more intense. She found herself thinking about him frequently during the day and asking herself how he would feel about this or that idea or plan and wishing she could talk to him about it. Since she could not call him on the phone, the only way she would ever be able to enter into any kind of a relationship with him was if she came out to visit him. When she saw how happy he was to see her, she was glad she had come.

"Joshua, I hope you don't mind my barging in on you like this," she said in halfhearted apology.

"Not at all. In fact, nothing seemed to be going right today and I was feeling down. I'm glad you came."

"I know that you are an intense person," Marcia said, "and have profound ideas on many things. I treasure your opinions and the unique viewpoint you express. My own work is very demanding and I am asked for my opinion on a variety of topics. I don't feel adequate sometimes and I only wish I could discuss some of these matters with you. I know you could offer valuable suggestions. For example, the other day at the United Nations Culture and Art Committee meeting the question arose over political ramifications of the various types of art and culture. The Russian delegates felt that Americans were having too much influence on other peoples, thus affecting their political sympathies. They sarcastically suggested that American art is decadent and brings out the worst in people.

"My feeling is that the United Nations organizations should be a forum for the expression of each nation's feelings. If a people feel drawn to American art, or to Russian art, that is a good thing because it creates a bond between those two peoples. If another nation is unhappy about that, it is only because they feel threatened by people becoming attracted to a nation they oppose. But unless there is freedom of expression in the United Nations, how can it survive? Some Third World countries jumped all over me, and I left the meeting depressed. The meeting was an important one because we have to make a decision on what programs we are going to sponsor and fund for the coming year. Not being able to agree on something so basic was discouraging.

"I realize this is probably all new to you, and maybe out of your field, but I thought perhaps you might have some suggestions I could bring to the next meeting."

Joshua looked at Marcia, or, more precisely, seemed to look right through her. His thoughts seemed a thousand miles away. She wondered if he even heard what she had so carefully tried to express. Then, after what seemed an endless silence, he said to her, "Marcia, you are innocently involved in a struggle to control the human mind. What you propose as a way of uniting people is seen as a distraction from a dark and devious scheme to dominate the minds of simple people. You are dealing with forces that want to control people's thoughts by controlling their art and other forms of culture. Since these agencies are dominated by political considerations, you can't approach issues from a purely artistic or cultural perspective, but you must be as shrewd as a fox. My suggestion is that you propose the development of emerging art forms from one of the Third World countries that is neutral rather than lobbying for your own artists. If you do this, your opponents won't dare oppose you for fear of alienating emerging nations. Then, when your proposal is approved, you have won important allies and can plan more long-range goals with your newfound friends. It can all be done very nicely and discreetly, with no one realizing what you have in mind. In situations like this you have to have short-term and long-term goals to keep your opponents in the dark. You can accomplish more this way than by direct confrontations."

When Joshua had finished Marcia seemed impressed. "You are a lot less simple than you appear, Joshua. How does the saying go, 'Simple as a dove, and as shrewd as a fox'? I suppose that's the only way to outfox our opponents.

It's worth a try. Now there is another question I want to ask you. It is more personal and I hope you don't mind my asking it."

Joshua nodded casually that he didn't mind.

"I don't know whether you realize it, but you have an extraordinary potential, not only as an artist, but also as a thinker and a philosopher. With the right connections you could have a devastating impact on society. I have already taken the liberty of talking about you to some of my friends, and they are anxious to meet you."

"Marcia, I feel honored that you think so highly of me. I am concerned about the healthy development of society, but each person is limited to the role in which he feels most comfortable. I don't look upon myself as one to influence the decision-makers of society but as a friend of ordinary folk, with whom I feel most comfortable."

"But, Joshua, you feel that way because you are so humble, and no one has ever pushed you to your full potential. I feel very close to you, and I can see that much of our thinking and feeling is identical. I really feel that, with the doors already open to me, we could do great work as a team. I know it's impetuous and presumptuous of me to intrude on your personal life like this, but I am very concerned about the problems of society, and we need men of vision like yourself to exert all the influence we can. I realize this is new to you, and you may not feel comfortable with it right now, but I do wish you would think about it and perhaps we could discuss it again."

"I promise to give it a lot of thought, and I would not be honest if I said it didn't have great appeal."

Having accomplished what she had intended by her visit, even though she had not succeeded, Marcia suddenly felt more relaxed. "I like your little house," she said as her eyes scanned the small living room. "It's a perfect setup for a bachelor, though it does look a lot more austere than I think you really are," she continued, trying to pry Joshua loose so he would reveal something about himself.

Joshua merely smiled at her playfulness. He liked that trait in Marcia so he went along with it and answered in equally playful fashion, "It is all I really need, and even though I would enjoy more artistic elegance and comfort, it serves a purpose in a practical way. I don't spend much time in the house anyway, so it never occurred to me to decorate the place. My dreams go a lot further than these four walls."

"You really dream?" Marcia said, surprised at this latest revelation.

"Of course, doesn't everyone? We would all love to see things different from what they are, and, being quite human, I am no different," he said.

"What do you dream about?"

"About people I meet, about things I would like to accomplish," he answered.

"I'm sure I never once entered one of your dreams," Marcia asked coquettishly.

Joshua smiled warmly. "Yes, I think of you, and I admire so many things about you. God has graced you with many gifts, and you are very dear to him because you allow him to use you as a partner in the work he has planned for your life. You are a rare person, Marcia, and I feel happy our paths have crossed."

She was hoping he would say something like that, and when he did her face lighted up. "I feel the same way about you," she responded. "I hope we can get to know each other better."

Marcia looked at her watch. It was getting late. She

didn't want to wear out her welcome on the first visit. As she started to get up and leave she said to Joshua, "I hope you enjoyed your visit to our temple Friday night. The people feel close to you and look forward to seeing you. You don't know how impressed they were with your dialogue during the social hour. Are you coming this week?"

"Yes, I'll be there. It's just as enjoyable for me as it is for the people. I feel very much at home, thanks to all of you."

Marcia started walking to the door. Joshua followed, saying to her, "I'm very grateful for your visit. It picked up my spirits, and I will think over what you proposed."

As they were standing on the porch Marcia turned toward Joshua and tilted her head slightly, offering him an opening if he wanted to kiss her good night. He placed his hands on her shoulders and kissed her warmly on the cheek. She responded, embracing him and kissing him affectionately. They both walked up the path to the car.

A streetlight cast eerie shadows through the moving trees. Marcia stepped into her Mercedes, waving a last good-bye as she did so, and drove off.

As Joshua turned to walk back to the house he noticed the shadows of two figures across the street. They seemed to be two of the people who had accosted him earlier in the day.

12

BY MONDAY MORNING gossip had spread all over town that a woman had stayed at Joshua's overnight. Though some disagreed and said they had seen a woman leave at a respectable hour, others denied it and insisted she stayed all night. When Joshua went to the store later in the morning, people were polite as usual, but he noticed a change. One woman, who was part of the group that had confronted him, was talking to another woman and every now and then would look furtively in Joshua's direction.

Joshua knew full well what was going on and that there was very little he could do about it. He was open and friendly as usual, and acted as if he was oblivious to all the undercurrents of rumors.

When he returned home he put away his groceries and went back to work. He finished up the little jobs and had already started work on Peter the Apostle. He had picked up special wood for the job, as he had to fit pieces together for a bas-relief. As the statue was more like a scene than a simple figure, he needed well-seasoned wood that wouldn't crack or separate when it was finished.

Later in the day he took a trip to the mill to get more wood. On the way he came across the children he had made the figures for. They turned the other way when they saw him. Joshua said hello to them, but they did not answer. He continued on his way and later returned home and spent most of the day working on the figures. By late afternoon rough outlines were beginning to appear.

On Tuesday he had his meeting with the clergy. It was held at the social hall at the Presbyterian church. All the clergy in town were there, including Father Pat. His pastor didn't attend these groups. He felt the Catholic Church had the truth and there was no point in fraternizing with ministers. The meeting started with a prayer asking God's guidance on their work and petitioning the Holy Spirit to use them as instruments of peace and love in the community. Joshua bowed his head as they prayed.

"Joshua," the president of the group began, "we appreciate your coming to this meeting. We feel it is important because there has been considerable confusion since you came to town and we would like to get some things straightened out before the situation gets worse. We are concerned, first of all, with your remarks about religion. From what I have heard you have been critical of the way the churches practice religion. Is this true?"

"First of all," Joshua began, "I don't set out talking about religious matters. People come and talk about many things, and in the course of the conversation questions will come up about religion. When they do I answer simply and matter-of-factly. In fact, religion is not practiced the way Jesus preached it or intended it to be."

"Why do you say that?" Reverend Engman asked.

"Because religious leaders have imitated those characteristics of Judaism that Jesus attacked so vigorously."

"Like what?" Reverend Engman continued.

"Like making religion an artificial observance of practices contrived by religious leaders. Take the Christian denominations. It is not their following of Jesus that makes them different from one another. It is the denominational practices that you have created that make them different from one another and keep them apart. This has brought ridicule on Christianity and destroyed the united influence you could have on the world."

"I would agree to that," Reverend Engman responded.

But the others were not so agreeable. One of the ministers asked him if he had any theological or scriptural training. He had not. Where did he get his information from if he had no training? The scriptures are quite clear to anyone who is willing to read with an open mind, and history speaks for itself was Joshua's reply.

When the Presbyterian minister asked him why he went from one church to another and didn't join a particular church, Joshua replied, "I like to pray with all people who sincerely worship God. Each of your churches preaches a variation of what Jesus taught, but you have strayed far from his original message. Jesus prayed fervently that his people would be one, and you have torn it asunder with your bickering and petty jealousy. You have kept the Christian people away from one another and forced them to be loyal to your denominations rather than to Jesus. That is the great sin. You make null and void the teachings of Jesus and his commandment of love by forcing allegiance to your own traditions."

They were all stung by what he had said, and when Joshua finished there was an uncomfortable silence. In the course of the discussions that followed Joshua pointed out the history of each of their religions and their break with the body of Christ in order to start their own versions of what Jesus taught.

The meeting ended badly. The clergy were so angered

by his stinging criticism of their denominations that it was difficult for them to be civil to him. They ended up by agreeing that Joshua would no longer be welcome in their churches until he made up his mind as to which religion he really belonged. Reverend Engman and Father Pat were the only two who did not go along with the consensus, and afterward they told Joshua privately that he was welcome in their church any time he wished to come. Father Darby had to leave the meeting early, so he was not part of the decision. Reverend Rowland did not attend these meetings, so he had no part in what took place.

Joshua walked home calmly, seemingly undisturbed. As soon as he got back to the house he continued working on his figures. He worked hard the rest of the day and the next few days, and by the latter part of the week he was well along on both figures. Though the subject of both statues was the same, the portrayal of each took an entirely different turn. In fact, the contrast was remarkable, as if the artist was delivering different messages through the different renditions of the same personality.

In the middle of the week the TV station aired the special program on Joshua. There were interviews with the artist in his workshop, scenes in the garden, and a beautiful pastoral scene of Joshua walking across the field with Joe Langford's sheep walking beside him. That was the first shot the camera crew took, because on their arrival Joshua was walking in from the meadow. It had not been staged, but it was so like him that it might have seemed so. There were also dramatic shots of Joshua carving intricate details of various figures. The highlight of the feature was the interview with Joshua himself in which he answered pointed questions about his life and his ideas.

He was frank and honest as ususal and became eloquent when speaking about religion.

When they tried to pin him down to which religion he belonged, he responded, "I feel very much a part of the whole Jewish-Christian tradition, and with the message that that tradition teaches. But that message has been fragmented and torn apart, so its clarity has been fogged by those who preach one message by their words and another message by their actions. I feel drawn to all those people who are trying to bring love and unity back into the human family, wherever I find them."

When asked about attending the synagogue services he answered that he enjoyed them and felt they were very much a part of Christianity because Judaism was the root from which Christianity sprang. His view of religion was stripped of all the fracturing pettiness that characterized most committed people's view of religion. He saw the overview of God's people trying in their own well-meaning ways to honor God and serve one another. He looked upon religion as people rather than as structures and saw no contradiction in being part of all believing people. It was very simple to him and, as one interviewer remarked, "an unusual point of view and quite beautiful."

When asked about the obstacles to unity among Christians, he was incisive and blunt. "Many religious leaders don't want it. They talk about unity and dabble in it, and feign attempts at oneness, but deep down they don't want to give up what they have so they postpone critical commitments to unity. They also contend that differences in belief are the great obstacle to unity. They say this because they presume purity of beliefs among their followers, which is false. People don't all believe what their leaders teach them, nor do all Catholics or Lutherans or Methodists believe the teachings of their bishops. Charity should be the first step to unity. Then, when people are worshiping together and working together as a Christian family, their love will make possible a unity of belief and a willingness to accept the guidance of Peter. There may still be some whose beliefs have strayed too far from Jesus' teachings. They will have to ask themselves where they really belong."

The whole interview lasted almost an hour and gave a fair picture of Joshua's life-style and a cursory glimpse into his unusual philosophy. The interview was well received and brought Joshua to the immediate attention of the religious leaders of Auburn. People from the synagogue thought it was a sympathetic portrayal of a sensitive, compassionate artist who was also a deep-thinking philosopher. They certainly did not consider him a theologian.

Christian leaders were divided in their reaction. Those whose denominations had little doctrinal content were impressed by his open-mindedness. Others found his mentality bordering on religious anarchy and a definite threat to simple believers. Father Pat said in his sermon the next Sunday that he thought Joshua to be a rare, authentically religious man and one of the few persons who truly understood religion.

There were some who thought Joshua was just another crackpot artist who was hooked on religion and had a big enough ego to peddle his own peculiar brand of it. Not too many took him seriously. Joshua became more the butt of jokes among the clergy than a serious threat.

The week passed rapidly and by Friday he was pretty well finished with the rough work on the figures and was well into the details. Friday evening Aaron came on schedule, and together the two men went to the temple. The evening was a happy one. People talked excitedly about the TV interview and congratulated Joshua on becoming a celebrity. They were proud he was their friend and exuded happiness for him. During the social hour he was more popular than the week before. His circle in the corner grew wider each week, and even the rabbi, who jokingly said he was a bit jealous, came over and joined the group. He and Joshua exchanged stimulating ideas, and, although they did not always agree, they respected each other and became very close. The rabbi whimsically remarked that night that he was even beginning to like the statue of Moses, and now that he was getting to know Joshua, could understand Moses better. Joshua laughed heartily.

Marcia's mother and father came to the synagogue that evening. Marcia introduced them to Joshua. They were proper, refined people. Joshua's casual dress didn't impress them, but Marcia had praised him so highly, they couldn't restrain their curiosity to meet him. It didn't take long for them to detect Joshua's innate refinement of personality, and they wondered, if he was not a rebel, why his dress was so casual and so unconventional. They came away with the distinct feeling they had met a person who seemed to walk through the world untouched and unspoiled by the greed and pettiness that poisoned the lives of so many. They sensed a purity and an innocence that was uncommon and realized their daughter had found a person much like herself. But the relationship confused them. They were practical people and could see nothing coming of it other than a broken heart.

On the way home Aaron and Joshua talked calmly and casually about a variety of topics and eventually came back to the same theme as the week before, Aaron's inability to feel the same way that Joshua did about life. Joshua told him he was too impatient There really had been a big change in him over the past month, even though he didn't see it himself. This was the first time Joshua had seen Aaron's car not highly polished. Joshua laughingly said, "That's progress," to which Aaron replied, "I forgot about it."

Joshua told him he wouldn't have forgotten about it before, but now it wasn't that important to him. Joshua also heard, during the social hour, about Aaron hiring heads of poor families to work in his steel fabricating plant. Those incidents alone showed important changes in his life. We all have to be content with slow progress, Joshua reminded him. Human beings are like plants. They grow in stages and those stages can't be accelerated. In due time plants bear their fruit, and with human beings it is much the same. In the proper time and at the proper pace we grow into what God intends us to become. Events take place and strangers cross our path that force us to think. All these things God uses to teach us and suggest a different way of understanding things. So we grow, gradually, imperceptibly, under the subtle guidance of God's own spirit. Being conscious of our success is not important. The left hand shouldn't know what the right hand is doing. That can lead to vanity.

What Joshua said made Aaron feel better. He had done the things Joshua had heard about. He *was* a little less attached to his car. He even began to take little walks by himself and think about God. He found a real good feeling of peace when he withdrew into this world of the spirit. But he still felt he wasn't doing enough.

Joshua liked Aaron. He was a naturally good man with noble ideals, even if they weren't the same highly spiritual ideals that drove Joshua. These long weekend drives to the city and back had a big effect on Aaron's life. He never looked upon Joshua as belonging to a particular religion. Joshua was too big for that. Aaron saw him as a giant of a man whose life transcended denomination or religious affiliation. He was just a healthy person who had a supremely well-balanced view of life and whose relationship with God was well integrated into the fabric of his personality. To Joshua, God was like the air he breathed. It was so much a part of him that he didn't need to be aware of it. It was this carefree lightheartedness that had attracted Aaron to Joshua in the first place.

As he lay in bed that night Joshua's thoughts drifted across the centuries to the synagogue in Nazareth that he knew and loved so well. The whole scene passed vividly before his mind: the attendant handing him the scroll, the dead silence of the audience, the nervous reading of the text, "The Spirit of the Lord is upon me . . . to bring good news to the poor . . . to proclaim release to captives and sight to the blind; to set at liberty the oppressed, to proclaim the acceptable year of the Lord, and the day of recompense." It had been a hot, sultry morning, and the synagogue was packed. The air was tense. These were the people he had grown up with, and they were surprised at what they were witnessing. They weren't ready for it, and they resented it. "Is not this the carpenter's son? Where did he get all this from?" After a few brief moments the young preacher was being dragged bodily from the building. Only because of the confusion was he able to slip away and escape.

Tears came to Joshua's eyes as he lay there in the dark. "How different from the big-heartedness of the people at the synagogue this evening," he thought. These people responded in a way that was new and different from all his past experiences. He went to sleep feeling good, and grateful to his Father.

By Saturday morning the figures were taking shape. The one for Father Darby was almost finished. The one for Reverend Rowland was not far behind. Joshua spent the better part of the morning working on that one. Both figures were almost five feet high and wide enough to include considerable detail. Joshua worked assiduously, bringing meaning and messages out of the lifeless wood that were bound to cause conflicting reactions in the viewers. But that was what he wanted to do. Works of art that merely evoke admiration rarely stimulate the mind and have little effect on behavior. His work was, therefore, strongly suggestive, and no one walked away from his creations unmoved.

He worked late on Saturday and slept soundly that night. Early Sunday morning he walked down the back road to the Pentecostal church where Reverend Rowland preached. The building was a simple wooden frame structure. There weren't many people in the congregation; there weren't many black people in town. Some of their members came from a distance to attend services at this church, and they made great sacrifices to keep their community together.

When Joshua came walking up to the church Reverend Rowland warmly welcomed him and introduced him to the handful of parishioners standing with him. The minister asked Joshua how the statue was coming along. Joshua said it was coming nicely and should be finished by Friday. If he came late Friday morning, it would be ready for him. The man was delighted and made no attempt to hide his pride at the thought of having a figure of the Apostle Peter in his church. Even though statues were frowned upon, the minister managed to convince his people that Peter was a symbol of the rock foundation of Christianity and would be a constant reminder of the fundamentals of their faith in Jesus. The group felt all authority rested in the Scriptures. The authority of religious leaders was merely human, and they were disinclined to place much authority in the Church. For them the Scriptures were the real touchstone of faith, not the Church. While this approach had its pitfalls in the confusion it occasioned over meaning of important parts of Scripture, and the splinter groups it gave rise to, the people themselves were simple and well-intentioned. Above all they took their faith seriously and were an inspiration to the rest of the community for the charity and honesty of their personal lives.

The service in the church was informal and joyful. The people sang and prayed aloud and gave touching testimonies to the wonders that took place in their lives when they gave themselves over to the Lord. Joshua was moved by the simple sincerity of the people. The minister welcomed the visitors and guests and singled out Joshua, the accomplished artist who was carving the figure of Peter the Apostle for their church. A lady prayed spontaneously for the Spirit to bless his hands, so he would put into the figure a message that would touch the hearts of everyone in the congregation. Everyone responded by proclaiming a loud "Amen."

After the service the people filed into the little hall that served at different times as classroom or meeting room. The friendly smell of coffee and pastry floated around the room, putting everyone in a congenial mood. A group of men gathered around Joshua and asked him how he liked their service. He was honest and told them of the thoughts that had passed through his mind during the service.

The Reverend Rowland also came over and told Joshua how happy he was to have him meet his people and that he was welcome to their service at any time.

The social hour ended and the group broke up. It had been a long session, almost two and a half hours in all. As Joshua walked home a handful of people walked down the street with him, then separated as they reached a corner, each going his own way.

Joshua spent the afternoon relaxing in his backyard. Pat Zumbar and Herm Ainutti stopped over with a friend they wanted Joshua to meet. His name was Woozie. That was not his real name, but it was what he had been called since boyhood so he still used it. He was shaped like Pat and could double for him in other ways. Woozie was earthy and practical, and his goals in life were simple. He had a gruff exterior but underneath was a kind man who would do anything for a friend. Joshua grinned broadly as he was introduced to him, as if he already knew all about him.

When the trio went into the kitchen Woozie eyed everything in sight. "You can tell a woman never touched this place," he commented. There was a coat of dust on practically everything, which was obvious to any visitor, though it was of little importance to Joshua.

"You really live alone?" Woozie asked, skeptical that a fellow as young and good-looking as Joshua really lived by himself.

"I'm never alone," Joshua countered, "but I am very contented living by myself. Some people can't live with themselves, and they find it impossible to imagine anyone else living by himself. When you are at peace you can enjoy the opportunity of living with your thoughts."

Woozie was interested in Joshua. "How come you moved up here all by yourself? You have to get away from someplace?" he asked Joshua as soon as they were all seated. "I can't understand why anyone would want to live in this godforsaken place," he continued.

"Maybe because people are so nice and friendly," Joshua shot back.

"That'll shut you up," Pat said to Woozie with a great belly laugh.

"You know, you're getting to be quite a celebrity," Herm continued. "I saw you on the television the other night. You should have been a politician, the way you handled the tricky questions. You looked right at home. Were you nervous?"

"Yes, a little. It was a new experience, but it gave me a good chance to say a few things I felt were important."

"You did a good job, even though I hate to admit it," Pat said.

"How come they put you on television?" Woozie asked.

Pat was quick to respond. "Because he's a good artist. He even carved a statue for a synagogue in the city. In fact, it's the synagogue Silverman belongs to, the one who owns the television station. I hear you've been going to the services every Friday night, Joshua."

"The people have been very gracious in inviting me, and I enjoy being with them. They are God's chosen people, you know."

"They were, you mean," Woozie interjected. "They had their chance when Christ came, and they blew it."

"They didn't all reject him," Joshua answered. "In fact, a great many of those who rejected him perished in the destruction of Jerusalem. Those who accepted Jesus took his advice and fled to the hills and were saved when the Roman armies came. The Jews of today are the descendants of Jews who lived throughout the Roman world. They never knew Jesus. Their descendants today are still God's chosen people. God never takes back what he gives."

The three men were surprised at Joshua's understanding of history. Even a historian would have been shocked at what Joshua just said because it revealed a knowledge of something historians would not have known.

Joshua took the men into the shop. It was cluttered with a variety of pieces in different stages. The two figures of Peter the Apostle stood out, and Woozie asked about them.

"They are both of Peter the Apostle," Joshua said, "for two different churches."

The men were impressed. Even Woozie, who prided himself on his ability as a craftsman, admired the perfect detail of Joshua's work.

CHAPTER

JOSHUA worked hard all the next week, trying to finish the figures of the Apostle Peter on schedule. Monday afternoon two boys from a local commune came to visit Joshua with a tale of woe. They and their friends had a little farm that they had been working. Their equipment was primitive and not in good shape. This morning, while they were working, a wheel on their wagon broke. They tried to fix it but couldn't. Would Joshua be kind enough to help them? They brought the wheel with them. Joshua looked it over and smiled. It brought back faint memories of so long ago, when he was just a young apprentice working for his father.

"Yes, I can help you," Joshua told them. "Come back tomorrow and it will be ready for you."

The free spirits left and talked about Joshua all the way home. He was freer than even they were, yet his life seemed so well-ordered, unlike theirs. They sensed a peace and a contentment in Joshua that they lacked, and also a joy that they had never known. Their simple life came from a discontent with society, and it didn't bring them the peace they thought it would. Joshua chose the simple life, obviously because it gave him the freedom to expand the breadth of his inner life. Externally his life and theirs were much the same. Internally there was a world of difference. They envied him.

Joshua worked on the wheel during the breaks in his other work. It was less tedious and even relaxing. He hadn't worked on a wheel in ages, and a train of memories flooded his imagination. Now and then a tear collected in his eyes as he thought of tender memories of long ago. They were good days, when he was just a boy learning about life. His mother was never far away, sometimes hovering over him like a mother hen, too protectively, as if some impending calamity would occur at any moment. His mother was a happy person, always humming to herself as she went about her household chores. He could hear her out in his father's shop. He remembered his father remarking one day, when they were carving an ox yoke, "How come your mother doesn't sing like that when we're around the house?" They both laughed. He remembered his mother forever trying to keep him away from bad companions. She never had much success. How many things have happened since then!

Joshua had to send for Woozie to help him finish the wheel. He needed the iron band welded. Woozie came and asked Joshua who the wheel was for. When Joshua told him he went into a tirade about those weirdos who don't know whether they are men or women. Joshua just listened and helped as Woozie welded the band on the wheel.

When Woozie left Joshua went back to the two figures. He had come a long way in the past week, and in another couple of days he would be finished.

The next day the boys and two of their friends came for their wheel. They talked with Joshua for over an hour, trying to understand something of his life. "You seem to have achieved in your own life something we struggle for constantly, but it always evades us, and that is peace and contentment. What is your secret, Joshua?" a tall, lean young man with full beard and overalls asked him.

"My peace comes from within," Joshua told them. "The simplicity of my life reflects what I possess inside. The simplicity of your life does not come from within. It is an escape from the world around you, a denial of what you have been a part of and been hurt by. I have no such problem in my life. I do not let myself be hurt by events. I realize all humanity is in a process of growing and, of necessity, will always be imperfect. It can never be any different. I understand that and accept it, and love people for what they are, and I find them enjoyable because our Father made them that way. Find God and learn to love people, and you will find the same peace and harmony with nature."

The young men were impressed, even though he criticized their values. They appreciated the insight. They thanked him for spending time with them, as well as for fixing the wheel. Each of the four fellows had a gift for Joshua. One was carrying a rooster under his arm, another a fat hen. One of the others had a jar of jam his girlfriend had made. The fourth had a basket of eggs and a small bag of flour he himself had ground. They were all deeply grateful to Joshua for what he had done for them. Joshua told them about Woozie welding the band. When they heard Woozie's name they were amused. They knew Woozie. They had had more than one encounter with him. They laughed over Joshua conning Woozie into doing a job for them. They took the wheel and left, rolling the wheel down the street as they went. Joshua watched them, smiling.

He went back into the house and worked zealously on the figures. He knew things about Peter no one else could ever imagine and incorporated them into the personalities emerging from the lifeless wood. Each figure was strikingly different, so much so that, although the features were perfectly similar, the character traits were so paradoxical that they gave the feeling of two different persons. That was the way Joshua had planned it. There were two distinct messages he wanted to express through these statues, and there was no mistaking them. Whether they would be understood by the two clergymen was another matter, and if they understood them, would they accept what they saw? But Joshua continued to work, chiseling away at all the fine details.

By Thursday afternoon he was finished with both of them. He sanded them down to a satiny smooth finish, then stained them with a deep color that brought out the rich grain of the wood. He then waxed them and set them aside. These were to be the last of the masterpieces Joshua was to create. His life was becoming increasingly complicated. His personal life was simple enough, but people would not allow his life to remain that way; their varied reactions to him were too intense. And there were some who did not feel at all comfortable with his presence in the community. They were determined to do all they could to get rid of him.

Joshua slept soundly that night, but dreamed strange dreams: of Nathaniel cynically questioning his origins, of James and John conniving for positions of authority, of Peter fearful of being identified with Jesus, and Judas meeting with temple officials. All the human weaknesses of the apostles that would forever be ingredients of those who shepherd his people. As they gave him trouble then, so the pattern would be repeated again. As long as people were human he would be too much for them to cope with. He complicated their lives too much, just by being himself.

Joshua woke up early. Birds were singing outside his window. He sat at the edge of the bed with his head in his hands. He was still tired. He had slept soundly enough, but the intensity of his dreams had drained him. He finally pulled himself up, dressed, and made breakfast. He didn't take his walk that morning. He puttered around his garden, harvesting the ripened vegetables, which had grown large and full. There wasn't much time left. He had planned his garden well, and was now picking what little was left of the first big crop.

While he was still working he heard a car pull up in front of the house and voices exchanging greetings. He walked out and saw the two clergymen coming up the path together.

It was Father Darby who spotted him first. He couldn't resist the remark that jumped out as he saw Joshua again with his garden tools, "Well, our famous artist has been working in the dirt again. I can't help but feel you would have made a better gardener than a sculptor. It seems you enjoy it more." The Reverend Rowland was shocked at the priest's behavior.

"The earth is where all life originates," Joshua countered, "and even the best of us can never be so proud as to believe we're above it. It is very much a part of us all." The black minister thought that was a fair rebuttal and justly deserved. The priest didn't accept it too graciously and his face showed his disdain.

Joshua walked to the porch and opened the door for the two men. Then, excusing himself, he returned to the living room carrying one of the figures. He left again to get the other one. When he brought it in the men were struck by the similarity of the features, but did not understand the wide difference in the bas-relief scenes. Neither had known what the other had commissioned.

The priest eyed the one he thought was his and admitted Joshua did not do a bad job—for a gardener. Joshua smiled at his attempt at humor.

"Gentlemen," Joshua said, "I was not expecting you to come together. It is a coincidence that both of you ordered a likeness of Peter. I tried to honor your requests and carve what I thought would be aspects of Peter's personality that would be of significance to your people." Taking the sculpture depicting Peter on his knees, caressing the head of a dying beggar, his three-tiered tiara lying disrespectfully on the ground, he lifted it up and placed it near the Episcopal priest. The man was horrified and deeply offended. "That is not the great Apostle Peter but some pious servant saint whom I do not even recognize," the priest said angrily.

"On the contrary," Joshua said, "that is Peter at his greatest. It was not part of Peter's personality to serve. He was born to rule, and that dominated his whole personality. As he grew spiritually to more resemble the Master, and realized his real role as the servant of God, he became much more humble in his attitude toward those he considered inferior. This figure depicts the moment in Peter's life when he had finally overcome nature and realized what Jesus meant when he washed the feet of the apostles and told them they should be the servants of God's children."

The priest was impressed with Joshua's logic, but unmoved by his explanation. He was still angered by what he saw, as if Joshua had hit him with a sledge hammer. The other clergyman was just as dismayed by the other figure, which he realized was his. He could understand the one Joshua had given to Father Darby, but this one was incomprehensible, with Peter standing in toga and stole, his left hand firmly gripping a shepherd's staff and his right hand gesturing with great force and determination to a crowd that included, obviously, the other apostles. It was everything about the Church that Pentecostals dislike, particularly the strong authority. Reverend Rowland was very uncomfortable with the scene. When Joshua placed it near him he was embarrassed.

"Joshua," Reverend Rowland said as politely as he could, "I think, perhaps, you have made a mistake with these two figures. It seems that Father Darby would be much more happy with this statue, and I love the message in the one you did for him."

"If each of you likes the other's statue," Joshua replied, "I have no objection, you may exchange them."

The two men exchanged statues. Reverend Rowland took out his checkbook and wrote out a check for the exact amount he and Joshua had agreed to, $100. Father Darby was surprised.

"Why is the sculpture you made for me so much more than the other one?" the priest asked. He had agreed to pay Joshua $135 for his figure. Joshua didn't charge the Pentecostal minister as much because he knew his congregation was poor, and it would be difficult for them to come up with much money.

Joshua looked at Father Darby with a trace of impatience. "Did we not agree that a fair price would be one hundred and thirty-five dollars?" Joshua asked him. "If you want to exchange costs between you that is your right, but that is between the two of you."

The priest was visibly angry, but was reluctant to show his pettiness in front of the minister, who, in his heart, he looked upon as inferior both professionally and socially. He merely told Joshua he would receive his compensation in the mail, as all his church bills had to be paid through the proper channels.

With that both men left, carrying their statues with them. Joshua accompanied them to the gate, where the chauffeur met his master and relieved him of his burden. The priest apologized to the minister for not being able to give him a ride, as there was not sufficient room in the car. Joshua watched both of them with an impish smile, as if he was aware of something no one else knew. He had carved those statues for a reason and that reason was not going to be frustrated, no matter how those two men felt about them. He went back into the house with a sigh of relief.

The workshop looked bare with the big carvings gone. Joshua went to work on several small pieces he still had left. When he finished them he set them aside. There weren't many left. It was almost three-thirty when Joshua finished the day's work.

It was Friday and Aaron would soon be over to pick him up. He quit early to prepare supper so he could be finished by the time Aaron came. While he was getting ready he was interrupted a number of times by people who came to pick up their pieces. They were all grateful for what he had done for them and for the reasonable prices. One man came in after the others had left. His name was Dick De Ratta. He had ordered a special piece as an anniversary present for his wife. He had liked Joshua ever since meeting him at the mill one day when he went to get some wood. The two would meet every now and then and talk about a whole range of things. Dick taught history at the university and practiced law. He was fascinated by Joshua's intimate knowledge of historical events and his ability to give unusual slants to events that differed radically from what was accepted by historians. Dick's respect for Joshua's judgment was such that he incorporated many of Joshua's interpretations of history into his courses. What Joshua said made sense and provided a better logic to the underlying social and political currents that crisscrossed through history. They seemed to provide the missing link between many heretofore unrelated facts.

Dick belonged to the Presbyterian church in the village. He was active in the congregation and, being a friend of the pastor, was privy to much of the "official" gossip around town. Joshua was a topic of that official gossip of late, and it had Dick worried. He was torn between loyalty to the inner circle of his parish and his friendship with Joshua, who he saw as very much alone in the community and quite vulnerable. Dick had heard things about Joshua he didn't like, but was confused as to what he should do about it. He finally decided to tell him in a way that would not violate his loyalty to his pastor and, at the same time, perhaps help Joshua.

"Joshua," he said, "I know you, and I understand your feelings about things. I know you share my own misgivings about religious leaders' abuse of authority. But you are in a much more difficult position than I am. I can talk about religion within a framework of history and disguise my criticism. When you express what you think it is looked upon as just that, an expression of your own personal views, and people judge you from where they're coming from. Most people do not have much understanding of things, and they are shocked by rumored versions of what you were supposed to have said. Unfortunately it gets back to the pastors, who are none too pleased with what they hear."

Joshua listened attentively. Dick was right. This was always the problem. Joshua spoke honestly, the way he believed about things, and few people had the experience necessary to understand him. But it was still important that he say it. At least people would be forced to listen and think about what he said. In due course it would have its effect, but unfortunately it would not be until after he was long gone.

"I know you are right, Dick," Joshua said, "and I appreciate what you're telling me. I've thought a lot about what I should do and say, and always come back to the same conclusion—nothing that I say will be heard or understood in the same way by those who hear it. But that is true of everyone's ideas. Mine are no exception. The difference is that what I have to say affects people's lives, their children's lives, and their relationship with God. They must have a clear understanding of these matters, so I really don't have much of a choice. In time, when the wind dies down and the chaff is blown away, the kernel will remain. But it will always be that the prophet is the first victim of his own message, and only later do people say, 'Oh, now I understand.' But he is already gone."

Dick listened in admiration of Joshua's insight and his cool courage in the face of approaching storms. It showed that this was not the first time Joshua had been through situations of this type. He turned his attention to the work of art Joshua had carved for him. It was a figure of a man standing near a fence playing a flute. Little children were looking away disinterestedly, while birds sitting along the top of the fence listened attentively. A woman stood near the fence looking admiringly at the man. Dick recognized his family and couldn't help but laugh at Joshua's insight into the problems he was having at home. "Joshua, how clever," he said, "and perfect in every detail! How do you find the patience to work on such minute details? It would drive me to distraction, even if I had the ability."

Dick tried to pay Joshua for the work, but Joshua wouldn't hear of it. Dick had said it was his own anniversary present to his wife, and he wouldn't feel right if he didn't have some part in it at least paying for it. The love Joshua expressed in the work was itself a treasured gift to both him and Elizabeth. And he hoped the kids would get the message. Dick was so appreciative, he gave Joshua a big hug, and tears ran down his cheeks at the thought of Joshua understanding his family so completely and the affection shown in the carving.

He picked up the carving and shook his head in bewilderment as he walked toward the door with Joshua. They went outside together. Dick chuckled as he got into his car, thinking about what his wife's reaction would be when she saw the gift.

Aaron came on time. His car was washed and shining again. He did it just before he came because he knew Joshua would notice. Joshua was waiting on the porch and walked toward the car as soon as Aaron stopped. He was embarrassed whenever Aaron got out of the car to open the door for him. This way he could avoid all the fuss. "I'm glad you cleaned your car," Joshua said as he got in. "I couldn't imagine what it would look like after not being cleaned for two weeks."

Aaron laughed. "You're sharp, Josh. Why do you think I had it cleaned? I couldn't drive a fashion model like you up to the synagogue in a dirty car."

Joshua slapped Aaron on the knee. "I earned that one," he said good-humoredly.

On the way Aaron confided an interesting bit of information to his friend. A group of well-placed persons in the synagogue had approached the rabbi during the week with a proposition. Lester and Marcia and a few others were behind it. When Joshua asked him what it was Aaron beamed but said he couldn't tell him. It had to come from the rabbi. He just hoped that Joshua would be amenable to the proposal. Joshua didn't pry any further.

When they arrived at the synagogue they were, as usual, greeted warmly. Aaron left Joshua by himself and an unfamiliar man walked over and introduced himself. He heard Joshua had been coming to the synagogue each week and was warmly received. He didn't like it one bit. That was why he had come this evening. He and his family had been persecuted by Christians as long as he could remember, and he couldn't stand the thought of a Christian being welcomed so cordially by his people. He accused Joshua of a whole variety of charges, saying that he shared the guilt of all the people who had persecuted his people and killed them in the concentration camps.

Joshua pitied the man's tortured spirit and felt it would be cruel to counter him. Then, impulsively, to the man's utter disbelief, Joshua put his arms around him and hugged him intensely, asking him for forgiveness for all the meanness his people had done to his family and all other Jews throughout the centuries. The man was so overcome by the sincerity of Joshua's compassion that he broke down, threw his arms around Joshua, and cried like a baby. In a moment all the bitterness and rage had left his troubled spirit, and his body went limp with the release of years of pent-up hatred and sickness.

People who knew the man and had avoided him because of his bitterness were dumbfounded at the change that came over him in that brief instant. Everyone watched as the two men walked into the sanctuary, hand in hand. The incident was not soon to be forgotten.

The man sat with Joshua during the service and was shocked when he heard Joshua saying the prayers and singing the hymns in perfect Hebrew. After the service they walked out together. When Joshua's admirers gathered around him for their weekly conference, the man joined the circle and found Joshua to be a beautiful person in his understanding of human nature and his insistence that people will find peace only when they are ready to lay aside pettiness and prejudice, even those prejudices that have been consecrated through the passing of centuries. Only an open mind is capable of developing the attitudes necessary for peace. The things of this world cannot give peace; it must come from our ability to rise above material things and reach a point where we don't crave them. Even God's people must realize that each people is chosen by God to fill a different role in the destiny of the human race, and only by accepting other peoples as equal partners in God's plan can they hope to find acceptance by the rest of the human family.

These were bold ideas that Joshua put forward. But as strong as they were, some of the older men and women, who had suffered much in their long lives, were shaking their heads thoughtfully and knowingly. Where you want to find love and acceptance, you may first have to show love and acceptance, because love can be returned only when it is given. No one took offense at what Joshua said. They had come to know him and realized that what he said had great depth of thought and feeling and came from a profound understanding of life. Everyone was willing to listen to what he said, and many were inclined to agree.

One of Woozie's friends was at the service that night, a man by the name of Phil Packer, and his wife, Ada. They unobtrusively joined the little circle. They came over with Marcia, who was a friend of the family. During the discussions they did not take part, just listened. Marcia almost said something a couple of times, but realized her questions would have been of little interest to the others so she didn't ask them.

When the social hour was over Marcia introduced Phil and Ada to Joshua. They became fast friends. Phil was open and outgoing. He joked with Joshua right from the start. "How did a nice guy like you ever get to be good friends with Woozie?" Joshua laughed.

"Rather easily. With Woozie what you see is what you get. There's no guile, no deceit. There's no fine print, no hidden pages. There should be more people like him."

"You really like him, don't you?" Phil asked, not too surprised.

"Why shouldn't I?" was Joshua's simple return.

"Just testing. You're okay, Josh. You're my kind of man too. If ever I can do anything for you, just call, and I'll be there." When Phil said that, that was the seal of friendship. He and Woozie, and the Sanders and, in fact, the whole gang, were much the same in their code of honor. It was real. It was sincere and it was rugged love. Joshua thought of the apostles and the rough ways and shocking language when they thought Jesus wasn't listening.

While they were talking Aaron came over, waited till they stopped talking, then told Joshua the rabbi would like to see him. A broad grin lighted up his face, and when he noticed Marcia he winked, as if she would know what it was all about.

The rabbi's office was well-appointed. He was a scholar, and most of the books that lined his walls he had already read, not like so many who buy books for decoration. A russet-colored shag rug stretched from wall to wall. Deep maroon, velour-covered chairs flanked the rabbi's desk.

When Joshua entered the rabbi stood up and welcomed him. He offered a chair to Joshua and both men sat down.

"Joshua," Rabbi Szeneth began, "I appreciate your coming to see me. I know Aaron takes you home every Friday night so I won't keep him waiting. What I have to say won't take long, and I hope you will be able to oblige me."

Joshua listened as the rabbi continued, "Our people have come to love you over the past few months. They are very impressed with your little talks each week. They have never met a person quite like you, and I must admit, I share their admiration. You have been an inspiration to all of us. During the week some of my board approached me and asked if you could be allowed to speak to the whole congregation. I was happily surprised because the same thought was going through my mind, but I was a little reluctant to suggest it. I told the group there would be no objection and that I thought it was an excellent idea. They asked me to discuss it with you and ask if you would be willing. So, Joshua, my dear friend, I would be honored if you would accept our invitation to speak to our congregation at next Friday's service."

Joshua beamed his delight. Tears came to his eyes as his thoughts went back to a similar invitation so very long ago. "Rabbi, you have no idea what this means to me,"

Joshua said. "I am the one who is honored by your warmth and goodness. I would be more than happy to speak to our people next Friday."

"Is the notice too short? Do you need more time to prepare?" the rabbi asked.

"I need no time to prepare. I have been preparing for a longer time than you could imagine."

"Well, it's all set then, next Friday night." The two men shook hands, and the rabbi walked out with Joshua.

14

JOSHUA worked all day Saturday, finishing most of the remaining jobs. They were neatly arranged along the top of the workbench. Late in the afternoon, lying under the tree near the pond, he thought of the talk he was to give at the synagogue and smiled at the chain of recent events that had brought about this startling decision. He thought about the synagogue and others he was familiar with. They hadn't changed much through the centuries. They are still constructed much the way they used to be. Men and women sit together now. The scrolls are still enshrined in the ark, though they are not used anymore. Lectors read from printed versions. There are no scribes or Pharisees, or priests strutting around in flowing robes wearing broad phylacteries, looking like peacocks among the common people. But common people are not too common anymore either. He thought of the man who accosted him at the synagogue last night and reminisced about the man with the speech impediment from whom he had driven the devil. Devils were more visible in those days. Today they are subtle, disguised as advanced, compassionate thinkers who want to revolutionize society, sowing seeds of doubt about all that is sacred, or as religious leaders inciting their followers to hatred of their fellow man and even murder in the name of God.

Then he thought of Marcia, her work at the United Nations, and the good she was trying to accomplish among so many whose objectives were dubious. She stood out as a pure and innocent dove among a pack of vultures. Perhaps the beauty of her innocence would melt more hearts than the most devious political maneuvering. He thought of Mary of Bethany. Marcia was different, though they both loved with the same intensity. His feelings for both were the same.

Returning home, Joshua encountered a young boy walking off the porch. They met at the gate.

"Can I help you, young man?" Joshua asked.

"The pastor, Father Kavanaugh, wants you to come to the rectory. He wants to talk to you," the boy answered.

"Now?"

"No, he's busy now, and tomorrow he's busy. He'll see you on Monday morning at nine-thirty."

"Thank you, son."

The next morning Joshua went to the Episcopal church for Mass. Father Jeremy offered the Mass and spoke about the new statue of the Apostle Peter, which had been installed in the niche at the side altar. Joshua noticed the English flags all around the big church, betraying the denomination's focus of allegiance. He tried to pray, but found it difficult. The music distracted him beyond even his own power of self-discipline. The organist, Mr. Walls, pounded out in mechanical perfection two-hundred-year-old hymns from another continent and another part of history. The service was technically perfect, but worship rang hollow. Father Jeremy went on orating in well-cadenced elegance about the moving symbolism of the liturgy and how wise the Church was in incorporating artistic richness into the liturgy. It was a fitting tribute to the awesome majesty of God.

Joshua was glad when the Mass ended. The chauffeur met Joshua outside the church and made a big fuss over him, pointing him out to all his friends and introducing him as the artist who had carved the new statue. The people were nice to him, and congratulated him on his ability, and asked how he liked their church. Joshua told them the ritual was beautiful and he had noticed some people in church who seemed to be deeply absorbed in worship and felt they were the source of blessing to their community.

At that point Father Jeremy emerged and heard Joshua's remarks. Joshua turned and greeted him. The priest stayed where he was and merely nodded curtly, waiting for Joshua to come up to him, which he did not do. The priest turned and began talking to other people who were waiting for him. When the chauffeur saw the priest coming out of the church, he slipped away.

Joshua walked down the street. Some of his friends were leaving their churches and they stopped to greet him. Phil, the manager at the mill, came over and put his arm on Joshua's shoulder. "You're just the man I wanted to see," he said. "How about coming over to my house for breakfast?"

"Okay," Joshua replied, and the two men walked over to Phil's family, who were walking down the church steps. They all walked around the corner to the house.

When they went inside Phil took Joshua into the living room while his wife cooked breakfast. He had a few questions he wanted to ask Joshua. He hadn't seen Joshua lately and had heard all kinds of rumors. Was Joshua all right?

How was his business? He hadn't been using as much wood lately and Phil was worried that he might be having problems.

Joshua was at a loss as to how he should answer. Yes, things had changed considerably of late. He had been very busy filling orders for people, but other aspects of his life were beginning to take precedence over his carving, and he wasn't taking any more orders.

Phil knew some people were making life difficult for Joshua and tried to reassure him that the majority of the people loved him and supported him.

Joshua told him he could read the signs of the times and could pretty well tell how events were shaping up. He told Phil not to be concerned, he was confident of the future.

The delicious odor of pancakes and sausage and bacon filled the house. Ellen, Phil's wife, called everybody to the table. Joshua went in with Phil and sat next to him at the table. The serious talk stopped, and after prayers everyone dug into breakfast. The hot coffee smelled good and tasted even better. The food disappeared as fast as Ellen could put it out. Joshua ate heartily, enjoying everything. He was glad there were so many good people who liked him and cared for him. It helped to dispel some of the gloom.

Ellen was a good woman. She had come from Germany as a young girl and still had a trace of an accent. Her ways were very much old country. The way she kept the house, the way she raised the children, even the way they dressed was in good taste but simple in an old-fashioned way.

Joshua talked to each of the children while they ate. They were not as demonstrative as the children on the back road, but they liked Joshua in their own way and were glad he had come to breakfast. Their father had told them so much about Joshua that they looked up to him as sort of a local hero.

The breakfast ended, and each of the children set about performing his and her chores. Joshua stayed a few minutes talking to Phil and Ellen, then went back home.

The rest of the day passed by slowly. Joshua didn't have the zest that characterized his carefree behavior of a few weeks before. He was still at peace. He still enjoyed his walks out past the Langfords'. He was still thrilled when a beautifully colored pheasant jumped up in front of him and flew off. But he seemed preoccupied with an inner world, where a drama was beginning to unfold. It was as if he was waiting for things to happen. He knew he could influence those events, but chose not to. He allowed himself to become an actor on a stage set by others.

On Monday morning Joshua went up to the rectory for his meeting with Father Kavanaugh. The receptionist greeted him cordially and took him into the office. It was a large room, well decorated, with a large mahogany desk at one end and high-back chairs along the walls. Behind the desk was a picture of the Pope, and on either side a picture of the bishop and the pastor. Off on the side wall was a large map of what appeared to be Auburn and its environs. Father Kavanaugh was sitting at his desk.

"Young man," the pastor started, "I have been hearing many things about you of late. You have quite a following for a person who has been in town for only a short time. One of the matters that has been brought to my attention is your discussions about religion."

"Could you be more specific?" Joshua asked.

"Yes. I have heard you have taken it upon yourself to teach religion, and from what I gather, a not-too-healthy version of religion at that. Quite a few of my people are very disturbed about it and asked me if I approve. I told them, of course, that I did not approve and that I did not even know you. It seems also that you have been telling people that religion today is not what Jesus intended, and that religious leaders are not much different from the religious leaders in Christ's day. Is that true?"

Joshua looked at the priest with compassion in his eyes and answered simply, "Not exactly. I do not set out to teach religion, but when discussions get around to those topics I speak freely about what I know. And, yes, it is true, Jesus never intended that religion become what it is today. Jesus was free and preached to people that they are God's children and that, as God's children, they are free. They are not slaves. Jesus also intended that his leaders be humble men and allow people to enjoy being free. Unfortunately not many religious leaders feel comfortable with people being free but enjoy more exercising their authority over the people. They like to make rules and laws that burden people's lives and decree that, if they are not obeyed, they sin and are liable to punishment by God. That is so unlike Jesus."

The pastor was becoming uneasy and irritated by what Joshua was saying.

"How do you know what Jesus intended?" the priest interjected.

"Aren't the Gospels clear in showing Jesus' attitudes on these things?" Joshua asked calmly.

"What Jesus taught is one thing, but it's another thing for a layman with no training in theology to criticize the Church's practice of religion," the priest objected.

"I know what I say is true, and the Scriptures are solid evidence. You know that Jesus preached humility to his apostles and told them they were to exercise authority with gentleness and meekness. He even washed their feet to impress upon their minds the importance of serving people, not ruling them."

"I don't like your attitude, young man, and I resent the way you presume to preach to me. I also resent you talking to my people, and I will not permit it."

"Who are your people?" Joshua asked caustically.

"You see that map on the wall?" the priest said, pointing to the large map. "All the people living in the territory marked out on that map are my people, and I have jurisdiction over them. No one is to speak to them without my permission."

Joshua was visibly angry. "They are not your people," he said sharply. "They are God's children, and as God's children they are free. It is shepherds like you who have stripped God's people of the freedom and joy they should experience as the children of God and returned them to the status of slaves, no longer free to follow their own consciences, or to listen to their inner voices, or even the voice of God. It is shepherds like you who are so taken up with your own authority that you resent people even talking to others about the things of God without your permission. It is men like you who have destroyed the good name of Jesus' message and have bound up people's lives in shackles and fear of punishment, not because you care for people, but merely to protect your authority. Jesus taught his apostles to love and to serve, but you have never loved your people because you cannot love in the normal way men love. You rule them and force them to serve you instead."

The priest was livid. He stood up and walked over to Joshua, who also stood up. The priest knew that Joshua knew him inside and out, although he had never met him. He was also afraid of him and, at this point, only wanted to get rid of him.

"Young man," the pastor said sharply, "this discussion is ended. I don't know what you are up to, but I cannot imagine it as anything good. I would prefer that you did not attend my church again. I do not see how you or my people could benefit from your presence. I intend to tell my people to avoid your company." With that the pastor ushered Joshua to the front door and went upstairs to his room, slamming the door behind him.

Joshua walked out and down the street. Some little children were playing in a vacant lot along the street. When they saw him they ran over and walked down the street with him, telling him about all kinds of trivial things that were important to them. Joshua forgot his own hurt and put his arms on the children's shoulders, telling them they should enjoy their childhood and not grow up before their time. "You are God's children," he told them, "and you are free. Let no one on earth take that freedom from you."

"We won't, Joshua," they responded, not really understanding what he meant, though the words would stick in their memories for years to come.

While Joshua was walking with the children Father Kavanaugh had gone to his room and paced back and forth, contemplating what he should do about this impudent fanatic. He certainly could not let Joshua get away with this unforgivable affront to his dignity. Since he could not control him himself, he would see to it that something was done. He reached for the telephone and called the bishop's office.

"What's the problem, John?" the bishop asked.

The pastor was enraged, and it showed in the stream

of accusations he made against Joshua. "There is a man in our parish, a newcomer, who has a powerful influence over a great many of the people here. He has a thing with religion and is turning the people against the Church. If we don't stop him, he will undermine my position here and do irreparable damage to the faith of the people. I tried to talk to him in a nice way, but he insulted me and told me I was unfit to be a priest."

The bishop listened attentively, then, when the pastor finished, responded, "You are no doubt talking about Joshua."

"Yes, he's the one."

"What can I do?" the bishop asked.

"You might call him in and talk to him."

"What makes you think he would listen?"

"At least it will show him he can't get away with his impudence."

"And if he doesn't listen, then what do we do? His influence is not limited to Auburn, you know. We have already received a batch of letters from people all across the area as a result of his interview on television. He is fast becoming a celebrity."

"That's all the more reason to stop him now, before it is too late. Mark me, he's dangerous. If people pick up his ideas there's no telling what will happen to our churches. It's hard enough now getting people to come to church, and if his ideas take hold, our churches will be empty."

"Aren't you exaggerating, John?" the bishop asked. "Do you really think he is that important?"

"See for yourself, Bishop. If you talked to him, you might change your mind."

"But he is only a layman. We can't come down as hard on him as we could if he was a priest. However, if it will put your mind at rest, I'll see him."

When Joshua reached home after leaving the rectory he spent most of the day thinking. He took a walk out to the high meadow. The sun was hiding behind thick leaden clouds. The birds were quiet. Even the woods were silent. Joshua fell on his knees and sat on his heels, his hands folded tightly, resting on his lap. He looked out across the horizon, not seeing what his eyes saw but a vision of something far beyond the colors and sights of matter. He knelt motionless, transfixed, for almost an hour, as if his soul had momentarily left his body and only the shell remained. Tears flowed freely down his cheeks, then stopped. The sun played games with clouds as a single ray shone through an opening, lighting up Joshua's face, transforming his delicate features into radiant beauty. He knelt there still, in profound thought. Then his face relaxed, and tense muscles melted into peaceful calm as a faint smile hinted at messages only he heard.

15

LATE that afternoon Father Darby received a phone call from the Reverend Rowland. He felt very uncomfortable with his statue of the Apostle Peter. He liked the art work, it was beautiful. He liked the message that spoke so clearly from the living wood, but he already knew that message. There was something missing, as if the figure had become dumb and no longer spoke. He felt uneasy having the figure in his church. Would the good Father consider exchanging statues again?

Father Darby was surprised by the call, but it saved him the embarrassment of having to make the same call. He, too, was having uncomfortable feelings about his statue. It fit only too well into his stately church, but, fitting in so well, it said nothing. It was as if his good friend, the Apostle Peter, refused to speak. The statue, too, had turned dumb, and just didn't seem in place in the church. He would be very happy to exchange it with his good brother. "I'll have my chauffeur drive us down right now," he said, referring to himself and his friend, the Apostle Peter.

In no time Father Darby was at the little church. He was surprised at the poverty of the minister and his family. This humble minister was a true Christian. The priest took the wood carving from the minister and gave him his. "Osgood," the priest said humbly, "I'd be honored if you and your family would come to my place for supper some evening this week."

"We would like that very much. My wife will be thrilled."

The chauffeur drove the car past Joshua's house. The priest was still angry at Joshua and resented his being right about the statues. He also felt an uncomfortable sense of guilt that Joshua should know him so well as to carve a statue like that for him. To make up for the insult, he had decided not to send the check for the statue, at least not right away. Now it bothered him that he hadn't, but he still couldn't get himself to relent.

They reached the church and went in to put the figure in place. When they had it positioned they stepped back and looked at it. It was a powerful and moving sculpture. It spoke with a force that would move the hardest heart. The dented tiara lying in the dust spoke powerfully of Peter's final triumph over nature and the conquest of grace. The face of the dying man Peter was attending struck Father Darby. He looked at it more closely. He looked again in disbelief. It was himself. He cringed at the thought of the great apostle on his knees caring for him. It was beneath him. And then he realized it really wasn't. Tears filled his eyes as the meaning of the statue hit him full force. The chauffeur was embarrassed and politely turned away so the priest wouldn't think he had seen. The priest knelt, not to the statue, but to offer a prayer, asking God to forgive him for his aweful pride and to help him to be more like the real Apostle Peter, whom he loved so much.

The two men left the church. The priest took the chauffeur's cap and, like a true actor, opened the rear door of his Mercedes and gestured, with a flourish, for his chauffeur to enter. Arthur was embarrassed but obliged.

The priest put on the cap, took the wheel, and drove the chauffeur home.

The week went by slowly. Joshua finished his work on the remaining figures and people came by to pick them up. These people loved Joshua. They had come to know him as a friend. They told him their problems. They shared with him the funny things that took place in their lives and they joked with him about events in town.

As people came and left over the next few days, they couldn't help but feel a sense of sadness for Joshua. He wasn't the same happy person who had come to town just a short time before. Oh, he laughed and joked with them as usual, but there was a melancholy that seemed to hang over his cottage. The shop was no longer filled with figures.

On Wednesday, Lester Gold came to see Joshua. He was a good friend of Aaron Fahn, who had told Lester practically everything he had learned about Joshua. Lester did volunteer work with a group of blind people and wondered if Joshua would accompany him on a visit to their meeting. He had told the blind folks about Joshua and about the figure of Moses he had carved. He had even brought some of them to "see" the figure, allowing them to run their highly sensitive fingers across the features and hands. They couldn't wait to meet Joshua. Would he come? That is, of course, if he wasn't busy. Joshua grinned. He was glad to see Lester. Aaron had told Joshua a lot about him and his family. Lester was now in the state legislature and was rising rapidly in the Democratic Party. He had just given a passionate speech in the Senate against the death penalty. Joshua was pleased when he heard that. How far Jews have come from the days of old, when the law and the death penalty were so much a part of life.

Without realizing it, through the centuries they have absorbed the real spirit of Jesus, while Christians were so often inclined to abandon that spirit and return to the rigid strictness of the old law. It was a strange paradox.

Joshua told Lester he would be glad to go with him. He wasn't busy so it wasn't an imposition. He just asked for a few minutes to wash up.

A short time later the two men drove to the city. When they arrived at the meeting hall Lester took Joshua to the president of the organization and introduced him. The president, Thelma Bradford, was a woman with great dignity and a ripe sense of humor. Lester had told her all about Joshua and she knew, if she kept pestering Lester, she would get to meet him someday.

After introducing Joshua to the rest of the officers, Thelma asked Joshua if he would talk to the group for a few minutes. They were dying to meet him and ask him questions. Joshua consented and was led to the head of the room. After a short introduction he rose to speak. There were about a hundred people in the audience, men, women, and even some children.

Joshua scanned the audience. They knew where he was without seeing him. The room fell silent.

"My dear friends," he began, "and I call you that even though you have never met me, because I know you, and I know that you are special people. As Lester was driving me through the country on the way here, I looked across the fields and saw all the things you have longed all your lives to see. I thought of all the things that you do see, things which we who have sight will never see, and I realized the strange goodness of God. The vision of things that pass so quickly is indeed a fleeting vision and an illusion of real things. But the things that you see are the reality beneath the illusion. What you see is real. We see merely the appearances. And we are indeed to be pitied because so few of us ever find the reality beneath the lights and colors. Your vision pierces the surface and sees the substance of life, and you can much more easily see things the way God sees them. You have a role in life that is precious. You can share with others the visions of things you see, which others cannot.

"I realize the shock of not seeing is hard to accept, but if you can trust God, and know that he has a unique work for you to do for him, then you can understand the value of your role in life. You may be tempted to compete in areas where the sighted thrive, and that is your right, but there are unique contributions to humanity and to the understanding of life that only you can make because you have resources that others do not have. Listen to the voice of God, and do not be afraid. Let him take you by the hand and guide you. Let him be your staff, and the lamp at your feet. The world needs what only you can teach them. Find what that is for each of you, and you will find overwhelming contentment."

Joshua went on talking about other things, but that was the main thrust of his message. It was well received, and the people felt they had known him all their lives, his warmth so touched their hearts, like a soothing balm that nursed many hurts and bruises they had carried with them for years.

During the time after the talk they asked him a barrage of questions, about where he lived, where he was born, about his parents, and about his work as an artist, and where he learned to carve. He answered them all simply, with the same answers he gave others, but they saw more to him than other people did and realized that, in spite of his simple ways, there was more to him than meets the eye, and he was a very different kind of person. They wished they could get to know him better.

Informal and more personal conversations followed, and Joshua became acquainted with many of the people. Sensing his compassion, they told him of many of their trials and tragedies. He listened and encouraged each one. As he and Lester were walking toward the door afterward, a young girl in her twenties was introduced to Joshua. He talked to her for a few moments. She told him of her elderly mother she was caring for, and how difficult the situation was becoming, and that she was worried about the future. Joshua listened and sensed the impossibility of the girl's predicament. He talked to her briefly, and then reached out and placed his hand on the girl's head as he said goodbye, and told her to trust in God's goodness—he would not fail her.

"I do trust him," she replied. "He is my only hope."

When Lester and Joshua went out the door and were busy talking, they were unable to hear the commotion inside. The blind girl let out a scream that sent chills up and down everyone's spine, causing many to panic. "I can see, I can see. I could never see in my life before, but now I can see," she kept saying over and over. The crowd gathered around her and asked her what had happened. All she could say was, "I don't know. I was talking to the artist, and when he was leaving, he touched me. He touched me, and now I see."

Everyone was happy for her, as if they had been blessed just as much as she. They had felt that way since Joshua had begun speaking to them, and when they went home that afternoon they felt as if something wonderful had touched each of their lives.

Outside, Joshua and Lester kept talking as they walked toward the car, unaware of what had just taken place inside. It was private for those who were there, and Joshua did not want it to go any further.

By the time Lester dropped Joshua off in Auburn and returned home, his phone had been ringing constantly and his wife had a pile of calls for him to return. As he called each one they told him what had happened. They were so grateful for Lester bringing his friend to them. They would never forget what had happened that day.

When Lester had made his last call and hung up, he fell back in his green velvet armchair and cried out loud, "That fox, that consummate fox! He knew all along what was happening inside that hall and never let on. Wait until I see him on Friday night. I'll give it to him good," he said with a big laugh. But then his wife came in and sat down to talk to him. Several of the people had told her what had happened. She asked Lester what it all meant and what he thought of Joshua. They talked till well past midnight and couldn't wait until Friday night to hear what Joshua would say to a congregation full of Jews and a host of visiting rabbis. They were proud that Joshua was their friend, but they were beginning to have second thoughts as to his real identity. He was not just a simple wood-carver. There was much more to him than he let anyone know. They were just beginning to pierce the veil of mystery surrounding him.

When Joshua returned home he found a letter in the mailbox. Looking at the return address, he read, "Office of the Bishop," with the address beneath. He opened the letter and read it while walking into the house. It was a formal letter and from the bishop himself. "Dear Mr. Joshua," it began, "It has come to our attention that you have been expressing interest in religious matters and have shared your ideas with certain people in the parish community of Auburn. We would like to discuss this matter with you and have scheduled a meeting for this Friday morning at ten-thirty. We will expect you at that time." The letter was signed, "Cordially in Christ," followed by the bishop's signature.

Joshua saw through the unpolished attempt at formal protocol. He realized all too well not just the purpose of the meeting but how it had come about. "Obey them, because they occupy the chair of Moses" crossed his memory. He knew the bishop and the pastor were friends, and that the pastor must have insisted that something be done with him. Joshua did not like the arrogant way he was politely ordered to appear. There was no room for question, no consideration for any possible inconvenience to him. He was merely told what to do and was expected to comply.

That evening Joshua went to bed early. He was weary, with a tiredness far different from the kind that came from carving wood for long hours. That was a satisfying tiredness. This was the wearying fatigue of a harried man who was not allowed to rest in peace. He slept soundly and woke, as he did every morning, as soon as the sun rose.

It was still early when he arrived in the village for breakfast. The crew was at the diner and kidded him about all the rumors going around town. He just laughed and commented, "Well, I guess I'm finally accepted as one of the family, the way they're all talking about me."

"You sure are," Moe said. "In fact, they're already arranging your marriage, and it ain't to Mary either."

"Moe, I thought you were nice. You're being wise," Mary said, then continued, "I don't believe a thing they're saying, Joshua, and don't you pay any attention to it either.

They'd crucify Christ all over again if he came back here, and then they'd be sorry over it two days later. They just like to talk, but they're like dogs without teeth. They can't hurt you." Joshua laughed and ordered his breakfast.

He returned home to finish the last of the figures. The people who had ordered them picked them up in the early afternoon. By two o'clock they were all gone and the shop was clear of everything. Joshua looked around and thought of all the activity of the past few months and how much fun it had been. He felt a twinge of melancholy at the thought of how kind and friendly the people had been and the good times they had had together.

He cleaned the house for the first time in weeks and tidied up the yard. The two chickens had had the run of the place the past few weeks because Joshua had been too busy to do anything with them. He found a nest the hen had constructed and noticed three eggs in it. He decided to wait and see if they would hatch. He cleaned the grill and wondered what he should have for supper. The priest still hadn't paid him for the statue, so he didn't have much money. What he got from the other statue went for food and to pay for the wood. He reached in his pocket and took out a handful of bills, totaling $175. He needed most of that for the rent, but still had a little money for food. Some people still owed him money for work he had done, but he wouldn't get that till next week. He wished Father Jeremy would pay what he owed him.

16

THE WALK to the city took Joshua almost four hours. It was almost ten when he reached the outskirts. Now he had to find the bishop's office. It was a hot day and he was sweating profusely. After asking directions from several policemen along the way, he finally arrived at the bishop's place.

It was more like a modern office building than a traditional chancery. Joshua went inside and announced himself.

The place was cold and stiff. Joshua felt ill at ease and out of place. It was not his style and it brought back poignant memories of temple porticoes and flowing robes, and solemn clergy preoccupied with the same business of religion, and all its irrelevant legalities.

Joshua sat in the hall and waited. Priests and other functionaries walked back and forth looking very busy, going from one office to another. Joshua could hear conversations from each of the offices as they discussed the business matters of the diocese and the various parishes and agencies. They were very much involved in their work, and Joshua couldn't help but notice their deep interest.

Parish life was audited through this office, and financial reports were monitored with a fine-toothed comb. Monetary matters were, as in ages past, the prime occupation of religious leaders. There was no way to monitor spiritual matters anyway. That was God's business. Running the kingdom of God on earth was the noble task of ecclesiastics, and they thoroughly enjoyed this great work for God. Joshua shook his head in bewilderment. "How much they enjoy the business of the kingdom!" he thought. "If only they could become fired up with the same zeal for souls."

After waiting for almost half an hour, Joshua was finally ushered down a long corridor into the bishop's office.

The office was spacious. A deep red rug covered the floor. A golden coat of arms had been woven into the rug and looked impressive but commercial. A hand-carved desk stood at the far end of the room, and behind it sat the bishop. He stood when Joshua approached. They shook hands and the bishop gestured for Joshua to be seated. The bishop was a tall man, quite stout, and balding. His gold-rimmed glasses gave him a worldly appearance, and his mannerisms betrayed a refinement befitting his station.

As Joshua sat down his eyes scanned the ornately decorated room. Costly antiques placed tastefully here and there displayed one of the bishop's interests. A magnificent chandelier hung from the ceiling, its pendants sparkling as the sun's rays coming from a window bounced off various glass objects in the room.

The bishop thanked Joshua for coming and, as his time was valuable, got right down to business. "Joshua, I have heard many things about you the past few weeks. We have also received quite a few letters from people who are concerned about what you have been saying."

Joshua doubted very much what the bishop was saying. He knew full well the only reason he was here was because the pastor in Auburn had complained about him. Joshua also knew that, if people did take the time to write about him to the bishop, they would have said nice things, but the bishop found it difficult to let anyone know the nice things people said. It gave him a psychological edge.

"Where are you from originally?" the bishop asked him.

"Bethlehem, a little place with a lot of friendly people," Joshua answered.

"Oh, I know that community. I have some friends there. It's an-up-and-coming area," the bishop replied.

Joshua relaxed, knowing his response went right over the bishop's head.

"I have heard you like religion, and are a religious person, and enjoy talking about theological matters with people," the bishop said.

"I think you may have been slightly misinformed. I don't set out to talk about religion. I am not really interested in religious matters as you understand them. I feel strongly about God and I like people, and I am very much interested in people's relationship with God. That is different from the business of religion."

"But you have been talking about religious matters and things involving the Church, is that not true?" the bishop insisted.

"Insofar as Church people say and do things that affect people's relationship with God, yes," Joshua replied.

"What are some of your ideas about God?" the bishop asked.

Joshua looked at him and could see the emptiness of his spirit. Perhaps he was a good administrator, but there was very little spiritual depth in this man whose life was consumed with his position in ecclesiastical politics.

"How can one describe God in a few words?" Joshua said, almost bewildered over the uselessness of the question. "If you want to understand God, you have the full expression of the Father in Jesus. He is the living expression of the Father's love, unbegotten from endless time and born into this world in time to manifest God's love for all his creatures."

"What do you believe about Jesus' ideas about religion?" the bishop then asked, getting closer to the point.

"Jesus was not interested in religion as you understand it. For you religion is the passing on of finely chiseled doctrines and rigid codes of behavior. For Jesus religion was finding God and enjoying the freedom of being close to God—seeing Him in all creation, especially in God's children. Perfecting those relationships was Jesus' understanding of religion. In the mind of Jesus the Church's great concern should be to foster people's relationship with God and show people how to work together, caring for one another and building trust and love among the families of nations.

"Religion has not done that too well. Religious leaders have spent too much time and interest in setting up structures to imitate worldly governments. In running people's lives by law they have severely restricted the freedom Jesus intended his followers to have. Instead of inspiring people to be good, they have tried to legislate observances like the scribes and Pharisees. In running religion this way they have created more tensions and added to the barriers separating people from one another. Jesus intended that his message bring joy into people's lives, but too often religion has brought misery and guilt and made people see God as severe and critical."

"Where do you get your ideas from? Have you studied theology?" the bishop asked, trying to disguise his discomfort.

"I speak of things I know, and I know what I say is true. You also know that."

The bishop was irritated that this uneducated woodworker should preach to him, and it showed in his next question. "Have you been telling people that they are free of their pastor's authority?"

"I told them they are free, and that no one can take that freedom from them. If they feel their pastor deprives them of their freedom, they have made that judgment, not I," Joshua answered sharply.

The bishop began to realize he was not dealing with an illiterate. Joshua was shrewd, and the bishop couldn't help recalling the saying "Simple as a dove, but as sly as a serpent." He knew it would be futile to pry any more information out of this man without having a thorough examination by professional theologians and scriptural scholars. He saw that what Father Kavanaugh said was true. This man could be dangerous. If his popularity spread and his message of freedom took hold, it could cause a schism and severely damage the Church.

"The pastor in your church is very concerned about what you are teaching his people," the bishop continued, shifting responsibility for this meeting from himself to the pastor. He didn't want Joshua to think ill of him and tried to get on Joshua's good side. "I realize you are a learned man, Joshua, and beneath your simple ways you have a profound understanding of the things of God and a deep feeling for people. There should be more Christians like you."

Joshua said nothing, realizing the bishop was not being honest.

The bishop looked at his watch. It was almost lunchtime. He stood up, thanked Joshua for coming, and said that he had other appointments, ushering Joshua out.

As Joshua walked down the hall alone he walked past several priests and lay officials. He smiled hello, but they were too busy with their work to notice. He was famished from the long walk, and didn't have money to go to a restaurant, and the walk home would be long and hot.

As he left the chancery and was walking down the steps, he noticed a vendor selling hot dogs across the street. He reached into his pocket to see if he had any money. He had just enough to buy two hot dogs and a bottle of soda. The vendor was friendly enough, and Joshua talked to him while he ate his lunch. He then wished the man well and started on his long trip home.

In the meantime the personnel in the chancery were gathering in the dining room for lunch. When the bishop entered the chancellor met him and asked how he made out with that "oddball" from Auburn.

"He's a shrewd fox," the bishop told the chancellor. "John was right," the bishop went on, referring to Father Kavanaugh, "this guy is dangerous. We've got to get rid of him."

"How are we going to do that? He's popular, and the Jews love him. And if they suspect we're doing something to hurt him, it's going to seriously affect their donations to our charities," the chancellor suggested. He was used to carrying out unpleasant tasks that might tarnish the bishop's image and was quite adept at shrewd behind-the-scenes maneuvering.

"Call a meeting of the consultors for this evening," the bishop said. "But don't call Bob or John, they'll have conscience problems, and I don't need that. If they ask why they weren't called, tell them you weren't able to get hold of them. Don't take any excuses from the others. If they say they can't come, have them call me personally. I don't want to take the blame for this. It'll look better if the decision seems to come from them."

The chancellor skipped lunch and started making the phone calls. By the time lunch was over he had contacted everyone. Then he went back into the dining room, where the staff was relaxing after their meal. He told the bishop everyone had agreed to come. "Some of them gave me a hard time in the beginning, but when I told them they had to call you if they intended not to come, they gave in, even though it would mean changing their schedules."

The dining-room table in the chancery was the grand tribunal where personalities were discussed and reputations of priests made and destroyed. The chancery regularly reviewed the latest gossip about various priests, and as there wasn't any deep interest in the work the priests were doing as long as they were on schedule with the assessment payments, they enjoyed the pastime of discussing the latest scandals and rumors about priests. Most of the talk got back to the priests eventually and created deep resentments, which rarely surfaced. Priests knew which chancery officials said what about whom, and one day it would all erupt. Father Pat had always thought the comptroller was a good friend of his. Little did he know that everything he told his friend in secret became fodder for discussion at the chancery table.

The talk about Joshua was typical. There were rumors and jokes and casual remarks made about him, and the bishop and his staff were content to allow Joshua's reputation to be determined by these remarks. It showed the poverty of their concern for the real life of the community and the little value they placed on reputations.

In the meantime Joshua's walk back to Auburn was slow. He was tired from the long walk in the morning. The day was hot, and he hadn't eaten enough to give him the stamina for such a long hike. When he reached the outskirts of the city he rested under a fat maple tree in front of an old Victorian house. No sooner had he sat down than a crotchety man in his sixties came out of his house and, with a rake that he had picked up from the porch, walked over and told Joshua to get off his grass. Joshua assured him he would do no harm, but the man was in no mood to listen. He just raised his rake threateningly. Joshua picked himself up and walked down the sidewalk to a tree in front of the house next door.

Some kids were selling refreshments down the street and saw what had happened. One of the boys came over to Joshua with a tall glass of Kool-Aid. Joshua was sitting in a niche between the roots with his legs outstretched. His clothes were soaked with sweat. When the boy offered him the drink Joshua reached into his pocket, but the boy seemed hurt and said, "No, mister, it's free. You look sad, as if you've had a tough day."

Joshua thanked him, and took a deep draught of the refreshing drink, and sighed with great pleasure. The boy beamed his delight that he had given a stranger such comfort and sat down beside him. "What's your name?" he asked Joshua.

"Joshua," he answered.

"Where you from?"

"Auburn," Joshua said, almost too tired to talk.

"Do you work?"

"Yes, I carve wood."

"Don't mind that man next door. He's mean. He's always been mean. When I was a little boy he hit me with a stick for walking on his lawn. He hurt me too. So don't feel bad."

Joshua just smiled and said it didn't bother him. He was used to people like that. He reached out and put his hand on the boy's head and thanked him for the delicious drink, then got up and started on his way. "God bless you, Peter, and don't ever lose your kind feeling for people." The boy walked him as far as his Kool-Aid stand. As Joshua continued walking the boy watched him and wondered how he knew his name.

Not too far down the road a car drove past, stopped, and backed up. It was some of the crew from Auburn returning from work. They had finished a job and were going home early.

They were surprised to see Joshua walking along the road and were delighted to pick him up. Joshua was just as pleased. He had not been this tired for as long as he could remember.

That evening Aaron arrived at six-thirty sharp, as he did every week. Joshua ached all over and was limping slightly as he walked toward the car. Aaron asked Joshua what had happened. Joshua just laughed. "I'm getting old," he said. "I walked to the city this morning, and I'm just not used to those kinds of trips anymore." He thought back to long ago, of walks for days on end along rocky roads dry with dust, speaking in villages all along the way, with little time to eat or rest. But that was long ago.

"All ready for your talk?" Aaron asked as Joshua got into the car.

"I suppose. I had an unusual week and didn't get too

much chance to think about tonight. I did get some time
to think today when I walked to the city, so I suppose I'm
as prepared as I'll ever be."

"Lester called me early today and told me all about
what happened at the meeting of the blind people," Aaron
said, thinking Joshua would follow up and tell him the
whole story. But Joshua just kept looking out the window,
as if it was all news to him. He merely said, "Yes, it was
a nice little meeting. Those people have a lot of courage,
but it will not go unrewarded."

Then Aaron asked him point-blank, "What happened
to the young blind girl?"

Joshua thought for a long time. Aaron just waited. He
wasn't letting Joshua off the hook over this one. When he
finally realized he was trapped Joshua laughed and said,
"Oh-h-h, Aaron, you and Lester are going to get the best
of me yet. Why do you think I had anything to do with
that blind girl?"

"It happened right after you put your hand on her
head."

"Why would that have anything to do with it?"

"The coincidence is mighty strange. You touch her,
and she immediately begins to see. And she had been blind
from birth."

"I do admit I did feel sorry for her, and realized how
impossible it was for her to care for her invalid mother,
and I did pray for her. I guess it was quite a coincidence."

"You know damn well that was no coincidence, Joshua.
Why don't you square with me? I thought by now we were
friends," Aaron said in a hurt tone of voice.

That got to Joshua. He remembered words spoken long
ago: "I call you friends because I tell you all things and
keep nothing from you. You are no longer servants, but

friends." If anything Joshua knew, it was how to be a friend. He felt bad; things were different now.

"Aaron," he said, "you are my friend, and you already know what happened Wednesday. It's difficult for me to talk about things like that. All I can say is that I am, and always have been, close to God, and He always hears me. Besides, that girl had great faith, and that had a lot to do with what happened."

Aaron seemed satisfied, but both men were quiet for a long time. Aaron felt bad for pumping Joshua and for using that event as a test of their friendship. He realized he had embarrassed Joshua, but Joshua's answer put him at ease and made him realize he understood. They looked at each other and laughed heartily over the incident, then talked about something else.

When they arrived at the synagogue the parking lot was full. There was an unusually large crowd filing their way up to the building. "Looks like you're pretty popular, my friend," Aaron said, looking at the crowd. "I have no doubt you will have them spellbound before they even know what hit them. And you don't even seem nervous. You certainly are a phenomenon," Aaron said good-naturedly.

"I really am a little nervous," Joshua told him. "I haven't done this in a long time, and I'm hoping this time will be different." Joshua's mind wandered far away and recalled many similar occasions, most of them pleasant. He thought of scribes and Pharisees. There were none here today. No institution, no structure in Judaism like the old days. The Church has assumed that role now. Too bad the Church didn't develop more like the synagogue. But Jerusalem had to be destroyed before that could happen.

The two men walked inside, mingling with the crowd. Aaron knew most of them, though tonight there were many strangers. People spontaneously greeted each other and introduced their friends. Lester and Marcia were waiting with Rabbi Szeneth. They greeted Joshua enthusiastically. They were ecstatic there were so many people. Even rabbis had accepted the invitation to come, and already there were a number of them in the crowd.

Marcia asked Joshua if he was nervous. She put her arm in his and held him tight, as if to reassure him. Joshua smiled and admitted he was nervous. He wanted so much for everything to go right. Marcia put a beautifully embroidered yamulka on his head, and over his shoulders she placed a prayer shawl that had belonged to her grandfather. It helped to cover his frightfully underdressed look. In fact, he looked quite attractive in his own rugged way.

The services started late, which was unusual for the rabbi, who was always most punctual. But people were still pouring in after seven o'clock so there was little else he could do but wait. Finally everyone was seated.

Aaron, Lester, and the rabbi walked with Joshua from the study out onto the platform and the service began.

Joshua was sitting on the left side of the ark, next to Rabbi Szeneth, who was sitting in the middle. After a silent prayer the rabbi began prayers and readings. Aaron then got up and read an appropriate text to suit the occasion. Joshua was shocked at the one he had picked.

"The spirit of the Lord is upon me," he read from the prophet Isaiah, and went on, "because he has anointed me. He has sent me to preach to the meek, to heal the contrite of heart, to preach release to captives, and to give sight to the blind; to proclaim the acceptable year of the Lord, and the day of visitation of our God, to comfort all who mourn."

Aaron closed the book and went to his seat. Joshua

stood up and walked calmly to the lectern. Silence overcame the spacious sanctuary. Joshua put his hands on the lectern and gripped it firmly. The muscles in his strong arms rippled.

"My people," he began, then paused. The words resounded through the room. The people could not possibly imagine the full import of those words or who it was who said them. They could only sense the infinite tenderness with which they flowed from Joshua's lips.

The pause was only for a few seconds, but it seemed endless. He then went on, "Those words of Isaiah have more meaning today than they have had for centuries. God has not abandoned his people. He has been with you through all the joyful and tragic events that you have endured. You may have felt abandoned. You may have wondered what happened to Yahweh, who spoke with such tenderness in times long past and has been silent now for so many generations. You may have wondered what happened to the Anointed One he promised to send. You may have wondered if, indeed, you were still his chosen people, his bride he promised never to forsake or to cast off. You may even have felt as if you had been cast off when you were scattered among the nations and despised by the rest of humanity.

"But open your ears and open your hearts and hear me well. You have never been forsaken. Nor was God far away from you, even in your darkest hours. You are still his chosen. You are still his beloved, dear to his heart, and are still the apple of his eye.

"You may ask, 'Why did he treat us the way he did, and for so many centuries? Why was his voice silent and his powerful arm not outstretched to help us?' But I tell you, let the tragedies and the lonely wanderings speak for themselves. God gave your forefathers the key to understanding his signs and his messages. They speak no less clearly today than in ages past. Listen to them and hear what they say so clearly and so loudly. But more important, continue to trust God. What he promised he will carry out. What he has sworn to, he will fulfill. And though you may have walked from his paths, he will still be faithful.

"But you must not look for him and his salvation in the world around you. Nor will you find salvation in accumulating the goods of this world. You become what you love, and when you love the things of this world you lower yourselves to the level of those things. It is unworthy of you to crave them and set value on them as if they bestow upon you a dignity. They have value only as reminders of the world where God lives. To love them in themselves is to drink from the polluted well Jeremiah talked about.

"In spite of what you have suffered you have remained faithful. But it is important for you to remember that God is so far above you and his being is so far removed from anything you have ever experienced that you should not be shocked when he manifests himself to you. His love for you is so tender and so intimate that should he manifest himself to you in a way that is personal, in a way that expresses his desire to be present in your midst, you should not be scandalized. He is, as Isaiah said, your 'Emmanuel,' God in your midst. If this forces you to alter your understanding of the nature of God, then open your hearts and listen. Your minds must not be closed to a deeper and wider understanding of God than you may have known before. Though God is one, his oneness is far different from any kind of oneness you have ever known because he is unique. He is himself. His oneness is not like the oneness of man's nature. The sun is one, yet there is the source, the light, and the warmth of the sun, all one, but each a different facet of the one existence. Do not judge God by what you see in man. Even though man is, in a way, God's image, the image is reflected in man's soul. There is his soul, and his mind and his will, all distinct, but one."

As Joshua looked across the audience their faces were deep in thought, tears of understanding flowing down the cheeks of some. He went on, "You are destined and chosen, not just to bring material blessings to humanity but to be the instrument through which God will speak to people of all nations, helping them to come to a wiser understanding of Himself and his plans for mankind. Be true to that call, and never, never doubt that Yahweh is ever at your side. Do not try to find your Messiah or your salvation in a worldly kingdom. God alone is your Messiah, and only in him will you find peace and fulfillment of your long-sought destiny."

When Joshua finished there was a deafening silence, then the whole congregation arose and clapped their wild applause. Joshua beamed his joy and bowed slightly, acknowledging their response. They finally stopped and settled down. Joshua went back to his seat. Rabbi Szeneth shook his hand, as did Aaron and Lester, their cheeks wet with tears.

The rabbi walked to the lectern. "I must admit," he said, "that I do not know what to say. I could not help but feel, as our beloved friend was speaking, that I was hearing the voice of another speaking through him, and that what he said was not his own but a message sent through him. We have indeed been honored and privileged these past few weeks to know Joshua. Our lives are richer and more filled with meaning than ever before. We hope that, whatever the future brings, we will never lose the closeness and the love we have known on these Shabbat nights. May

God bless our friend and be with him along whatever road he may travel."

The rest of the service moved along smoothly. At the end everyone filed out into the vestibule and down to the meeting room for their social hour. Joshua was a celebrity that night. They told him he was inspired, and they, too, felt inspired by his vision of God's people. They were impressed with his radically new concept of God's people and his plan for their lives. It would provide food for thought and discussion for months to come. They were, most of all, grateful to him for having given so much of himself to them. They were, for all anyone knew, strangers to him, and he had no responsibilities or commitments to them whatsoever.

Aaron and Lester hugged him affectionately. The rabbi kissed him on both cheeks and introduced him to his rabbi friends. They each expressed their evaluations of his talk, and even though they may not have completely understood what he was driving at, they thought his ideas came from a heart filled with love for people and gave them much to think about and search their consciences over. They promised to talk about his ideas when they returned to their own congregations.

Marcia came over and threw her arms around him possessively, and she kissed him, overjoyed at the success of his talk and the wild response of the people.

"Joshua," she said as she helped him take off his prayer shawl and yamulka, "I thought what you said was beautiful. You have to be inspired to talk about something so delicate among Jews and to say it in such a way that they not only did not take offense but applauded what you said and the way you said it. I was so proud of you. I can easily imagine God taking on a form that we could understand to assure us of his love. He has done it in the past. Jacob fought with him in the dark of night. Even Abraham saw God in the three strangers who came to visit him. I am so glad we have come to know you as a friend. We are all honored and proud of you."

Everyone socialized for the next hour. Many of the visitors were introduced to Joshua and told him they had heard many good things about him. The crowd in the hall was so large, it was difficult to talk in much depth about anything, or even to answer questions without being interrupted time and again. Finally the hour came to an end and everyone went home. Aaron, Lester, Marcia, and Joshua left together.

Aaron had listened intently to the talk Joshua had given in the synagogue and had some questions. "Joshua," he said, "when you were talking about the presence of God becoming manifest in a personal way, what were you driving at? I am sure most people thought what you said was beautiful, but knowing you the way I do, I see a lot more in your apparently simple remarks and I am intrigued by that particular statement. I wish you would elaborate."

"Aaron," Joshua responded, "I don't know who gives me a more difficult time, you or Lester. You are forever probing and questioning. Can't you take things on face value and just use them as reference points for your own meditation rather than have everything spelled out for you in detail?"

"With anyone else, yes, but with you, no. You speak in such riddles, you defy us to challenge you. I always knew there was more to you than meets the eye, and when you speak it is the same. There is more to you than meets the ear as well. So don't sidetrack me. What did you mean?"

Joshua laughed. "God is not limited in his presence.

People are so frightfully rigid and limited in their under-standing of things. Do you not realize that God can be present in many different ways? In whatever form he uses we should be careful not to prejudice ourselves and say, 'He can't come in that form, or in this form,' because if we do, then we reduce God to our own limited image, and in doing that run the risk of rejecting him if he comes to us in a way we don't expect. God may be one and he may be simple, but he can also manifest himself in many facets of his greatness. Look at the sun. The sun is one and it is simple. However, there is the sun itself, and there is the heat and the light that touches our lives. We know the sun when its rays disperse the darkness of night. A blind person knows the sun by its warmth. They are dif-ferent, but they are expressions of the same being. It is the same with God. His oneness cannot be defined by our understanding of oneness."

Time passed quickly as they drove along. Marcia just listened, happy to be close to Joshua. She was content just looking at him when he spoke, trying to absorb all the meaning from his every word. In no time at all they were in Auburn. They drove down the street to Joshua's place. Joshua thanked them all for their kindness in coming so far out of their way to take him home and then got out of the car before Aaron got a chance to open the door for him. As he was getting out he put his hand on Marcia's and wished her good night. Lester jokingly remarked how dark Joshua's house looked and suggested that Marcia should be his housekeeper. "I'd be delighted," she said, half jok-ing, "but I don't think he'd want anyone around to distract him." Joshua smiled at Marcia, but said nothing. After telling Aaron he'd appreciate his picking him up next week, he said good night and went into the house.

THE NEXT FEW DAYS were
quiet. The workshop was empty, and Joshua took advan-
tage of the lull to rest. The frenetic activity of the past
two weeks had taken its toll on him, and he was glad he
had no deadlines to meet, no schedules to keep.

On Thursday, Father Pat brought Reverend Joe Engman, the Methodist minister, and another priest friend of
his to visit Joshua. His name was Al Morris.

Father Morris was a middle-aged man, good-humored,
perhaps overly conservative in his thinking, but because
he was so kind his parishioners loved him and overlooked
his shortcomings. Joe Engman was a friendly, stocky man
with curly hair. He was a good family man whose devoted
wife, Mary, was his greatest inspiration. He had a ready
laugh and was very open in his faith. Occasionally Joe
would attend morning Mass, if Father Pat was saying it,
and would receive the Eucharist, about which the priest
never made an issue. The parishioners thought it was
beautiful.

Joshua enjoyed Pat's two friends. They all had a good
time helping him put the supper together, one making
the barbecue sauce from ingredients he had brought with
him, the other preparing the meat and another the salad

from Joshua's garden vegetables. They laughed and joked as they reminisced over the events of the past few months. They kidded Joshua about taking the village by storm and stirring up a hornet's nest. He enjoyed their humor. They didn't talk about anything serious, they just had a good time.

After the party broke up Joshua went back into the house and went straight to bed. It was well past midnight, and he fell sound asleep as soon as he hit the bed. His last thought as he drifted off was the bishop. During the course of the interview the bishop had told him a number of times the things he was teaching were not really new. Joshua could detect a put-down. He also knew he had been the butt of jokes at the table after he left. Father Pat got some information about what happened and had passed it on to Joshua. He told Joshua it was too bad they didn't take the time to get to know him themselves rather than make decisions based on rumor and jokes. Pat was not a favorite of the chancery. His criticism of their pettiness and politics had gotten back to them. One night he had called them all phonies, accusing them of not really being interested in the Church or spiritual things but just public display and power. That was just before they transferred him to Auburn.

The consultors' meeting had taken place as planned. The bishop and the chancellor made believe they were asking the consultors' advice but shrewdly insinuated their own predetermined plan. The consultors perfunctorily fulfilled their accepted role and approved what was presented. It was decided that any handling of Joshua locally would meet with opposition, since he was popular, especially with the Jewish community. To antagonize them would be to jeopardize considerable contributions to the bishop's programs.

Since Joshua was docile, he could be counted on to cooperate, even in his own downfall. They decided to send a complaint to the Vatican telling about the spurious ideas of this man whose popularity was growing to such an extent that they feared the possibility of a schism. It was not true, of course, but it sounded intelligent, and as they knew which buttons to push to cause concern at the Vatican, they knew their strategy would work. It was decided the chancellor would write the letter and send it immediately, suggesting that, perhaps, a doctrinal proceeding might be held to look into these matters. This way professional theologians could carefully dissect Joshua's ideas and show him how uninformed and ignorant he really was and convince him he was over his head—dabbling in matters which were best left to the professionals who ran the Church.

Joshua found out from Pat what had happened and now all he could do was wait patiently. The drama was about to unfold. The stage was being set, and the actors were making last-minute preparations.

It didn't take long for the Vatican to respond. The bishop had contacts, carefully cultivated over the years. It was hardly two weeks later that Joshua received a very important-looking letter. Charlie, the mailman, couldn't just put it in the mailbox. This one had to be hand-delivered. He was dying to know what was in it. Not that Joshua would ever tell him, but he would at least see Joshua's reaction.

Joshua answered the door and smiled when he saw Charlie. Charlie couldn't hide his feelings, and it didn't take much for Joshua to guess what Charlie was excited about. As expected, Joshua invited him in, and they sat down and talked while they had something to eat. To Charlie's supreme disappointment, Joshua just took the letter from him and put it on the table, not opening it until Charlie left.

When he did finally open it it read:

Dear Mr. Joshua:

We have been informed by your bishop of certain religious matters you have been discussing and disseminating among the Christian people in your community and in other places. The bishop is quite concerned. Because of the serious nature of these matters and the doctrines involved, as well as our continued concern for the faith of the Christian people, we are requesting that you appear before this Congregation for a hearing. We hereby set the date for this proceeding as August thirteenth of this year of Our Lord, one thousand nine hundred and eighty-three, at 9:30 in the morning in the Palazzo del Sant' Ufficio in The Vatican. We hope these matters can be happily resolved to everyone's satisfaction.

Sincerely yours in Christ,
Cardinal Giovanni Riccardo,
Secretary,
Sacred Congregation for the
Doctrines of the Faith

Joshua thought over the content and tone of the letter and its meaning. The bishop had told him he was impressed with him, and that there should be more Christians like him. Then why report him to Rome and demand an investigation? The memories of long flowing robes and broad phylacteries again crossed his mind and brought back a train of images, of men trying to hold on to power.

Joshua looked around for a pen and some paper. There was some good stationery left by the previous tenants, which Joshua found in an old desk. He sat down at the kitchen table and wrote a brief response.

Dear Cardinal Riccardo:

I feel honored that I have been invited to come and meet with Peter. While I find it difficult to fully understand the purpose of the proceeding to be held on August thirteenth, I would be most happy to comply. However, I do have a problem. I am a poor man, and do not have the means to make a voyage like this. Even if I were to save what little I make, it would take me a very long time to save what would be necessary. If you could help me to solve this problem, I would be more than happy to cooperate.

Sincerely,
Joshua

Joshua sealed the envelope and walked down to the post office to mail it himself.

From then on things happened rapidly. It was only ten days later that a messenger arrived from the chancery summoning Joshua to meet with the chancellor. He wasn't going to go through that routine again. He asked Father Pat to drive him. He was delighted and changed his schedule accordingly. On the way Joshua told him about the letter from the Vatican, which had surprised him, since the bishop had given him no indication that he was displeased with him but even seemed to approve. Pat just laughed.

He told Joshua what he had learned. "The bishop was ordered to pay your fare to Rome. Afterward he told the chancellor he'd be damned if he was going to give you a free trip to Europe so he made arrangements with a friend of his, who is captain of a tramp steamer, to take you on his ship and make you wait on tables to earn your fare. That ship is supposed to depart in just three days."

Joshua laughed. "That's going to be fun," he said.

When they arrived at the chancery Pat waited in the car while Joshua went inside. As Joshua entered the vestibule the bishop was walking across the hall. When they saw each other the bishop was caught unawares and looked sheepish, making believe he hadn't really noticed him. The chancellor called Joshua in immediately. He was short, rather stocky, and balding none too gracefully.

When Joshua entered the room the chancellor was sitting behind his oversized desk. Joshua wanted to laugh at the sight. The chancellor almost disappeared behind the huge desk, and as the chair he was sitting in was extra large, to compensate for his short stature, Joshua could see his feet dangling a clear two inches above the floor.

Joshua walked to the desk and stood there, looking straight at the priest sitting insecurely in his high chair. The chancellor slid off the chair as he introduced himself and shook Joshua's hand. He told Joshua to be seated, then proceeded to tell him why he had been called.

"The bishop asked me to inform you that he had been requested to make arrangements for you to go to Rome and meet with officials of the Holy Office. Accordingly, he has very generously arranged for your trip with the captain of a very fine ocean liner. The captain will provide you with passage, and you in turn will earn part of your way by working in the dining room on board ship."

"I thought the bishop was impressed with me?" Joshua told the chancellor. "How come he praised me when I was with him, then a short time later I am summoned to Rome for an investigation? It doesn't make sense."

The chancellor could not look at Joshua. He told him he didn't know anything about that.

"When does the ship leave, and from where?" Joshua asked.

"This Friday morning. The name of the ship is *Morning Star*. The captain's name is Captain Ennio Ponzelli. The ship will be leaving from Pier Forty in New York at nine in the morning."

The priest then gave Joshua an envelope with all the papers he needed. The bishop had had to use his influence to get the passport, as there were so many unknowns in Joshua's life. They had used a picture taken of Joshua at the synagogue by a man who was a friend of one of the chancery staff.

When the chancellor finished he wished Joshua a good trip and saw him to the door.

Pat was sleeping when Joshua came out. When Joshua opened the door he woke up and rubbed his eyes. "This is always a good place to sleep," he said caustically.

Joshua smiled and commented, "The Church would function better if it were closed. Like Judaism, once Jerusalem disappeared, the spirituality of the Jewish people began to thrive."

"Well, what's the verdict, Josh?" Pat asked as they drove.

"I leave Friday morning."

"Did they tell you or ask you?"

"Told me, but I didn't object. I've been looking forward to this for a long time. I can handle myself, and there's nothing they can do without my permitting it, so don't worry, Pat."

"How about lunch?" Pat asked.

"Good idea, sounds like fun," Joshua replied.

"Where will it be," Pat asked, "the kosher deli or Gino's?"

"Let's try the deli. I haven't had kosher in ages." The remark went over Pat's head.

They drove around for a while just talking and looking at the sights, then headed for the deli. They were a strange couple as they entered the restaurant, but no one paid much attention. They sat down and ordered a beer while they decided what they would eat. Joshua felt right at home, ordered a Reuben sandwich on rye and another mug of beer. Pat ordered the same. They sat and talked about a thousand things while munching on their sandwiches.

It was almost two-thirty when they finished. They took a roundabout route back to Auburn. Pat was beginning to realize the implications of the events that were about to unfold. He asked Joshua if he would be coming back to Auburn after the affair in Rome. Joshua told him honestly that he didn't think so. What would he do and where would he go? Joshua liked Pat and answered him truthfully. His work was reaching its conclusion and his future was in his Father's hands.

Pat dropped Joshua off, then went back to the rectory. The pastor was furious. "Where have you been all day?" he demanded.

"In the city, at the chancery," he answered.

"What were you doing there? Never mind, it's none of my business. I want you to help the janitor in the cellar. He needs a hand bringing wood up for the bazaar."

"I'm sorry, Father, I have some important things to do that can't wait," Pat replied. It was the first time Pat had had the courage to refuse the pastor's orders.

Father Kavanaugh was enraged at the insubordination. "Do you know who you are talking to?" he demanded.

"Yes, unfortunately. To a man obsessed with a sense of his own importance who hides behind his priesthood to dominate other people. I'm sick of it. So leave me alone or I'll walk the hell out of here, and, with your reputation, you won't get a replacement."

Pat was angry because it was the pastor who had caused all Joshua's troubles. Rather than get in deeper, he went up to his room. The pastor was speechless. Like all bullies, he didn't know how to react when someone crossed him and showed he wasn't afraid of him.

What was so important to Pat was contacting all of Joshua's friends and letting them know he would be leaving in a few days. He wanted to at least give him a decent send-off, in spite of all those phonies who had done him in. He called Aaron and told him the whole story of what had happened. Aaron called Roger Silverman and Lester, and then broke the news as gently as he could to Marcia. She broke down and cried but got herself together and called the rabbi and a few other friends. Before the hour was over the whole Jewish community knew about what had happened. They were furious with the bishop. They had thought him a decent man and honorable. Now they knew. This would cost him a small fortune in donations.

After calling Joshua's Jewish friends Pat then called the Sanders and told them to pass the word around town that Joshua was leaving and that they were having a surprise party for him at his place on Thursday evening. He didn't tell them the whole story for fear of shaking their faith. They loved Joshua and could never understand how a religious leader could be so callous as to hurt anyone so good.

The party Father Pat was planning was to be in Joshua's yard. It was plenty big enough, and if the weather was nice they should have a great time. All the village would be able to see how much the people loved Joshua.

After Father Pat had called Roger Silverman, Roger called Larry Schwartzkopf, the news director, and told him to get a crew over to Joshua's place at five-thirty on Thursday night. "But that's almost air time," he protested.

"I don't give a damn if the President's coming to town, I want a crew over there at five-thirty," Roger insisted. He wasn't ordinarily that way with his men, but he was really disturbed over this whole matter.

Although there wasn't much time to prepare a party, the people loved Joshua so much that they would drop everything to make sure they'd be there.

After Father Pat had dropped Joshua off on their return from the city Joshua went into the house and surveyed the place, wondering what last-minute business he had to take care of. He had already paid the rent and told the landlord he'd be leaving within the week. There were still some vegetables left in the garden. He went out and picked them, intending to give them to his friends on the back road. The rest of the afternoon he spent doing little things around the house. After supper he walked up to the high meadow and just thought, planning his moves for the days to come.

The next day Joshua was at peace. Now that the future was decided and the course plotted, he rested in the assurance that everything was ready for the next act of the drama. He crossed over to the side road toward where the Langfords lived.

When he reached the place the children were playing back in the yard so they didn't see him. When he knocked on the door Margaret answered. She was surprised to see him. "My goodness, what do you have there?" she asked.

"Just some vegetables from my garden, and a few chickens I won't be needing anymore as I'm going on a trip. I thought you might be able to use them. They're all special-grown and fresh-picked," he said with a grin. After he put the bags on the table Margaret kissed him and the two sat down to talk. She offered him a cup of coffee, which he accepted.

Anxious over what he had just said, she questioned him further. He told her he was taking a trip to Rome. She was glad for him but said she would miss him terribly. She promised the family's prayers for a safe journey.

At that point the children came in carrying the chickens, which were clucking and squawking angrily. The kids were happy to see Joshua and asked if he had brought the chickens. Yes, they were presents for them. Their mother told them about Joshua's trip. They were glad for him and wished they could go.

Joshua didn't stay long. He told Margaret to say goodbye to Hank, and after kissing her tenderly, he left.

When Joshua reached his house all was still quiet. The house was empty and neat. It was early. Joshua packed a lunch, took a towel, and walked out to the pond to take a dip. He stayed there all afternoon.

It was around five when he returned and he was surprised to see cars parked along the street and people standing around on his front lawn. He was surprised to see all of his friends, some of whom were carrying dishes of food or bottles of one sort or another.

When he appeared around the corner they all turned toward him and together cried out, "Surprise!" It was a surprise, and a strange sight, all these people, so many of them not even having met each other before. Joshua was baffled by the spontaneous show of enthusiastic affection from such a large group of people who just three months before had been total strangers. They gathered around him. Some embraced him, some kissed him, some shook his hand warmly. There must have been a hundred people in all, and more were coming. Joshua spotted Aaron and Lester, and Marcia and Rabbi Mike Szeneth, Father Darby and his chauffeur, the Reverend Rowland and the Reverend Joe Engman, all standing and talking together. Then he saw Father Pat in the middle of the group, beaming from ear to ear. It finally dawned on Joshua just what was going on. Pat had organized the whole affair. He just hoped he hadn't told everyone the whole truth of what had happened. Joshua was concerned for people's already fragile faith.

Walking over to the group, Joshua asked Lester what this was all about.

"I guess you wouldn't have the slightest idea, would you, Josh?" Lester said playfully.

Joshua looked Pat straight in the eye, and the priest broke down and confessed what he had done. "Well, I didn't want you to just disappear without saying good-bye to all these people who love you so much. That would have been cruel, and knowing how sensitive you are to people's feelings, I knew you wouldn't mind. So enjoy it and let them show you their love. It's good for everybody."

Joshua realized they were right. He had never experienced anything like this, except on that one occasion at Bethany so long ago. But that was only a family affair. This was a grand testimonial.

Joshua still had the towel over his shoulder and his hair was all mussed up, so after smiling across to the crowd he excused himself and went inside to comb his hair and make himself more presentable. Father Pat led the crowd around to the backyard, where there was more privacy and the atmosphere more relaxing.

Some of the women were barging into the kitchen asking to borrow things. Arthur, Father Darby's chauffeur, and Woozie, and his friend Tony were busy trying to get a fire started in the grill and they were looking for charcoal. When Joshua went out Phil Packer confronted him. "Josh, you're like something from another age. Don't you have anything modern? How are we going to get this grill going?"

"Use Woozie's torch," Joshua replied. "If that doesn't work, rub two sticks together. That's always worked."

At that moment Moe Sanders and his brothers came, all of them this time, including his brother Freddie. Moe told Joshua there was a television truck out in front and a reporter was looking for him. Joshua went out front and they were all ready for him. The reporter had his pad in his hand and started firing questions at Joshua. What happened? How come this sudden turn of events? Is it true the bishop reported you to Rome and you're being investigated?

Joshua had to be shrewd this time. To be honest and truthful was one thing, to damage the Church or the people's faith was another. Out of a sense of loyalty to the shepherds of the flock, Joshua tried to put events in a light that would be more understandable. But the reporters saw that he was evading them so they zeroed in and asked him if what he taught was objected to by officials. Joshua told them that it was always difficult to agree on matters of belief:

"Church officials are concerned about order among the people, prophets are concerned about people's relationship with God. There will always be tension between the two. Only when officials try to suppress the voice of prophets is real damage done to people and to God's message. This tension would be lessened if spiritual leaders were as knowledgeable about spiritual things as they are about the worldly business of the Church. The real key to progress in the kingdom of God is not in legal structures but in allowing people to enjoy their freedom as God's children and to grow as individuals, not constrained by rigid laws that prevent growth. The Church has to get away from the role of universal moral policeman and judge of human behavior. She must learn to guide by inspiring people to noble ideals and not by legislating human behavior. The sheep will always flee when shepherds try to bully them. Human behavior must be free if it is to be pleasing to God."

"Is it true," the reporter asked, "that you have been summoned to Rome for official proceedings?"

"Yes."

"What have you said that is so wrong?" the reporter probed deeper.

"The words of Jesus and what they imply are never too popular. People get angry when they interfere with the way they are used to doing things. No one likes discipline, but, unlike other people, religious leaders see criticism of traditions or suggestions for change as attacks on doctrine. That is not necessarily true. The Church must review its relationship with God and His people honestly if they are to remain faithful to their trust."

"What are some of the words of Jesus that are not being observed?" the reporter continued.

"Jesus preached poverty and humility. That is never popular so it is ignored. Jesus also preached gentleness and meekness among his apostles. That is also ignored. When it is criticized the criticism is resented."

"Is that why you are being called to Rome?"

"I don't know, I haven't been told."

"Didn't the bishop tell you when he was talking to you?"

"The bishop told me I was a good man and there should be more Christians like me."

"So you have no idea what their complaint is?"

"No."

"Since you are not a priest, can they order you around like this?"

"They presume jurisdiction over all baptized persons. I have no objection to meeting with Peter."

"Thank you, Joshua," the reporter said in ending the interview. Roger Silverman was standing nearby and told the reporter not to edit the interview but to televise the whole thing. The crew stayed around for a little while talking to people and getting their reactions to Joshua. They then left.

The people were watching Joshua. You could see the affection in their eyes. He had been in their midst only a few months, but he had captured their hearts. His quiet, unassuming ways, his sincere feeling for people, his concern for even the simplest, his gracious manner with rich and poor, the powerful and the lowly, attracted people to him like a magnet. He fascinated them and bewildered them. Who was he really? Was he just a wood-carver? Where had he come from? There were so many mysteries about him that it made people even more curious. But they loved him and now they were showing that love.

Joshua was gratified by the people's response. It made him realize how people could react to a shepherd who guided them the way Jesus intended. Father Pat was at home with all these different people. In situations like this he really shone. He liked people and he wanted this occasion to be special. All during the evening he didn't touch a drop of liquor. Pat Zumbar kidded him about it, and he told him that Joshua did so much for him, in helping him to understand himself and his work, that out of friendship he had sworn off the bottle. He no longer needed it. And it didn't go unnoticed by Joshua either, even though he seemed so occupied with others that it could have easily escaped him.

It had been arranged by Father Pat that no one would bring any gifts. Joshua would want it that way. It would also embarrass the poor. Only Father Jeremy K. Darby violated the agreement. He approached Joshua when he was alone and gave him two one-hundred-dollar bills, which he said was for the statue of the Apostle Peter. He also admitted it was a masterpiece of psychological insight. While he was talking he pressed into Joshua's hand a tiny gift-wrapped box, which he told Joshua not to open until he was on board ship. Jeremy was visibly shaken by the prospect of Joshua's leaving, but like a true Englishman he was not one to get emotional—no matter how he felt inside.

Joshua thanked him and looked deep into his eyes. Messages passed that needed no words, and Jeremy understood. He smiled and wished Joshua bon voyage.

Most of the activity during the rest of the evening centered around the grill. Everyone was either sitting on the grass or on the steps, or on whatever chairs there were available. They were all talking excitedly and in good humor as they got acquainted with their newfound friends. Pat Zumbar's voice could still be heard clearly above the rest. The Jewish people were more sophisticated than the other villagers but they were intrigued by their simple warmth and sincerity and many new friendships were made that night.

Marcia stayed in the background, though she was dying to know about Joshua's future. Only well into the evening did she finally approach him. She told him she cared for him deeply and would miss him more than he could imagine. Joshua told her he loved her and would think of her always. When she asked if he would be coming back he said he thought not, though he did not know what God had planned for him. He always left his future up to his Father. He told Marcia not to worry about her work. She was a light in darkness, and God would bring her work to fruition. What she had to offer mankind would stand out clearly, even when she seemed not to succeed. Success is measured in different ways. Her life's work would be a great success and would affect the lives of many people.

She told him she would pray for him every day and would never forget him. She doubted if there would be any other man in her life. He had made too deep an impression, and no one could ever take his place. She hoped their paths would cross again, but if they didn't she wanted him to have a little keepsake. She took his hand and pressed a gold medal and chain into his palm, asking him if he would wear it. It was her most precious possession, and she would be so proud if he would accept it. Joshua looked at it. It was a figure of the sun on fire, with a man standing in the middle of it. It had been given to her by an African king during a United Nations tour one year. The medal, for some reason, reminded her of Joshua. Joshua accepted it gratefully. Tears were beginning to well up in Marcia's eyes so she wished him well, kissed him affectionately, and walked back to her friends. Joshua watched her as she walked away. She was beautiful and rare. He did love her, and would never forget her.

The party went on until late in the evening. Then, as people had to get to work the next day, they began taking their leave and departed one by one, thanking Joshua for his friendship and wishing him well. Aaron, Marcia, Lester, their wives, as well as Father Pat and Reverend Joe Engman, were the last to go. Aaron mentioned to Joshua that Rabbi Szeneth's son, Michael, would be working on the same ship that he was taking to Rome. Aaron and Lester thanked Joshua for all that he had done for them. Not only their lives but the lives of many people would be affected by what he had taught them by his words and example. They would never forget him. Marcia looked at him sadly but said nothing. She just smiled and kissed him good-bye and left with the others. Joshua had tears in his eyes.

Reverend Joe Engman and Father Pat had earlier offered to take Joshua to New York. It was a good three-hour trip east by turnpike. Joshua was grateful for their offer. They were the last to leave with the Sanders and their buddies. Finally the place was quiet. Joshua went to bed, his work finished.

CHAPTER 18

JOSHUA rose at four-thirty, precisely as planned and without an alarm. Father Pat and Reverend Joe Engman arrived at five-thirty, right after Joshua had finished breakfast. They had a cup of coffee with him, shared a few jokes, and started out. Joshua looked around the house with a touch of melancholy. He took a hammer and chisel off the workbench and gave them to Pat, and another set and gave them to Joe, without saying a word. He picked up his little pack containing all his worldly possessions and looked out the back window across the meadow. Through the slats in the picket fence he could see three sheep looking into the yard. He walked out the back door, over to the fence, and petted the sheep, affectionately pulling their ears like he always did, then went into the house and out the front door with his two companions. They saw tears trickling down his cheeks but said nothing.

The car rolled quietly out of the village. Most of the people were still asleep. The golden rays of a blood-red sun cut like lasers through the trees. It was chilly. Joshua was wearing his sweater. It was a perfect morning for a long ride. Down the country roads to the turnpike they went. In no time they were at the tollgate.

"Getting an early start today, Father?" the toll collector asked as he gave Pat the ticket.

"Yea, got a long trip ahead," Pat responded sleepily.

The trip to the city didn't seem long. Once they were fully awake the men talked all the way. They stopped at the service area near the last exit to get gas and another cup of coffee and a doughnut. Traffic in the city was not heavy yet and they arrived at the dock in plenty of time. The ship was all ready to leave. It was an old ship but presentable. As the three men walked up the plank to the deck the captain greeted them. He was a pleasant man, good-looking, and spoke with a refined Italian accent. He looked distinguished in his naval uniform. He presumed Joshua was the passenger, being accompanied by two clerics, so he asked for his papers. Joshua took them out of his pocket and handed them to him. He looked them over and welcomed Joshua coolly, then called a deckhand to show Joshua his cabin. Pat and Joe followed. Down the stairs to a back corridor they walked. The room was by itself. It was the only one left by the time the bishop made the arrangements. It was a room not ordinarily used. The deckhand opened the door and let the men pass into the room. It was small, but neat and freshly painted. There was one bunk, a chest of drawers, and a bathroom. They all laughed at Joshua's luxury apartment and went back upstairs together.

It was almost sailing time, so Pat and Joe said goodbye. It was a difficult parting for all of them. They had become close and had similar approaches to life. Pat told Joshua he would pray for him. Joe did the same. Joshua told them to be true to themselves and follow their convictions and not become discouraged because people did not understand them. Things that are of value are usually out of the ordinary. Same with ideas. To lead people you can't think the way they do. So don't expect them to understand. You are doing God's work, He will give the reward in good time.

The two men hugged Joshua and left the boat. The gangplank was lifted and the ship's whistle blew. Slowly the huge boat slipped away from the dock. From down below the men waved to Joshua. He waved back. He looked a sad, lonely figure all by himself on the big ship. That was the last his friends saw of him.

Joshua was assigned duties in the dining room. He was to report to the cook at six in the morning to set the tables for breakfast, then wait on people during breakfast. He would again come to the kitchen at eleven and do the same for lunch. Supper would be at six o'clock, so he would be ready at five to serve that meal. Otherwise, he was free.

When the sailor finished with the instructions Joshua walked back on deck and looked across the water toward the land. It was moving farther and farther away. A trace of melancholy passed over him as he thought of all the goodness and beauty he had found in so many of the people he met during his brief stay in Auburn. He thought also of the pastor and the bishop, and pitied them. Their lives were so shallow and empty. They had little to give people. He looked out to sea and wondered what the next few weeks would bring. Would it be pleasant or disheartening?

In no time it was eleven o'clock. Joshua went to report to the cook. He told him to put out the water and set the tables. He showed him where the serving dishes were and told him to bring them over to the counter so he could put the food in them. He then told him to cut the bread and put it in baskets. By that time the passengers were entering the dining room. They were friendly and asked Joshua his name. He told them, exchanged pleasantries, and helped them to their seats. The cook gave Joshua a serving towel to put over his arm.

"What's that for?" Joshua asked.

"In case you have to touch anything hot, or have to brush crumbs from the table, or open a bottle of wine and prevent it from dripping on the tablecloth."

Lunch went easily. There were only some twenty-five people in all, including the captain and his officers. Joshua was sharp. He watched and anticipated each little need, and if someone wanted something he would approach the person and courteously ask if he could help. The women, particularly, were impressed with the delicacy of his manners and how prompt he was in noticing when anyone needed something.

Supper was much the same. It didn't take long for some of the more observant of the guests to notice Joshua and the graceful dignity that flowed with such ease from his personality. They were tempted to ask him questions to learn more about him but decided against it, thinking it more courteous to respect his privacy. But as he became the topic of talk at the tables the curiosity deepened. By the second day of the voyage people were keenly aware that this was not just an ordinary ship's servant. There was a majesty about him even when he served that belied the simplicity of his appearance. Although it was not his place to talk to the guests, they could detect from the way he answered questions that he was highly intelligent. From conversations with him on deck between meals they got to know him more intimately and developed a respect for him that embarrassed them when he waited on tables. He sensed this and tried to put them at ease by telling them what nice people they were and how much he enjoyed waiting on them.

There was only one person who gave Joshua a difficult time. He was a rough, boisterous man who found fault with just about everything. Joshua tried hard to please him and, to the admiration of everyone, never lost his cool. The man seemed to become even more obnoxious when he noticed it didn't bother Joshua, who just smiled and ignored his remarks. The other guests were embarrassed for Joshua, but enjoyed noticing how little the man's manners bothered him.

On the third day of the voyage, while Joshua was sitting on deck with some of the guests, a tragedy occurred below. One of the cabin boys fell down the stairs. They took him into the sick bay and paged the doctor. He rushed down and examined the boy. His neck was broken, and there was little life in him. The doctor did what he could, but it was of no use. The boy died a few minutes later. The doctor examined the X-ray he had taken and found a fracture in two of the upper vertebrae. The boy's name passed quickly around the ship. His name was Michael Szeneth.

When word reached Joshua he said nothing, just excused himself from the little circle of guests and went below deck. As he walked along the corridor the captain was leaving the radio room. He saw Joshua but paid little attention to him until he noticed he was heading for the sick bay. Then he became curious. He watched him from a distance and saw him enter the room where the dead body lay. There was no one else in the room, and as Joshua had left the door half open the captain could see everything.

Joshua walked over to the table where the corpse was lying, lifted the sheet from the boy's head, and called out to him, "Michael, wake up!" Shivers went up and down the captain's spine. After a moment the boy's eyes opened. He looked at Joshua. "Sit up, Michael," Joshua told him. The boy did as he was told and sat up on the table. The captain was overwhelmed and didn't know whether to scream with joy that his friend's son was alive or to fall on his knees. The boy's father had been a friend for years, and he felt terrible about what had occurred. But now his joy was a thousand times greater than his grief, and he was thrilled beyond measure. Joshua, in the meantime, was telling the boy to eat a piece of bread he had just handed him. Michael asked what had happened. Joshua told him he was all right, that he should go about his work and not tell anyone about what had happened. Joshua then left the room and went back on deck as if nothing had happened.

The captain went immediately to the doctor and told him the boy was sitting up. The doctor said that was ridiculous, the boy was dead. The two men ran to the sick bay, and when the doctor saw Michael standing near the bed he was beside himself. He told the boy to get back on the table.

"But why? I'm all right."

"Sonny, you were dead. What happened?" the doctor asked.

When the boy said nothing the doctor insisted. Even the captain didn't feel he could tell the doctor what had happened. The doctor insisted on taking another X ray. The X ray showed nothing, no fracture, no trace of a fracture. He couldn't have made a mistake. He impatiently grabbed the first X ray, looked at it, compared it with the second, and, with satisfaction in his voice, showed the captain. "There, his neck was broken. See. But what happened? How did it heal? I can't understand this."

The doctor released the boy and told him if he had any

feeling of weakness or nausea to come back immediately. When Michael went upstairs he became an instant celebrity. Everyone wanted to know what had happened. Michael told them nothing more than what he himself remembered, about falling down the stairs and faint recollections of people gathering around him, but nothing more until he woke up. Did he see anything when he was dead? Did he hear any music or voices? Did he see God? The boy protested that he didn't know a thing until he woke up.

The captain didn't know what to do. He had to make a full report, but what could he put into the report? Should he tell just what he had witnessed? Who would believe it? But he had no choice. He could only write what he saw. If they believed it, all well and good. If they didn't believe it, that was their problem.

The doctor had more of a problem. He could not account for the few brief moments between his leaving the dead boy and seeing him standing up a few minutes later. The captain was no help, though later that night he confided to the doctor what he had witnessed. The doctor scoffed and was still at a loss as to what he should write in his report.

The incident happened in the middle of the afternoon. Captain Ponzelli was deeply affected by the event. He began to wonder about the real identity of this humble waiter who took such delight in serving the guests. The bishop had told him a few details about Joshua, but none of them seemed to fit the man he had come to know the past few days. He became nervous at the thought of Joshua waiting on tables, especially waiting on him.

The captain called Joshua to his quarters. When he

arrived he offered him a seat and treated him graciously. "Joshua," he said, "I've decided to take you off dining-room duty."

"Why, Captain?" Joshua asked, concerned. "I enjoy waiting on the people. They are good people and I like doing things for them."

"Joshua, I saw what happened this afternoon. I know you and understand you better than I did. You are a lot different from what I had been told about you, and I really don't feel comfortable allowing you to do this menial kind of work."

"But Captain, that was my agreement with the bishop and I would like to keep my word."

The captain thought for a long moment. "All right, but I don't feel comfortable about it." Then he laughed as he thought of something. "I have an idea. I love to cook, but I never have a chance. How about me giving the cook some time off and you and I will do the cooking and serve the people ourselves? I usually do it one night of each voyage anyway."

Joshua laughed and agreed. So the captain called the cook in and told him his intentions. The cook was delighted. He didn't mind at all. So at four-thirty Joshua and the captain went down to the galley. Joshua got the tables ready as usual, and found things in the cabinet for the captain, while the captain went through the refrigerator and the pantry looking for things he needed for the meal.

For appetizers he decided on German-style fish in sour cream, fried wonton strips with soy-lemon sauce, and slices of tomato pesto tart. The next course would be artichoke mushroom salad remoulade and midwestern green salad. The main course would be Indonesian sate, a Southeast

Asian version of kabobs, served with spicy peanut sauce and rice with turmeric. The dessert would be Gugelhupf cake served with apricot sauce and a variety of coffees.

The dinner started a little late, but no one minded. Word had gotten around that the captain was cooking so the passengers weren't expecting it to be on time. They were all delighted with the idea of the captain doing the cooking. And he really did look the part with his white apron and high chef's hat.

Joshua served the appetizers. The people raved about them. "The captain should stay on as chef," remarked the chef himself as he stuffed himself with wontons. The next course came out. The people couldn't get over the captain's flare for gourmet cooking. In fact, it was a stroke of public relations genius. The whole affair brought everyone closer together. When the main course and the big spread of desserts and coffees came out, that really impressed everyone.

When the passengers finished eating and Joshua had cleaned up the tables, the people just sat around in the dining room eating their dessert and sipping their coffee. The captain and his helpers all sat at the captain's table afterward, and ate their own supper. They were immensely proud of themselves, especially when the cook himself came over and praised them for the magnificent job they had done. "I couldn't have done better myself," he told them. They all laughed.

The whole atmosphere on the ship changed after that. Everyone seemed more relaxed and friendly. The crew, who ate in their own dining room, had the same food as the guests and they loved it. Their attitude toward the captain changed. They still respected him, but they now had a much warmer feeling for him, seeing that he could be so human. They showed their appreciation by doing many little extra things that weren't part of their duties.

Joshua could see a lot of goodness in the captain. That was why he was chosen to witness what he did. The next two nights the captain and Joshua did a repeat of the previous night but with different menus. The two men became close as they got better acquainted. The captain had not told anyone about the incident in the sick bay, except for the doctor. He was sorry he had told him. It upset the doctor, and he had been miserable ever since.

The incident also brought Michael and Joshua closer to each other. They shared a common secret. Michael, who knew the captain well, talked to him about what had happened and asked him what it all meant. The captain admitted he didn't understand it either and just felt that Joshua, for all his simplicity, was an unusual person who must be very close to God. Michael told him that he thought he was much more than that and proceeded to tell him about all the experiences at his father's synagogue in Auburn.

"You should hear him speak," Michael said. "He's inspired, I'm convinced. You should have seen what happened one night at the synagogue. This real nut from our congregation approached Joshua and lit into him for the way Christians have persecuted the Jews throughout history. Joshua just listened to him and then threw his arms around him. The two became friends immediately and walked into the sanctuary hand in hand. It was beautiful." The captain just listened, trying hard to understand and wondering why the bishop had shipped him off to Rome to be investigated.

The third day of the voyage passed without incident, though the sea was beginning to get rough. Joshua came down with a bad case of seasickness and had to miss lunch.

He tried to make it, and even appeared in the galley but when the cook saw him he called the captain. The captain ordered Joshua to stay in bed and had the doctor prescribe something to ease the nausea. "He can cure others, but he can't take care of himself," the doctor told the captain. Captain Ponzelli winced at the sound of those words.

The next day the ship was approaching the Azores. The weather was always unpredictable in this area, and Captain Ponzelli told the passengers that, if they were prone to motion sickness, they should see the doctor and perhaps take medicine to prevent nausea. The sea did become rough, and heavy dark clouds gathered over the horizon. The morning wasn't too bad, but by afternoon the waves were higher and heavy rains began to lash against the ship.

The captain called the radio room for a weather report. Heavy rains, severe winds. The waves were powerful and began rocking the boat. Even the gyroscopes had little effect. Sailors were securing everything that moved so nothing would be swept into the sea. Most of the people had gone to their cabins or to the recreation room, where *Return of the Pink Panther* was showing. Joshua stayed in his room and tried to rest. The heaving sea was too much for him.

By four o'clock the weather was much worse. The rains were beating against the ship with such force, you could scarcely hear anyone talking. The winds had risen to gale force, and radio warnings were telling ship captains not to leave port until the storm subsided. The captain worked his way to the front of the ship to be with the pilot. The pilot couldn't see a thing out the window. The ship was tossing mercilessly. At one point the captain lost his balance and fell against the wall, banging his head against an iron bolt. He mopped the blood off his head and put his hat back on over the handkerchief.

The waves were rising. They were already almost fifteen feet and still getting higher. The captain was beginning to fear the ship might not make it. It was an old ship, and had gone through many a beating before, but this was the worst and there was a limit to what the vessel could take. The pilot tried to steer the boat into the oncoming waves but the wind kept pushing the ship against them, which completely inundated the vessel, threatening to capsize it.

The captain looked out the windows for any indication of the storm letting up, hoping there were no other vessels on their course. Storms at sea make everyone feel helpless. A huge, powerful ship that glides like a sailboat during good weather is totally at the mercy of the elements as soon as the weather changes. It is tossed about like a helpless piece of driftwood. The most any captain can do is keep the vessel steady and prevent the passengers from panicking.

But Captain Ponzelli was becoming increasingly concerned. There were no signs of the storm letting up, and there was nothing more he could do. He sighed a quiet prayer and continued staring out into the wall of rain. He walked to the right side of the room and looked out onto the deck for any signs of damage. Nothing so far. It was hard to see clearly. He thought he saw something unusual. He looked again and could see the faint outline of a figure tugging on the railing as he pulled himself up along the deck. The captain gasped in disbelief. It was Joshua. What in God's name was he doing out there? One false move, one slip of the foot on that slick deck, and he would be swept into the sea. He started to open the window to scream down but realized it would be useless. What in hell was he up to? The captain just watched and kept what he saw to himself. He had come to love that simple, good-natured fellow and had enjoyed the happy times of the past few days. But why would he have to do a stupid thing like this? He said a silent prayer for the poor fool. What was he trying to do? Where was he going?

The captain stood there transfixed, watching breathlessly, as Joshua, soaked to the bone, worked his way up along the deck. Momentarily the wind shifted. The boat steadied itself for only a brief moment, allowing Joshua to stand up straight. He lifted his eyes to heaven and held out his arms as if giving command to the winds. His mouth could be seen screaming into the howling wind, as if he had gone mad. The captain felt pity for the poor fellow. Maybe this is what made the bishop nervous.

Suddenly the wind died down, the rain slowed, and the waves subsided altogether. The clouds began to disperse, allowing blue sky to appear and the sun to cast a bright ray through the opening in the skies. Joshua turned and walked back inside and disappeared below deck, into his room, to take a shower and dry off.

The captain covered his face with his hands, in awe at what he had just witnessed. The pilot thought he was praying his thanks that the storm was letting up. The captain told the pilot to go below and take a rest, he would relieve him for a while. The pilot thanked him. He sure could use a rest. He left and went below.

Left with his thoughts, the captain wondered about what he had just seen. He was more convinced than ever of the real identity of this humble, simple man. "But is it possible? Could it possibly be?" he wondered as the tears flowed down his cheeks at the thought that it could happen to him, unworthy as he was. His memory drifted far back into childhood, to when his uncle, a priest, told his family strange stories of things that took place in the lives of people with simple faith. But the captain was not a man of simple faith, at least he didn't think he was. He felt guilty he was not more religious. He thought of his uncle, who was now a cardinal at the Vatican. He would have to tell him all about this as soon as he landed. Perhaps he could tell him what it all meant. He couldn't wait until the ship reached port. He would call him immediately.

The pilot came back after his brief rest and thanked the captain.

"Did you get a rest?" the captain asked.

"Yes, and I was thinking about the storm and how fast it passed. I told the radioman. He said he couldn't understand how it could have cleared up here when he was still receiving severe storm alerts. There are storms and gale winds all around the area as far as the Canaries."

"I'm sure there are," the captain said simply, then left to find Joshua.

People were beginning to come back on deck when the captain came down. The sun was out and the air was beautiful. He asked if anyone had seen Joshua. Someone saw him soaking wet, a few minutes before, walking in the direction of his cabin. The captain went down below deck.

He could hear him inside singing an unfamiliar tune. He knocked.

"Come in."

The captain opened the door. Joshua was just taking his shirt off a hot pipe that ran through a space in the back of his closet. He put on the shirt and greeted the captain as if nothing had happened.

"Anything I can do for you?" he asked the captain.

"No, you've done enough already," was the captain's ready reply.

Joshua let the remark pass, not wanting to get drawn into the discussion that would inevitably follow.

"I just wanted to say thank you for what you did," the captain said humbly. Joshua just smiled at him with a strange, boyish smile as if it was nothing.

"Joshua, I don't know how to say this," the captain continued, "but I feel proud to have you on my ship. I really don't deserve what has taken place the past few days. But I know it will change my whole life. I feel bad about how it all came about, the investigation in Rome, the distrust of the bishop and the other authorities. I have an uncle in the Vatican. Maybe he can be of some help when you get there. I will give him a call as soon as I land and tell him to expect you. His name is Cardinal Giovanni Riccardo. He's a good man."

"Thanks, Captain," Joshua said, "I may need some help when I get there. I'm afraid they will have a difficult time understanding me. I don't have very high hopes."

"But how can they find fault with you? After all, it was you who started . . ." His voice trailed off before he finished, realizing he was on ground where he didn't belong. He had no right prying any further and knew Joshua wasn't going to open the door more than a crack. He had already heard and seen enough.

"But they won't have any idea, no more than you when I first set foot on your ship."

The captain blushed at the cool reception he had given Joshua when he arrived on board. Joshua reminded the captain it was almost suppertime and they hadn't prepared the food yet.

The two men walked out of the cabin, the captain asking Joshua if he was up to working in the galley after his last ordeal. Joshua looked at him sternly and reassured him how much he enjoyed waiting on the people. He hadn't had so much fun in a long time. Everyone has fun in different ways. He had fun making people happy.

"I suppose that's the way God is," the captain said with a grin. Joshua laughed at the captain's playfulness.

The dinner was late, but the people didn't mind. They spent an extra hour at the bar having cocktails and hors d'oeuvres and were just grateful the storm had ended. This was the last supper on board the ship and the captain outdid himself in spite of the strain of having guided the ship through the storm. The meal was a smorgasbord of all the guests' favorite dishes.

The dinner lasted till well past midnight. Since everyone was having such a good time, they turned it into the evening's recreation as well.

During the meal the doctor had been watching Joshua. He was more than curious. Besides, he had already had too much to drink and was determined to draw Joshua into a conversation.

When everyone was sitting around afterward he called Joshua over and pulled out a chair. After offering a drink, which Joshua politely refused, he asked him where he was educated. Joshua told him his education was extensive and he had the best of teachers, even though he had never gone to college. The doctor laughed at the flippant humor.

"You are quite an intelligent fellow," the doctor observed. "In fact, you have much more intelligence than most of the people in this room. You know, young man, what's your name, Joshua, you know, I haven't filled out the medical report on that boy yet," the doctor rambled on. "I'm frankly at a loss as to what I should put down. Perhaps you could help me."

"How can I help you, Doctor, you're the expert," Joshua remarked.

"I may be the expert, but there are some things that baffle me. And, I frankly admit, this is one of them. Do you believe in miracles, young man?"

"No."

The doctor was taken aback. He was expecting a pious lecture. "Then how do you explain what happened the other day?"

"A little thing like that stands out in your mind because you miss the much greater mysteries that take place continually every day. What happened the other day surprises you because it was unexpected. Look in the mirror when you go to your room tonight and you will see an evolution of wonders far more exciting than the healing of a broken bone and the revival of the spark of life. The whole course of each day is filled with endless wonder, which we take for granted because it all flows so smoothly as the ordinary course of life. But each tiny event, and each moment of time, is a miracle of creation."

"That's very poetic," the doctor commented, "but you presume it is creation. I take it then that you believe in God."

"No. We believe what we do not see. I know God is, just as surely as you know I am sitting here before you."

"What do I put down about what happened to Michael?" the doctor finally asked.

"Put down what you witnessed. It is very simple. It is because you don't believe what you saw that you are having trouble writing the simple facts," Joshua told him.

"I would be laughed out of the medical society if I wrote that down."

"But if it is true then you should be the one who is laughing at their ignorance. When you witness something beautiful you should be happy and proud, not ashamed and afraid."

"You're a strange man, Joshua. I don't know what to make of you. How did Michael get healed?" the doctor shot point-blank.

Joshua laughed. "When we pray God hears. When we need God grants. Faith is like the helpless look on the face of a deer in hunting season. God can't refuse."

"Joshua, I wish I had your faith, or whatever it is you have. You are so free and so happy. I don't believe in God. I guess I'm an atheist."

"No one who heals can be an atheist. Life just gets out of focus. You have become too used to seeing wonders slip through your fingers. When you take the time to put back together all the mysteries you have dissected, and stand back and take notice, you will see the reflection of God and His shadow passing by. Then you will have no more doubt. His healing power courses through your fingers every day, and you have never taken the time to sense his presence. You are God's hands. His very closeness has hidden him from you."

"Young man, you baffle me. I told you, you are smarter than most of the people here."

Joshua smiled and, after telling the doctor how much he had enjoyed talking to him, excused himself and left the dining room. It had been a long day, and, as free and casual as Joshua appeared, the day's events had drained him of every drop of energy. Tomorrow they would be arriving in Italy, and a new chapter would unfold. He needed his sleep.

When he reached his cabin and turned on the light, he noticed a little box that had fallen from the bag in which he kept his belongings. It was the present Father Darby had given him. He picked it up and opened it. Inside were two old Roman coins similar to the ones Jesus referred to when he made the remark "Give unto Caesar the things that are Caesar's, and give unto God the things that are God's." Joshua laughed. The priest had a good sense of humor. Joshua remembered the remark he had made on one occasion when talking to the priest about his church. He had said that in making the King of England head of the Church the bishops had not only violated the injunction of Jesus but betrayed their sacred trust and turned the kingdom of heaven over to Caesar.

19

THE *Morning Star* pulled into Ostia. It was late in the afternoon. The passengers stood along the deck, enchanted by the breathtaking scene, the ancient city rising from the shore. Houses seemingly sitting on top of each other. Beautiful pastel colors. The emerald green water clear to the bottom. A cool breeze sweeping across the water. The passengers were excited about landing so they could start exploring all the beauty unfolding before them.

The old ship dropped anchor. The captain said good-bye to the guests as they filed past. He shook Joshua's hand warmly, and at the last moment threw his arms around him and they embraced. Michael, who was standing next to the captain, did the same. They thanked Joshua for everything and wished him well. The doctor was going to Rome for a few days and asked Joshua if he needed a ride. Joshua was glad to accept. He didn't have much money and would have walked otherwise.

The ride to Rome was short. The doctor told Joshua he had thought a lot about the talk they had the night before and that he had written in the report the facts as they occurred. He felt good about it, though he wasn't sure what it all meant. He enjoyed the experience of meeting

Joshua and doubted he would ever meet anyone like him again.

Joshua told him not to be hard on himself. He was a good man and, in time, the pieces of the puzzle would all fall in place and he would find peace.

The doctor left Joshua off near St. Peter's Square. After saying good-bye, Joshua took his traveling bag and walked off into the vast square, looking wide-eyed at the grandeur and splendor of Christendom's tribute to the majesty of God.

The piazza, with its massive statues of the saints along the top of the porticoes, seemed to reach out as if embracing the world, the gigantic basilica rising high in front of him, magnificent in comparison to the temple in Jerusalem. His thoughts wandered to similar porticoes, infinitely smaller, crowded with people and priests and Pharisees in flowing robes. The memory of the woman caught in adultery passed across his mind. Everything then seemed miniature when compared with the dimensions of this vast monument to God's glory.

He walked across the cobblestoned piazza to the basilica. People were wandering all around, looking here and there, trying to absorb all their eyes scanned. Black-robed clerics carrying briefcases dotted the open space. Joshua walked up the few steps to the entrance and went inside the vast sanctuary. He noticed the statue of Peter, with the toe worn down from being touched. He smiled. He looked up at the ceiling and stood there in ecstasy at the pictorial portrayal of the whole Bible. He walked around the aisles, noting every detail of every painting and statue. Organ music played as the organist rehearsed for a concert or Sunday service. Above the main altar a massive sunburst reflected the glory of heaven. The imagination and genius of man would be hard-pressed to improve on this representation of heaven to the human eye. The artists had done well in portraying God's majesty. "But," Joshua thought, "why do people try so hard to reproduce heaven on earth and have such a difficult time absorbing the message of the stable? They find more meaning in representing God's majesty and find more comfort in being surrounded by power and magnificence than in living the simplicity of the real message. They have missed the whole point of the gospel. Even when they preach poverty and detachment, coming from this setting it negates the sincerity of the message."

He walked out of the basilica and headed for the side street where he was to stay.

The apartment house was an old stone building with a heavy wooden front door protected by iron supports. Joshua walked in and introduced himself to the little old man who tended the desk. The man filled out some papers and gave Joshua the key to his room, which was around the corner and up a short flight of stairs. It was the only room at the head of the stairs. In fact, it was a dead end. Joshua went up the stairs and entered the room. It was small, just enough space for a bed and chair and a dresser. There was a simple bathroom with a shower. It was all he needed.

He put his bag on the chair and fell down on the bed to take a rest. He was finally here. Tomorrow morning he would have his interview. In a few seconds he was asleep. As he drifted off he thought of Auburn, and the simple people there; he thought of the synagogue and Marcia and Aaron. He missed them and felt homesick for all the memories he had left behind.

He rested for only half an hour, then got up, washed,

walked out into the street, and wandered through the streets of Rome, watching vendors selling their wares, all charging different prices for the same things. He noticed little children, Christian children, in the center of Christendom, undisciplined, working at businesses no child should even know about. He was approached by exotically dressed girls inviting him to come with them. He was fascinated by the compact cars and mopeds speeding their way through narrow streets, miraculously missing little old ladies, frantically trying to cross the street. He saw robed clerics walking two by two, talking excitedly about the day's events. He was amused by the stately Protestant church with the bold sign in front, "Lux in tenebris lucet" ("A light shining in darkness").

A small restaurant attracted Joshua's attention. He walked over, looked at the prices on the menu in the window, which were a little high, but he was hungry so he went inside and sat down. A waiter wearing a black suit, with a white serving towel over his left arm, came over. Aware of Joshua's non-Italian features, he asked in broken English what he would like. A large dish of shell macaroni in marinara sauce and a glass of Frascati. The man took the order and returned with a small loaf of bread and a plate of salad.

Joshua looked around the room. There were pictures of Naples and Capri painted on the walls and small tables neatly covered with red and white checkerboard cloths. In the middle of each table stood a large Chianti bottle holding a lighted candle, which created a warm, congenial atmosphere. Two young lovers were sitting on the far side of the room in a corner talking intimately while they ate cannolis and sipped cappuccino. Joshua felt alone.

The waiter brought the steaming dish of macaroni and

placed it before Joshua. He opened the bottle of Frascati, poured a little in a glass, and offered it to Joshua to taste. Joshua approved and the waiter filled his glass. Joshua thanked him, tucked his napkin into his shirt, and went to work on the gigantic pile of shells covered with red sauce. He was hungry and ate with gusto. The waiter brought over a bowl of grated cheese and placed it on the table.

Every now and then Joshua rested and sipped his wine. He enjoyed the meal and told the waiter how good the food was.

After he finished the macaroni he had just a cup of espresso, then left a generous tip, paid his bill, and walked outside. It was almost nine-thirty. He walked around the streets for a while, enjoying the colored lights and watching people in the sidewalk cafes, then went back to his apartment and went to bed.

The next day was hot and sultry. Car and truck engines replaced the birdsongs at sunrise. Joshua woke up early, washed, dressed, and went to a small restaurant for breakfast.

His appointment at the Ufficio was for nine-thirty. It wasn't far away, so he had plenty of time. After breakfast he walked to the entrance of Vatican City. Two brightly dressed Swiss Guards asked for his identification. He told them his name and said he had an appointment with Cardinal Riccardo. He still had to have identification. The only identification he had was a letter from the cardinal. If he could show them the letter, that might do.

The guard looked at the letter, and allowed him to pass. He went up the stairs to the first office attended by a Christian Brother. Joshua told him who he was and why he was there. The brother made a phone call, then gave

Joshua a pass and told him where to go, sending an attendant with him to escort him through the palace.

Outside the hall where the Congregation for the Doctrines of the Faith held its proceedings a guard was standing on duty, checking the papers of those entering. Joshua showed his pass from the Christian Brother and was allowed to enter. It was exactly nine twenty-eight. The officials were standing around talking to one another. The room had a high ceiling, with ornate marble molding. The floor was also of marble, with a large Persian rug in the center. A chandelier hung from the middle of the ceiling.

A long table ran along the front of the room. It was covered with a thick maroon velvet cloth. A large bishop's chair stood prominently at the center of the table. Legal-sized writing pads and some pencils were neatly arranged in front of each place.

When Joshua entered no one made any effort to welcome him. A few men turned and looked in his direction and then continued their conversations. Two bishops wearing red-trimmed black cassocks looked his way, stared at the odd sight, and continued talking. Joshua felt uncomfortable.

Exactly at nine-thirty a tall, aging cardinal in a black cassock entered the room. He was a courtly looking man with a full head of white hair, which made him look much younger than his seventy-five or more years. When he entered everyone took his place, the cardinal taking the chair reserved for him at the center.

There was a bench in the center of the floor about ten feet in front of the table. One of the clerics gestured for Joshua to take his place there. The cardinal began by offering a prayer, asking guidance from the Holy Spirit upon the serious work they were about to undertake. He prayed that they would conduct the proceedings with charity and justice and that truth would prevail. This prayer was directed in Jesus' name. Everyone responded, "Amen."

"Sir," the cardinal said as he looked at Joshua, "my name is Cardinal Riccardo. These are my colleagues. Their names are inscribed in front of their places. Would you kindly give us your full name and address?"

"My name is Joshua. Until recently I have been living in a little village in the United States. But I no longer live there. My present address is Via Sforza Pallavicini, Rome, Italy."

"What is your last name?" the cardinal asked.

"Joshua is my only name," he replied.

Realizing he was not going to get any further answer, the cardinal continued, "Joshua, we have before us extensive reports that you have been discussing theological matters with Catholic people belonging to certain parishes. Is this true?"

"I do not understand, Cardinal, what you mean by theology. I have never set out to talk about theological matters. I just work at my trade as a wood-carver. When customers come to visit me we talk. We talk about many things. We talk about people, about people's problems, about God, and problems they face in trying to do God's will. I am a simple man and talk very simply and honestly when people ask me what I believe."

"When you talk about God, and the things of God, and the Church, that is theology. Do you talk about these things?" Cardinal Riccardo asked.

"When people are concerned and confused about their religion and ask me what I think, I tell them," Joshua answered.

"What do you tell them?"

"I tell them that Jesus came to bring meaning into people's lives and that his message should give them peace and joy. They should not be confused and fearful and filled with guilt because of Jesus' message."

"Is that all you tell them?" a middle-aged bishop asked.

"No. People ask me what I think of religion as it is practiced today and I tell them honestly."

"What do you tell them?" the prelate continued.

"I tell them that religion is not something separated from life. It is their life, either well lived or badly lived. Jesus told people they are free and that they should enjoy their relationship with God and find joy and peace in their lives. But often Jesus' message is taught as a set of lifeless dogmas and rigid laws demanding observance under frightening penalties. That destroys the beauty of Jesus' message and frightens people away from God."

"You are referring to the Church when you tell people that?" one of the theologians asked.

"I am referring to those who teach Jesus' message in that way. The Church teaches beautiful things, but it is all on paper. The love of God is not preached the way it should be preached, nor is the beauty of Jesus' life preached to people, so they grow up without the comfort of knowing that God cares for them and accepts them as a loving father or mother accepts a well-intentioned but wayward child. The Church is supposed to be the living presence of Christ among God's children, but often all the people see is the aloofness and arrogance of ill-tempered shepherds who have little feeling for the people when they are hurting or when they have fallen."

"Are you saying all priests are that way?" a young, balding theologian asked.

"Of course not," Joshua replied. "There are some priests

who give their whole hearts and souls to the genuine work of God but there are not too many. Far too many enjoy the prestige and honor of the priesthood and, like the Pharisees of old, enjoy places of honor in public and the power that comes with authority. They look upon people as subjects to be kept in place and told what to do. That is offensive, not only to people, but to God Himself. Even bishops enjoy acting like heads of state and have all but abandoned the local Christian communities, who are starving for direction and meaning to their lives as God's people and often are ruled by feelingless and arrogant shepherds who hurt the flock and do irreparable damage to God's people with complete immunity. That is because the Christian communities are not really important to the Church, which has become too preoccupied with the business of its far-flung empire of redundant charities. It is the function of religious leaders to inspire charitable works but not to abandon the Christian communities and set up their own massive operation. And it is the chief work of bishops to give guidance and direction to local shepherds but they spend little time sharing the burdens and problems of the Christian communities."

"To go a little deeper, Joshua," a shrewd older priest said, "do you feel this is just a peculiarity of certain individuals or the way the Church is structured?"

"I think it is probably both. Too many need power and authority to give meaning to their work. The spirit of authority seems quite deeply rooted in the Church and running institutions provides that feeling of authority."

"Are you opposed to authority?" the same priest asked.

"No, authority is necessary, but the proper understanding of authority is essential. Jesus' concept of authority is a radical departure from authority as the world understands it. Church leaders have been too eager to exercise authority as the world understands it rather than authority as Jesus taught it."

"You seem to know quite a bit about what Jesus taught and what he didn't teach," a nervous young theologian said sarcastically. "Tell us what kind of authority Jesus is supposed to have taught."

"Jesus taught that his apostles and shepherds should be like lights in darkness, giving light and inspiration to the flock and treating the flock, not as beneath them, as subjects to be ruled, but as brothers and sisters who need compassionate understanding and at times, rare times, firm admonition when they endanger others. That is different from looking upon people as subjects to be ruled by regulation and decree as civil officials do their subjects. There is no room for that kind of authority in the Church. It demeans people and creates a caste system, which is totally foreign to the mind of Jesus. Jesus could see this tendency in the apostles. That was why he washed their feet the night before he died, to impress upon their minds the lesson that they should be humble and not lord it over the flock but be servants of the flock. Not too many like to be servants."

Cardinal Riccardo was watching Joshua closely during all this interchange and saw the simple humility of the man and his total detachment from any spirit of argumentation. He did not appear to be in the slightest way opinionated but believed sincerely in what he said. But wasn't that true of all radical reformers? Their appeal to people was the very same sincerity. But Joshua didn't, for some reason, fit that mold. There was a genuine stamp of real understanding and caring that separated Joshua from radicals and malcontents. The cardinal's long years of experience taught him to see through people they were interrogating, but he felt the younger priests did not see what he saw in Joshua. To them he was just an intellectual opponent who had to be demolished or exposed as a fraud or a danger to Holy Mother Church. The old man did not at all like the turn the proceedings were taking. But there was little he could do, as everyone was free to express himself.

One of the bishops who had been listening directed a further question at Joshua: "Sir, I can see that you are deeply concerned about the Church. Is it your concern for people or your anger against Church leaders that prompts your remarks?"

The question was diabolical and Joshua knew it. It reminded him of the lawyers of old who delighted in setting traps. "I am concerned that the spirit of Jesus' love has been replaced by the law all over again."

"Do you feel that the Church has the authority to legislate and decree?" the bishop asked further.

"Jesus gave authority to bind and to loose, but it is an authority that is to be used wisely and with solicitude for the flock. It was not intended to be exercised in an arbitrary manner or as the ordinary way of relating to the Christian people."

"Do you feel it is used arbitrarily?" the bishop asked.

"When one looks across history it is hard to conclude otherwise."

"But times have changed," the prelate continued.

"Circumstances may have changed, but the urge to control and dominate takes on different forms."

"You seem to subtly include the Holy Father in this blanket indictment," the bishop said.

"I have never met the Holy Father, but judging by the

surroundings I have seen since I came to Rome, it is hard to see how the spirit of humility guides the lives of those who live here."

"Is that intended as a criticism of the Holy Father?" a priest asked.

"Not at all. I have never met him. I hear he is a good man and a dedicated apostle," Joshua said, carefully covering his tracks.

"You mentioned these surroundings. What are you trying to say to us? Do you feel these surroundings are out of harmony with the teachings of Jesus?" the same priest asked.

"You have said it. The houses people live in reflect their opinions of themselves. Jesus preached humility and simple living among his apostles and disciples. Even though those who live and work here did not build these buildings, they choose to live and work here and also live in a manner befitting these surroundings."

"Which means what?" the priest said caustically.

"That the style is little different from the palaces of kings and rulers of this world, which Jesus strongly warned against."

"You feel, then, that those living here, including the Holy Father, are living a life-style forbidden by Christ?" the priest asked.

"I do not presume to judge the way you live. Only you know whether you are true to what Jesus taught."

"But you state that anyone living or working in these surroundings of necessity lives a style befitting the surroundings. The Holy Father lives here and works here, so according to your own logic he is living a style of life out of harmony with the spirit of Jesus," the priest said triumphantly.

"You have said it, not I. A humble king can live in a castle and still be a humble man and unattached to his possessions. A humble successor to Peter can live here and, in spite of it, can still live humbly. But these very walls speak a message, a message of worldly power and authority. And that authority and power form the image of the person who lives here, so it is possible to give two messages, a real one and one not intended. That ambiguity is what confuses the people and clouds the purity of the message of Jesus."

Joshua was sharp. They couldn't pin him down to anything heretical or even rebellious. What was coming across loud and clear was that Joshua was highly critical of the way Church leaders lived and conducted themselves. There was no way he could avoid giving that impression, nor did he want to avoid it. He was here for a reason, and not just to joust or fence. He had a purpose, and that purpose would not be frustrated.

The questioning continued. "Did you, when you were back in your home town, talk about these matters to the people who came to visit you?" a bishop asked.

"No, there would have been no purpose to it."

"Did you tell the people that Jesus never intended that religion be taught the way it is today?" the same bishop asked.

"Yes."

"Did you tell the people that, as God's children, they are free and that no one can take that freedom from them?" the bishop continued.

"Yes."

"And did you tell them that their pastors were violating the teachings of Jesus by the way they ruled the Christian people?"

"No, that would confuse the people and would have been counterproductive."

"But you did tell the people that Jesus never intended that religion become what it has become today?"

"Yes."

"And in saying that you were telling the people that religion was not being taught properly. Is that not true?" the bishop continued.

"I did not say that," Joshua said calmly, indignant over the man putting words in his mouth.

"But it was clearly implied. What other conclusion can be drawn?"

"I did not say how religion came to be the way it is or who was at fault, whether it was parents or priests or teachers. And is it not true that many people do have false ideas of religion?" Joshua asked.

"We will ask the questions," the bishop reminded him sharply.

The younger men on the panel were becoming more and more agitated. The older ones had gone through these proceedings time and again, and they were all pretty much the same. They were immune to insinuations and implications. They were primarily concerned with whether a particular preacher was a threat to the faith of the people and whether his relationship with the Church and its leaders was hostile and ominous. The younger men were sticklers for the fine points of theology.

The young, balding theologian asked the next question. "Joshua, you mentioned before that the Church rules by legislation and decree. Can you give an example of what you mean by that statement?"

"Take the case of marriage. Jesus never said Christians had to marry before an apostle or a priest. Yet you legislate that if a Catholic does not marry before a priest, or marries before another without permission, the marriage is invalid and the couple live in sin. That is arrogant and denies people the freedom to make their own choice. Many people may have good reason for not wanting to marry before a priest. They may not be sure of their faith or their faith may not be mature. Or they may be conscious of the fact that they are not good Christians and a religious wedding would be a hypocrisy. How can you say that God does not accept their marriage or that they live in sin? It may be a beautiful gesture for a couple who are filled with faith and the love of God to make a commitment of their lives to each other in the presence of the Christian community and before a priest, but to force it is neither healthy nor inspiring, and when the lives of the couple are scandalous it is a mockery. Religion is beautiful only when it is free and flows from the heart. That is why you should guide and inspire but not legislate behavior. And to threaten God's displeasure when people do not follow your rules is being a moral bully and does no service to God. You are shepherds and guides, but not the ultimate judges of human behavior. That belongs only to God."

Everyone was shocked by what they heard. Even the cardinal winced but listened intently, realizing that he was not far from right. There really was no reason why the Church had to make such rigid legislation about marriage, and it does cause anguish in many lives. But he was on very dangerous ground, and this would do him damage.

"Are there other examples?" the same priest asked.

"Take the case of a married couple who are destroying each other. In the past you said they could not divorce. But now you say you will grant them an annulment so they may marry again. And you base your decision on the grounds that there was no real marriage and the relationship was destructive. And in the process you examine the intimate details of their sexual life and call in witnesses to discuss what they know of the couple's relationship. Yet you admit you do not give the annulment but merely decide there was no meaningful relationship to work with. Don't you think the couple already know that? And what is the benefit of priests monitoring the intimate details of people's lives? That's what the Pharisees did to maintain control over people and make them answerable to them for their behavior.

"And if a couple do not appear before you and divorce and marry again, you say they commit adultery. How can you say they commit adultery if they know in their hearts their previous marriage was unhealthy and was destroying them? Is it merely because you were not allowed to make the observation that their marriage was not workable? And how can you hope to maintain control over so many millions of relationships, and commit so many thousands of people to this work of such doubtful value, when there are countless millions of souls needing the Gospel preached to them and countless millions of Christians drifting away from God because of neglect? Is it not better to leave the judgment of the intimate details of people's lives to God and go about the work of bringing the message of Jesus to the millions who need to hear him?"

The logic was devastating. The panel had become very thoughtful while Joshua spoke, realizing there was much truth in what he was saying, and with no trace of arrogance or cynicism. His whole manner reflected a deep concern for the Church and for the work of the Church, which prompted the cardinal to ask the next question

"Joshua, what is your idea of the Church?"

"The Church is the handmaiden of Jesus. It is his chosen partner in bringing God's love and his concern into the lives of people. It is his living presence throughout history. And it is because of this that it must take great pains to show the gentleness and the solicitude of Jesus for those who are hurting and not emphasize its legal and judgmental power, which serves only too frequently to frighten people and drive the sheep away from God."

The cardinal was impressed, though he said nothing. He was becoming tense over the way the proceedings were going and was showing his discomfort by wringing his hands in his lap. He was an old man and wasn't up to all this tense confrontation anymore. And Joshua was different from the rest. There was a goodness and a concern about him that gave meaning to what he said. He was not out to destroy or to tear down but to make people think, and that was a good thing.

One of the younger men questioned Joshua bluntly. "If you have such a high idea of the Church, why are you so critical?"

"Because I care," Joshua said wearily.

"If you care, why did you cause such turmoil in the place where you lived?"

Before Joshua could answer, the cardinal, who was mopping his face with his handkerchief, had some kind of an attack and fell over. His head hit with a resounding thud on the hard velvet-covered table. Everyone gasped. The two bishops on either side of him turned toward him, not knowing what to do.

Joshua quietly and calmly arose from his bench and walked to the table, leaning over and putting his hand on the cardinal's head and caressing his face and cheek. The cardinal's left arm was hanging limp; one side of his face was sagging and misshapen. He had had a stroke.

When Joshua touched him the cardinal could feel his hand caressing him and began to feel the life come back into his body and the paralysis leave his arm. At the same moment the young theologian came over in front of the table and pulled Joshua away, telling him, "Get away from him and get back to your bench," and pushing him as he did so that Joshua almost lost his balance.

By that time the cardinal was able to raise his head and saw what had happened. His eyes and Joshua's met in that brief moment, and the cardinal knew. The thought crossed his mind, "My God, is it possible? Can it be that history is repeating itself?" And the cardinal saw himself in the role of the high priest, and the young theologian as the high priest's servant slapping Christ in the face. He felt ashamed and powerless.

He had sensed something beautiful about Joshua. He had sensed his calm dignity that almost bordered on majesty, but now he realized everything. The other members of the panel were for adjourning the proceedings, but the cardinal insisted he was all right. He looked at Joshua as he said it, then lowered his eyes in shame. "The proceedings will continue," he said.

From that moment on the cardinal was for exonerating Joshua and tried in a number of subtle ways to sway the thinking of the panel. But it was of little use. The questioning went on into the afternoon, then, when everyone was satisfied with the information they had accumulated, the cardinal brought the proceedings to a close.

As they all walked out of the room the cardinal walked over to Joshua and thanked him. Joshua smiled and told him to tell no one. One of the bishops distracted the cardinal and they became involved in conversation so Joshua walked out alone. No one seemed very interested in him after the proceedings were over. Their interest in him was professional and detached, and the job was done, so they had no further care for him, not even if he was hungry or would like something to drink. He was just a case. It was another example of the almost inhuman approach to religion that had become the way of life for so many who had dedicated their lives to the pursuit of a career in religion. People were not important, but loyalty to the institution and efficiency in showing that loyalty was important if you wanted to get ahead.

Joshua was told by the attendant at the desk that if he was needed he would be summoned again so he should stay close to his apartment. Joshua walked out into the sun-drenched piazza and looked for a place to eat.

After lunch Cardinal Riccardo requested an audience with the Holy Father. It was very important. He was told he could see him at four-thirty in his library. He couldn't wait to tell him what had happened.

The Holy Father was congenial and listened patiently. "Holy Father," the cardinal began, "I am most distressed over what happened in the proceedings today. They were different from anything I have ever experienced. This man Joshua, as he calls himself, appeared to be a simple, uneducated man, but when we questioned him he showed a profound understanding of the things of God and an insight which, I am convinced, was inspired. I realize the report will show him to be critical of the way we run the Church, but I can see that in practically every point he makes there is a great wisdom, and perhaps we should listen to him. I also have the feeling the panel will decide against him, and

I have a premonition that if we do it will be remembered in history as a dark hour for the Church."

The Holy Father watched the cardinal as he spoke. He had been around for a long time and had done his work well, but his age was showing. He had always been a compassionate man, but you can't run an institution like the Church on compassion. There had to be order and discipline. When the cardinal finished the Holy Father told him he would read the report carefully before making a determination.

Cardinal Riccardo realized he was being put off and told the pope what had happened to him during the proceedings. He listened courteously and diplomatically expressed his thought that, even though it may be important to the cardinal, it was irrelevant to the proceedings and should not be used to prejudice his decision. Cardinal Riccardo had felt he could talk to the pope man-to-man, but the pope's legal conditioning was an immovable obstacle. The cardinal asked if the Holy Father would at least meet with Joshua and talk to him himself. The pope finally consented and thanked the cardinal for his concern. The cardinal returned the thanks and withdrew.

Captain Ponzelli had been trying in vain to contact his uncle in the Vatican. The secretary kept telling him the cardinal was busy with hearings and would contact him as soon as he was free. The captain was disappointed because he was hoping his uncle could be of some help to Joshua, never dreaming that it was his uncle who was chairing the proceedings against him.

Now that the proceedings were over the cardinal contacted his nephew and invited him over to his apartment. He didn't have much time to talk then, but he would be able to spend the whole afternoon with him the next day.

The next morning a courier appeared at Joshua's apartment house. He left a pass for an audience with the Holy Father. Joshua was delighted. The audience was for eleven-thirty the same morning. Joshua had over two hours before the audience so he decided to take a bus up to the Janiculan hill, overlooking Rome. It was hard finding the right bus, but once he did it took only a few minutes to wind its way up the streets to the top.

Joshua got off the bus, saw a food stand, and bought a candy bar. He walked along the sidewalk until he came to a place that provided a panoramic view of the whole city of Rome. The whole history of Christian civilization unfolded before him. The view was reminiscent of the Mount of Olives, overlooking Jerusalem. Only the dimensions were different. Many Jerusalems would fit into this scene. Joshua thought for a long time. He thought of the infant Church struggling to survive. He thought of the persecutions. He thought of the forced conversions of the pagans to Christianity and the heresies, the invasions, the rise in political power of the Church, the investigations into the beliefs of suspect Christians, the imprisonments, the tortures, the pope-generals leading armies into battle, killing other Christians. He thought of the proclamation of dogmas and the condemnation and excommunication of those who refused to believe. He thought of St. Francis and the many saints whose feet had trod this sacred ground. He looked at the magnificent sanctuaries spread out before him and saw the simple faith of people whose genius had raised these monuments to faith.

Joshua remembered days of old and the sad vision of his beloved city. "Jerusalem, Jerusalem, how often I would have gathered you together as a hen gathers her chicks under her wings, but you would not. And the days are coming upon you when your enemies will build ramparts around you and beat you to the ground, leaving not one stone upon another, because you have not known the day of your visitation." Joshua wept. Jerusalem . . . Rome . . . The one did not recognize him in the flesh. The other did not recognize him in the spirit. Both rejected him in different ways, unable to comprehend the meaning of his coming or the spirit of his message. The legal system of doctrines and morals he fought so hard against in Judaism, and which brought about the final events of his life on earth, resurfaced in the Church and replaced the living spirit of the good news. His grand mission to give a new understanding to human living, to breathe new hope into civilization, showing the world that to be Christian was different from anything it had ever known, and that the family of nations could see in Jesus' message a new bond of love that could unite all men into one, that vision was imprisoned and shackled in a bureaucracy that merely mimicked the forms and ways of worldly governments.

The vision faded. Joshua realized it was getting late. He walked back to the bus stop and boarded the next bus to the city. He got off not far from St. Peter's and walked to the Vatican.

The Swiss Guard recognized him but still waited for Joshua to show his identification, which this time was his invitation to the papal audience. The guard read Joshua's invitation and then allowed him to enter. He was ushered through vaulting corridors and around corners until he reached the room where the Holy Father was working. An attendant took him inside, telling him to kneel as he approached the pope.

"Kneel, what for?" Joshua asked, bewildered.

"That's the rule, sir," the man answered politely.

"I cannot imagine Peter wanting anyone to kneel down before him," Joshua said, half to himself.

As he entered the room the pope was sitting at his desk at the other end. He was dressed in a white cassock. His head was bare. When Joshua was halfway across the room the pope stood and walked around the desk to welcome him. He was gracious. The attendant again told Joshua to kneel and to kiss the Holy Father's ring. The pope held out his hand. Joshua took it and shook it with deep feeling. The attendant introduced the visitor.

"Holy Father, this is Joshua," he said as the two men shook hands.

"Hello, Joshua," the pope said cordially.

"It is a great pleasure to see you, Peter," Joshua said, to the pope's confusion.

After talking about little things the pope told Joshua he had received a copy of the transcript of the proceedings. "I must admit, I am not at all flattered or pleased by what I read. Cardinal Riccardo was impressed by many things about you, but he is a kindly and compassionate man. Why do you feel you must say the things you do, young man?" the pope asked Joshua.

"I say them because they are the things Jesus taught, and they should be a surprise to no one. In fact, I can't understand why it causes such consternation," Joshua replied calmly.

"Have you studied theology and do you have a degree in theology?" the Holy Father asked.

"No, I did not think I needed a degree to talk about the things of God. They flow as naturally from the human spirit as the air we breathe. As God's children they are our common heritage and, indeed, our very life."

"Son, you certainly do not lack self-confidence. I notice in the transcript you criticize the way we live and the surroundings here."

"I did not criticize. I was asked to comment and said honestly what I thought. Jesus taught the apostles to be humble and to live humbly and simply, not in the palace of kings, nor to rule like kings. You have changed greatly through the centuries, Peter, and it is not all for the good. Remember, it is by humility and meekness that you will win souls to God, not by rising above people in self-glory. Jesus also established twelve apostles, not one. Their identity has been overshadowed and all but lost. That is not right. Each apostle must be free to work with his own flock, and solve the unique problems of his own flock, with the different cultures and languages and understandings of life. The Spirit must be able to move freely and exercise His freedom in different ways and in different forms, and freely express Himself through a variety of gifts and not through sterile uniformity, which merely satisfies man's need for security."

The Holy Father was embarrassed by the audacity of this simple man's rudeness in giving him a sermon. He blushed and told Joshua his name was not Peter. He told him he had a lot to learn about life and about the Church, and if he was willing to learn, he should try to practice humility and care for his own soul rather than involving himself in matters that are above and beyond him. The Holy Father told him that in the future he should refrain from talking about these matters and follow the directions the Congregation would be sending him. It is behavior like his that can do untold damage to the Church and lead simple people away from God.

The pope then gave an eye to the attendant, who came over and gently took Joshua by the arm. Joshua told the pope that he had done much good for the Church, and that he would suffer much, but that he should not be discouraged because his sincerity would give him occasions to make great changes among God's people that would bring honor to God. As he was leaving Joshua asked God's blessing upon Peter and thanked him for the chance to meet with him.

The pope watched Joshua as he walked out, wondering about what kind of man could have the boldness to preach a sermon to the pope. Yet Joshua was, as Cardinal Riccardo said, a humble man and not really arrogant or cynical. The pope wondered as he watched Joshua walk down the long corridor.

At the same time Joshua was in audience with the Holy Father, Captain Ponzelli was just arriving at his uncle's apartment.

"Uncle, it is so good to see you. It has been so long," the captain said as Cardinal Riccardo welcomed him and the boy who accompanied him.

"I would like you to meet a friend of mine, Michael Szeneth. His father is a rabbi, and we have been friends for years," the captain said as he introduced Michael to his uncle.

"Welcome, my son. I have a friend here in Rome who is a rabbi. Perhaps we can meet him while you are here. Now, Ennio, my dear nephew, tell me all about yourself. What have you been doing since I saw you last? My sister told me you were coming to Rome, but unfortunately I have been so busy with proceedings, I haven't had much free time."

"Uncle, I have so many things to tell you, I don't know where to start."

"Before you begin," the cardinal interrupted, "let's go out to a little restaurant I know. It is more relaxing than this place, with phones ringing and secretaries interrupting."

The restaurant was just around the corner. As soon as they sat down and ordered light refreshments, the captain began to pour his heart out to his uncle. He told him about his friend the bishop asking him to do him a favor and take a certain fellow on board ship and make him work his way over to Rome by waiting on tables. The man had been summoned by the Vatican for a doctrinal proceeding. The man's name was Joshua.

"I obliged the bishop, took him on board, and assigned him to waiting on tables. Taking my cue from the bishop, I was cool to him, thinking he was a troublemaker. Two days into the voyage Michael fell down the stairs and literally broke his neck. The doctor examined him, found his vital signs weak, and tried to do what he could. But Michael died.

"We all left the sick bay. I went to the radio room to send a message. When I was coming out of the radio room I saw this young man, Joshua, walking toward the sick bay. I stayed at a discreet distance and watched to see what he was up to. He entered the room, leaving the door partially open, and walked over to the table where Michael's body lay. Then, lifting the sheet from Michael's face, he called out to him and told him to wake up. To my complete shock, Michael opened his eyes and sat up. I thought I would faint."

The cardinal listened intently as his nephew recounted the rest of the details.

"But, Uncle, that was nothing. Two days later the most extraordinary thing happened. We had this violent storm at sea. There were gale winds and heavy rain. The waves were tossing the ship around like a piece of driftwood. I thought surely it was going to sink. Looking out on deck from the pilot's window where I had gone to encourage the pilot, I saw a figure walking up along the deck. I couldn't believe my eyes. It was Joshua. I thought surely he would be swept into the sea. But as the ship steadied itself for a moment, he stood up straight, stretched his arms out as if commanding the storm, and yelled something that I could not hear. Immediately the wind died down, the rain stopped, the waves settled, and the sun came out. Uncle, ever since then, I couldn't help but think, could it be? Could it be?"

"Ennio. Hearing what you tell me, and knowing what I found out myself, I have no doubt. I wished you could have reached me before I got tied up with the proceedings. The man we interrogated was Joshua. It went badly. No one could understand him, and they were cruel. Even I added my share, and I feel guilty. Let me tell you what happened.

"During the middle of the proceedings I was beginning to become quite impressed with Joshua and felt bad for him and the way he was being treated. It began to bother me so much, I could feel myself getting sick. Then, all of a sudden, I collapsed. I fell forward, and my head hit the top of the table. I was not totally unconscious, but I was dazed. I felt my left arm hanging, but I couldn't lift it. The one side of my face was paralyzed. I couldn't even move my tongue. I realized I had had a stroke. I just lay there, unable to help myself. Then I felt a hand caressing my head and face. It was Joshua's. As soon as he touched me I felt power and life come back into my body. I lifted up my head and looked up at him. At that same moment one of the priests pushed him away and told him to sit down. I was shocked and could only think of the high priest and his servant. I saw myself in the same role, and I felt a shudder of horror pass through me.

"I directed the proceedings to continue and tried to help Joshua. But there was little I could do. There were too many on the panel, and I couldn't tell them what happened. They wouldn't have believed me anyway. I realized that I really wasn't supposed to do anything, that it was all part of a plan. I just felt bad I had to be part of it. Yes, Ennio, in answer to your question, I have no doubt but that it was."

Michael just sat and listened, thinking over everything he had heard and experienced. His own life would never be the same.

"Uncle, where is he now?" the captain asked.

"All I know is that he is staying temporarily in an apartment on Via Sforza Pallavicini. I am thinking the same thing as I think you are thinking. Let us go visit him and apologize for his rude reception."

The captain put down the money for the pastry and coffee and they left.

They arrived at the apartment house in a few minutes. The doorman bowed obsequiously when he saw the cardinal. "Your Eminence," he said, "I am honored. Can I help you?"

"Yes, is there a man here by the name of Joshua?"

"Yes. In fact, he came in before you and just paid his bill. He is walking up those stairs there now. His room is at the top of the stairs."

"Which room?" the cardinal asked.

"There is only one room there. It is his. It was really an old closet, but it was all we had left."

The three men went quickly over to the stairs and ran up. The door at the top of the stairs was open, and they could see shadows moving inside. Thank God they had caught him in time. They went to the room and knocked. No answer. They knocked again. Still no answer. They couldn't understand. They walked in and looked around. There was no one there. The bathroom door was open. They looked inside. There was no one. The room was empty.

Over on the floor near the bed were two sandals. In one sandal there was a gold medal with the figure of a fiery sun and a man in the middle of the sun. Michael recognized it as the medal Marcia used to wear. In the other sandal were two old Roman coins.

The men somehow knew they would not find him. But what a strange thing to find the sandals and the coins, the only mementos of a reality that only the three of them knew and could share only with each other, for who would believe them? They would give the medallion back to Marcia and the coins to whomever they belonged. The sandals were prized keepsakes, which they would forever treasure.

EPILOGUE

Cardinal Riccardo processed the report of the Congregation. The vote for censure was six to one. The cardinal read the details of the report. "The young man, Joshua, showed a distinctly hostile attitude toward authority, which if allowed to spread would do untold damage to discipline and faith. His criticism of bishops, and the highest leaders of the Church, could imply, if not immediately indicate, a defect of faith, which may be symptomatic of lack of belief in the scriptural or dogmatic foundations of the authority of bishops and even the Holy Father himself. His attitude toward members of the panel seemed to support this observation.

"The man's criticism of practices in the Church shows a lack of understanding of the realities of life and seriously questions the ageless wisdom and prudence of Holy Mother Church. The propagating of those ideas could seriously damage the faith and trust of the faithful. Although he seemed sincere, he was misguided and too angry to be of much good. Although his ideas do not appear to be heretical, they are so highly critical of Church practices and policy that it could be said that he does not have a healthy understanding of the nature of the Church or its role as the authority of Christ on earth."

The cardinal turned to the section on recommendations

and censures. Joshua was directed to cease talking about these matters to the faithful under penalty of further censure. He was told that his attitude lacked the docility and humility that befits a Christian layman and that, in the future, he would do well to cultivate those virtues for the benefit of his own soul and the edification of his fellow Christians. And, since he was uneducated in matters of religion, he was unqualified to talk about these highly theological ideas he was circulating. He was also forbidden to discuss the sacred proceedings or anything that transpired during these same proceedings under penalty of excommunication. The report was signed "Cardinal Giovanni Riccardo."

There was an addendum to the report, which the cardinal himself wrote and in which he vigorously and bravely defended Joshua. He included this in the report as the minority opinion. The whole report, with the minority opinion, was delivered to the Holy Father. A copy was sent to the bishop of the diocese in which Auburn was located. In that copy the cardinal included a personal letter to the bishop telling him what had occurred at the proceedings and about what had happened to him personally. He told the bishop that he felt everyone involved in this matter had made a grave mistake and that they had not yet heard the end of it.

Captain Ponzelli also wrote a long letter to his friend Rabbi Szeneth and one to his good friend the bishop telling both of the events that had taken place on the voyage. The rabbi had already heard from his son, who, in his impressionable youth, had his own ideas as to the identity of Joshua. He had grown close to Joshua during the past few months and saw a striking similarity between what Joshua said and the Gospels, which he had begun reading since he left Rome.

Marcia also heard from Michael, who told her all that he had learned from the captain and the cardinal. Although she was deeply crushed over all that had happened, and sad that the medallion had been returned, she understood. She told Aaron and Lester, and her family, and other close friends of Joshua. She also told Father Pat, and as time went on, to keep the memory of Joshua alive, they would all meet and ask Father Pat to explain many of the things Joshua had said and done. On occasion they would read the Gospels together, feeling honored that they should have been graced with his presence during those beautiful moments in their lives. Word spread of the final days of Joshua, and the hearts of many were either soothed or grieved over what had taken place during that brief, bright summer in their lives.